ALSO BY COURTNEY HENNING NOVAK

Adventures With Postpartum Depression: A Memoir

The Distance Learning Activity Book For Parents Just Barely Holding On To Their Last Shred Of Sanity

W0010568

CONFESSIONS OF AN IMPOSTER ROOM MOM

A NOVEL

COURTNEY HENNING NOVAK

For my Grandma Shirley

Loving, fierce and a total badass to the bitter end.

1

Tonight is the most important night of my life, and I don't know what to wear. The outfit I choose will set the tone for the rest of the year. If I wear the right clothes, I'll make the right friends. But if I choose poorly, I might as well give away my earthly belongings and join a monastery on the top of a mountain. My dresses and shirts judge my ineptness as I flip through my closet's offerings for the umpteenth time. That's it. I'm calling the expert.

The expert answers before the phone finishes its first ring. "I was about to power down my phone."

"Zoe!" I yelp. "You're turning your phone back on tomorrow morning, right?"

"No," Zoe says, "next year. You know that."

I sit down on top of the nearest unopened box. "But how am I supposed to survive?"

"Elodie Jones, you are a capable and wonderful mother and you are going to have an amazing year. You don't need my parenting advice."

Zoe Ziegler has been my best friend since she rescued my dignity during our first week of college. While I was showering in the girls' common bathroom, my freshman roommate Ingrid left our room and locked the door — with my wallet and key sitting on my desk. Ingrid had marooned me. Then, a pack of freshman boys from the football team stormed into the hallway, blocking my retreat to the sanctuary of the girls' bathroom. Zoe saved me. She rushed from her room down the hall, screamed several choice obscenities at the idiot boys, loaned me clean clothes, and took me to the dining hall for ice cream.

Our friendship flourished. After graduation, we shared a tiny apartment in Brooklyn and took the subway into Manhattan: Zoe to her entry-level job with a big publisher, me to law school. Three years later, I began my career as a miserable lawyer and Zoe married her college sweetheart, Paul. One year later, Zoe popped out twins. Fast forward a decade, and we were both still living in Brooklyn with our respective husbands, and we ovulated and conceived within days of each. It was perfect. We went to prenatal yoga classes together, shopped for onesies together, and planned our children's future marriage when we learned I was having a girl and Zoe a boy. I did not have to bother making any mom friends because I had Zoe. Even better, Zoe became my go-to parenting expert thanks to her prior experience with the twins. My life as a stay-at-home mom was perfect.

Until now.

Now I am minutes away from beginning my life as a preschool parent in Pasadena, California with a group of strangers while Zoe begins a year of off-grid living in Alaska. Paul says he wants to write a book about their adventures. I say he's having a mid-life crisis and should have bought a Porsche.

"Why do you have to give up your phone?" I ask for the millionth time.

"Because," Zoe sings, "cell phones are an integral part of the grid."

"What if we just text?"

"Texting is definitely part of the grid."

I knew that, but a part of me hopes that if I keep asking, the answer will change. I groan. "What if I have a crisis? Should I send a letter by the Pony Express?"

Alas, I already know the answer to that question as well. The Zieglers are embracing off-grid living with a vengeance, which means my best friend will not even have an address for snail mail.

"You won't have a crisis."

"Of course I will," I insist. "I'm having one right now."

"What's the crisis?"

"I don't know what to wear to preschool orientation."

Zoe snorts.

"I'm serious!" My wet hair is getting my shirt wet. "I'm a preschool virgin. What do I wear?"

"Clothes," Zoe deadpans.

"What did you wear to the twins' preschool orientation?"

After a long pause, Zoe says, "I can't even remember if I went. It was eight years ago, but if I went, I didn't dress up. Stop obsessing over this. It's only preschool."

It's only preschool? Zoe just does not get it. She knows how to act and dress and talk with the other moms because she went to a normal preschool with normal kids who had normal, mainstream parents. The closest thing I had to preschool was a box of crayons and a circus clown named Chuckles. I need Zoe to impart all of her parenting wisdom, even if she thinks I'm obsessing over trivial matters, so I don't ruin my daughter's only chance at a perfect preschool experience.

"So, jeans and a t-shirt?" I sigh.

"Wear whatever you want."

I dig through my suitcase for clean jeans. The suitcase balances on an unpacked box in a room with pink walls. That's a lot of information, so let me break it down for you. First: the pink walls. We bought our house, a two story Victorian built a century ago, without seeing it in person. This seemed efficient; now I have regrets. The online listing revealed the prior owner had a thing for pink, but I swear, the realtor must have tinkered with the photos. Online, the bedroom walls looked cotton candy pink but in person, the color is much closer to fuchsia.

Second: the unpacked box. Luke moved to Pasadena a month ago while I visited my family with our two-year-old daughter, Madison. He installed satellite t.v., plugged in the microwave, stocked the freezer with frozen dinners and ice cream, and did nothing else. Oh wait, my bad — he bought paper plates and plastic cutlery.

I extract my cleanest jeans from my suitcase (which does not mean they are clean) and then remember it is late August and too hot for jeans even at night, so I grab a pair of black Capri leggings instead. I am already wearing black Capri leggings, but they feel gross after a day spent chasing a feisty two-year-old who hates napping. This is my version of dressing up.

"I'm sorry," I say. "I'm ruining your last night on the grid."

"You're not." Zoe's voice cracks. "I'm going to miss you and your drama."

"I'm going to miss you." Now I am on the verge of blubbering — but we did the blubbering thing a month ago in Brooklyn, and if I cry now, I'll never make it to orientation.

"I'll call you next August as soon as we return to civilization," Zoe says, "and then you can tell me all about Madison's first year of preschool, which is going to be amazing."

"Okay, I can do this," I say, trying (and failing) to give myself a pep talk.

"What can go wrong? It won't be like freshman year. Ingrid won't be there."

Zoe despises my freshman roommate Ingrid. Ingrid locked me out of our room while I was showering, humiliated me in front of my friends too many times to count, and criticized my wardrobe, complexion, and childhood, but Zoe — well, it's a very long story involving a table, a sequin tube top, and a sophomore named Craig, but Zoe despises Ingrid.

"Right," I exhale slowly, "Ingrid won't be there. She can't make me perform circus tricks on command."

"Don't knock the circus tricks. Preschoolers love—"

"Absolutely not," I interrupt. "I made that mistake already in college."

"I thought it was hilarious when you made the balloon penises at Felix's Halloween party."

That is a story I am not emotionally prepared to share today. Or possibly ever.

"Mama! I hungry!" Madison stomps into my bedroom wearing her tutu. She has taken off her shirt and tattooed her stomach with a green marker. The pink tutu, which she has been wearing nonstop since my sister gave it to her three weeks ago, is also stained green. I will sneak the tutu off Madison after orientation and give it a good scrubbing. Separating Madison from her tutu when she's awake is impossible. Believe me, I've tried.

"Don't worry about tonight." Zoe offers a last piece of advice to sustain me through the next twelve months. "At least you aren't living off grid in Alaska."

By the time we finish saying goodbye, Madison is kicking me.

"Grandma is bringing cookies." I try to sound sweet and unhurried while pulling my chestnut brown hair into a ponytail, but I'm overwhelmed and on the verge of a tantrum. Should I wear makeup? I forgot to ask Zoe about makeup, and now it is too late.

I rarely bother with makeup. In college, after Ingrid said something rude about my freckles, I layered my skin with creams and powders to conceal the constellations of freckles that cover my entire face. I also scrubbed my entire body with various natural remedies, from lemon juice to buttermilk, to lighten the freckles on my arms, and I may or may not have clogged the women's shower after I slathered myself with honey. Fortunately, I dated a narcissist in law school who had one redeeming quality: he regularly and sincerely complimented my freckles. Ever since our brief fling, I have embraced the night sky of freckles that adorns my face and only wear lipstick and eyeshadow on special occasions.

"I want cookies! Now!"

"Grandma will be here in five minutes."

Madison shrieks at an inhuman frequency. I jettison any thought of doing my makeup while stifling the urge to throw a tantrum myself. She cannot be hungry. She ate a hot dog, carrots, and a generous bowl of mac and cheese less than an hour ago. Besides, it's not like I am asking her to fast all day. I just need her to leave me alone for five minutes so I can finish getting dressed for orientation before Luke and his parents (our sitters) arrive.

My phone buzzes with an incoming text:

Sorry, hon. I won't be home for dinner.

No, no, no! Luke is our designated normal parent. I'm the imposter and can't go to Orientation without my wingman. I type:

What?! We have orientation tonight.

Luke responds:

Crap, I forgot. The owner is in town and wants a working dinner. I'll be lucky if I get home before midnight.

Luke and I met at law school, although we did not date until we both started working at crazy New York law firms. About six months ago, Luke lamented the fact that he got home after Madison went to bed and missed at least half our weekend adventures. We brainstormed different ways to escape the Manhattan legal scene. Then, out of nowhere, a partner at Luke's firm asked if he would be interested in working in-house for a company with offices in downtown Los Angeles. So far, Luke loves the job, but why must tonight be the night that the owner wants a working dinner?

"I'm hungry!" Madison wails.

The Universe might want me to skip orientation.

"Grandma will be here with her yummy cookies any minute—"

"Why isn't she here now?"

The phone rings. It's my mother-in-law Ruth.

"Hi, Ellie, you will not believe what happened."

My stomach does a backwards somersault.

"Everyone is fine, but we got in a fender bender."

"Oh no!"

"We got rear-ended by a semi on the freeway."

"Oh, my god!" My in-laws drive a Prius.

"We're waiting for the tow truck. We're in the fast lane still. I could walk to the next exit ramp and call a taxi."

"Oh no, Ruth, please don't do that. You stay safe."

Madison throws herself to the floor. "I WANT GRANDMA! I WANT GRANDMA!"

It's official: the Universe wants me to skip preschool orientation.

2

F orty minutes later, I skid to a stop at the entrance to Mountain View Co-op Preschool with Madison balanced on my hip. I take a moment to collect my breath, gather my courage, wipe a smudge of chocolate off Madison's cheek, and then march beneath a horseshoe arch covered with pink bougainvillea and enter preschool.

Like our house, I used the internet to pick Madison's preschool. Online, Mountain View Co-op Preschool looked like a calm sanctuary; right now, it's an absolute madhouse. White stucco buildings circle a courtyard with a playground in the middle. Folding tables crowd the courtyard, and signs on the tables say things like "Fundraising" and "Parent Education." Parents have gathered in tight clusters around the tables, talking, laughing loudly, and broadcasting the fact that everyone already has friend here — everyone that is except me.

I don't know where to start. Madison, overwhelmed by the cacophony, tucks her head into my shoulder, and I stroke her light brown curls. This was a terrible idea. She is the only child here. I should have skipped orientation and called the office with my profuse apologies in the morning; but since we are here, I might as well learn the lay of the land.

I turn toward the building to my immediate left. The preschool buildings are all one-story high except for this one. An outside staircase leads to an upstairs room with an open door. Light spills on to the landing, and there is a cheerful babble of voices. Someone propped open the gate at the bottom of the stairs with a large rock. I transfer Madison to my other hip, step on the bottom step, and—

A stern voice surprises me. "No children on the stairs!"

I twirl around. A woman wearing a polo shirt with the preschool's logo (a smiling mountain) glares at me, and my cheeks flush with heat. "Sorry. I didn't know. Sorry. I'm new."

The woman crosses her arms. Her name tag reads "Becky, Co-op President." While researching preschools, I learned that a co-op is a preschool owned by the parents. About a dozen parents serve on its board of directors and run the school. The co-op president is essentially the Parent-in-Chief. That means it took me less than five minutes on campus to annoy the most important parent at Madison's first school. Yay!

"What are you doing?" Becky spits out the words.

"I thought... I was... I wanted to check out the school."

"The upstairs room is for board business," Becky snarls. She pushes past me and hurries up the stairs. During my lawyer years, I encountered many nasty and scary folks, from judges to opposing counsel to a partner the junior associates nicknamed "The Bear." This woman terrifies me more than all of them combined.

I kiss the top of Madison's head, expecting her to be equally, if not more, traumatized by our encounter with

Becky. Madison, however, surveys the preschool courtyard with curiosity. "Playground!" she says, and before I can react, she has escaped my arms and dashed toward the middle of the courtyard. As I hurry after her, I hear a very loud, very distinct laugh from the upstairs room and freeze. I know that laugh, but it can't be. The Universe is not that cruel. I squeeze through the crowd of parents and reach the playground as Madison runs across a suspension bridge.

The playground groans ominously. This is not the playground pictured on the Mountain View website. The website features a colorful playground with plastic tunnels, metal supports and several slides, but this playground is a wooden structure with a single slide blocked off with cones and yellow caution tape. Madison runs back to the suspension bridge and jumps several times. My heart seizes. I half-expect the entire bridge to collapse, but Madison safely scurries to another platform. I knock on a nearby pillar. It sounds hollow and smells damp and musty.

"Babysitting crisis?"

I startle as a young woman — emphasis on the "young" — joins me. She has long blonde hair pulled into a French braid, and her skin almost glows. My obstetrician referred to my pregnancy as "geriatric" but this woman makes me feel like an ancient crone.

"Total babysitting debacle," I say.

"Hi, I'm Miss Blaire. I'm one of Miss Lucy's teaching assistants."

"Then my daughter must be in your class." I nod toward Madison, who is once again jumping on the playground's questionable suspension bridge. She is still wearing her pink tutu, but I convinced her to pair it with a pink t-shirt.

"I can watch Madison if you want to visit the tables."

"That would be amazing," I gush.

I hurry toward the closest table. Its sign says "Script" so I assume preschool has a drama class or perhaps a film club for parents. I scan a flyer and learn Script has nothing to do with theater and everything to do with grocery store receipts. Fantastic. Preschool is even more complicated than I imagined possible.

I grab flyers about school maintenance, family activities, and fundraising. At the fundraising table, a tall, curvy mom with lots of blonde hair, intense red lipstick and a breathy Marilyn Monroe voice boasts about a recent swimsuit photo shoot she did in Malibu. I cannot help comparing my uniform — black leggings, baggy black shirt, Birkenstocks — to her tight beige dress and stiletto heels. She looks ready for a party at the Playboy Mansion while I look like I just survived a natural disaster. I cringe, keenly aware of my lingering pregnancy pounds and the dark circles under my eyes. Before the swimsuit model completely annihilates my self-esteem, I scurry away to the next table.

Are you interested in becoming a room parent? asks a mom wearing a Super Mario Bros. t-shirt. Her name tag reads, "Monica, Vice President."

"What does a room parent do?" I ask, feeling like an idiot.

"A room parent is the teacher's right-hand man. Or woman! Usually, it's a woman, but we have to say 'parent' because every five years, a dad wants the job."

I laugh.

"The room parents organize potlucks and class gifts for the teacher, and they also help create an item for the auction in the spring. Last year, the room mom for my son's class put the kids' handprints on an Adirondack chair."

Something inside of me stirs. While growing up in an RV parked outside a striped circus tent, I daydreamed about a front lawn with Adirondack chairs and potlucks. And having an actual teacher to whom I could give apples and coffee mugs. Being room mom sounds like a dream come true.

"That sounds fun," I mumble.

"Gather around," a voice booms over a megaphone, with plenty of screechy feedback. Becky teeters on a stepladder outside the office. "We'd like to begin the evening's main presentation."

I hurry back to the playground, half-convinced I will find Madison in tears, but no, she is handing a plastic teacup filled with sand to Miss Blaire. Madison pats damp sand into a mystery baked good, and Miss Blaire feigns taking a sip of her sand tea. She pretends to swoon and says, "This is the most delicious tea I have ever had." Madison grins with utter delight. This woman is the preschool equivalent of a Disney princess who enchants woodland creatures by singing.

"Thank you, everyone, for coming to orientation. I'm Becky, your co-op president. I'd like to welcome all the new families and remind everyone that we are a nut-free campus." Becky pauses for a smatter of applause. "I am sure you are going to love our preschool family. Just remember: we are a nut-free family! Last year, I found a peanut in the sandbox, and that's unacceptable.

"As I was thinking about what I wanted to say tonight, I came across a quote from Winston Churchill..." Becky blathers on and on as my fellow parents stir and murmur. After an interminable amount of time, Becky shouts, "I would like to introduce our board!"

Parents stop chatting as Becky introduces a dozen moms and dads. "We had a vacant position for fundraising on our board. Fundraising is our most important and difficult position." Becky pauses for dramatic effect. "Lucky for us, a new parent volunteered to take on that role. Thank you, Ingrid Smith-Livingstone!"

This is a joke. Zoe arranged this. Any moment now, Becky will say, "Just kidding, Elodie, don't worry. Your freshman roommate is not a mom at Mountain View Co-op Preschool." Or it could be another Ingrid Smith. After all, Smith is one of the most common surnames in the United States. I heard that laugh from upstairs, but this must be some horrible hilarious coincidence.

A mom with long red hair and a pale complexion joins the line of board members standing behind Becky and waves like a politician. She is wearing a jersey wrap dress and heels. Now I understand why the Universe tried to keep me from attending orientation. It was not being petty and annoying. It was trying to save me from my freshman roommate Ingrid.

I take a seat on a chair designed for a preschool butt and gesture for Madison to sit in my lap, but she ignores me and makes a beeline for a play kitchen set. Miss Blaire gives me a warm, reassuring smile, so I let Madison go.

As parents fill the empty seats, I take quick peeks for Ingrid. I briefly but seriously considered grabbing Madison and bolting for the parking lot after seeing my freshman roommate. Pasadena has other preschools. But then Madison showed me a unicorn sticker on her t-shirt. "My teacher gave it to me!" she proclaimed. As I admired the sticker, I resolved to keep Madison at Mountain View. We already ripped her away from the life she loved in Brooklyn, and I will not subject her to more turmoil — even if my freshman roommate is in league with the devil.

The classroom fills, and there is no sign of Ingrid. Her child must have another teacher. Beautiful! Tomorrow I will get a haircut, dye my hair, buy enormous sunglasses and change my name. Ingrid will never know I'm here.

A nasally voice screeches, "Oh! Em! Gee! Is that Elodie Flimbizzle!?!?"

I shrink into my seat at the sound of my maiden name. "Ingrid!" I say, feigning enthusiasm. "It's Jones now," I add hastily.

"Elodie and I were freshman roommates in college!" Ingrid announces to the entire room. Then she adds, "At a very prestigious New England school."

At least Ingrid cannot sit next to me, because I am jammed in between a dad with a handlebar mustache and a mom bouncing her knees and biting her fingernails. Ingrid smiles at Handlebar Mustache. "Do you mind if I steal your seat so I can catch up with my roomie?" Handlebar Mustache surrenders his seat to Ingrid, and Ingrid wastes no time in sitting next to me and pulling me into a sideways hug. "Isn't this exciting?" she asks when she releases me. "We get to be mom besties!"

A tiny piece of my soul dies.

"Hi, everyone! I'm Miss Lucy!" A petite brunette about fifty years old waves. She is standing in front of an enormous sheet of blue butcher paper decorated with construction paper fish and mermaids. "This is Mr. Joe," she gestures to a young man with a goatee standing next to her. "And this is Miss Blaire," she gestures to Miss Blaire, who has joined Madison at the kitchen set. "We call Miss Blaire the 'preschool institution' because she first came to Mountain View as a toddler and started working here in high school with our after-school program. It's hard to imagine this place without her. I'm excited to have Mr. Joe and Miss Blaire as my assistants this year."

The classroom door opens. Monica stands at the threshold. "Sorry to interrupt, but we need a room parent for this class. One of our veteran moms, Natasha Brown, was going to be Miss Lucy's room mom, but her family moved to London for work. I was hoping I could convince a brave mom or dad to take the job."

A voice inside me shouts, *Yes! Do it!* If I am room mom, the other parents will have to interact with me. Then I might actually make some friends and I won't be stuck with Ingrid as my "mom bestie." But even if I don't make any friends, being room mom sounds fun. Also, if I'm being completely honest, Ingrid brings out my competitive side. If she is the fundraising director, I want to do something equally helpful. I can escape the anonymous crowd by being a room mom.

Ingrid's hand shoots up. "I'd love to be the room parent!"

"Oh no, we need someone other than our new fundraising director," Monica says. "That job will keep you plenty busy."

"Anyone?" Miss Lucy clasps her hands under her chin. "It'll be fun! I promise, I am not scary."

My right hand twitches. *Go on, do it*, my inner voice hisses, but another, meaner voice inside me bellows, *You can't! You fraud! You'll screw up the year for everyone!*

Ingrid nudges me with her elbow and whispers, "You should do it."

I ignore her.

Ingrid elbows me again. "You organized amazing potlucks freshman year, remember?"

I fold my hands together and keep them safe in my lap.

The silence continues. A parent coughs. Miss Lucy's shoulders slump.

"Excuse me!" A woman with hollow cheeks and a black fanny pack pushes past Monica and bounces into the room. "I was talking to Dr. Konig about gentle parenting techniques and the psychological damage inflicted by negative language. What did I miss?"

"Nothing," Miss Lucy says. "We were recruiting a volunteer to be our room parent for the year."

"I would love to do that!" The newcomer acts as if she won the lottery.

My body relaxes. I will not be the room mom. I will not ruin my daughter's first year of preschool. Still, my inner voice whispers, *Why didn't you volunteer first?*

3

"A martini for the gentleman," a waiter sets a V-shaped glass in front of Luke, "and Unicorn Tears for the lady."

"That looks appalling," Luke says.

I raise my flute in the air. "To us!" We clink glasses and I take a tentative sip of my pink bubbly concoction. "It's like cotton candy and lemon drops had a baby." I smack my lips. "Delicious."

It is the last Saturday of August, and Luke's parents whisked Madison away for a sleepover before she starts preschool on Monday. I admire the bar — it has a speakeasy vibe at odds with my pink Unicorn Tears — and then I admire my husband. Black glasses frame Luke's sapphire blue eyes; his salt-and-pepper hair is thick and wavy; and his nose has a ridge at the top, like Michelangelo's David. He toys with the olive in his martini. "I know you are less than thrilled about Ingrid's kid going to school with Madison."

Understatement of the century.

"But do you like the preschool?"

"I don't know," I confess. "I'm worried the other parents

won't like me because they'll think I'm best friends with Ingrid."

Luke laughs. "She can't be that bad."

"Have you paid attention to anything I told you about college?"

Luke makes a dismissive sound. "You were eighteen and jammed into one bedroom. It's part of the college experience."

I love and adore my husband, but he does not appreciate the gravity of this situation. His office job guarantees regular interaction with adults; so far, the stay-at-home mom gig only guarantees regular interaction with a sidekick who expects me to manage a shocking amount of bodily fluids. If I do not make friends with Pasadena moms, I might start talking to inanimate objects; and as much as I love my coffee maker, it is not known for its conversational skills. Preschool is the ideal place to make friends, but if Ingrid sucks me into her orbit, I'll be stuck socializing with insufferable moms like Becky. I take another sip of my Unicorn Tears to soothe my nerves and get date night back on track.

A nasally voice crows, "Elodie Flimbizzle!"

I close my eyes and will myself to be invisible, but when I open my eyes, Ingrid looms over our table.

"Danforth! Danforth!" Ingrid cries. A man wearing dark jeans and a *Star Wars* t-shirt saunters over and drapes an arm over Ingrid's shoulders. Ingrid is only five feet tall, but thanks to her stiletto heels, she towers over him. "This is my husband, Danforth Livingstone. We're like Molly and Arthur Weasley!" It's an apt observation: my red-headed freshman roommate married a man with beet red hair.

"Danforth," Ingrid continues, "this is Elodie Flimbizzle, my freshman roommate."

"Elodie *Jones*," I say through gritted teeth.

"Why on earth would you want to take your husband's name? 'Flimbizzle' is so unique. Of course, I took Dan's last name because you know I always hated being Ingrid Smith." Ingrid grimaces. "Don't you remember how much I hated my last name and wished I had a last name like 'Flimbizzle'?"

Ingrid is rewriting history. She said my last name as often as possible to get laughs from the other freshmen in our dormitory, but she never coveted it.

"And you must be Elodie's husband!" Ingrid takes charge of the conversation as she always does.

"No," Luke says, "I am her lover Pierre, but don't worry, Luke and Elodie have an open relationship."

Ingrid throws her head back and laughs her annoying laugh. "We're here on date night. You should join us! How fun! A double date!"

No, no, no! Not fun! Not fun at all!

"That would be great!" Luke says.

The traitorous bastard. I will have to kill him when we get home.

The hostess steps into the bar. "Jones? Your table is ready."

Ingrid beams at the hostess. "Margaret! You won't believe it! We ran into our friends at the bar! The four of us will take a table together. The patio, please."

I shoot Margaret the hostess a pleading glance, but she says, "No problem," and leads the four of us outside to a brick patio with a stone fireplace and a canopy of vines growing overhead.

"Isn't this delightful? It is so delightful," Ingrid says as we take our seats. A nearby heat lamp illuminates Ingrid's unblemished complexion. Does the woman even have pores? I wonder if her skincare routine is the same as it was in college. (Elaborate, expensive, and exotic.) A waitress with a pixie cut stops at our table, and before she can speak, Ingrid says, "Melody, so good to see you. We will start with a bottle of La Guiberte and the charcuterie."

I love charcuterie, but I still wish Ingrid had not ordered for the entire table. Maybe I wanted crab cakes.

The waitress smiles and retreats.

"Do you like Mountain View? To be honest, I think it's a bit proletariat, but Danny Jr.'s a legacy. Didn't you say it's gotten scruffy, Danforth?"

Danforth grunts without looking up from his phone.

"They still have the same play structure that Danforth played on. It's decrepit!"

"Hey," Danforth bumps their shoulders together. "I'm not that old. Just because I'm a few years older than you—"

"Oh darling, I was not making a joke about your age." Ingrid blows him a kiss and he grunts and returns to glaring at his phone. "There's a dedication plaque by the bridge that I'm sure Elodie saw." I did not. "It says the Howard Family built the bridge in 1972. I think it has termites."

Our waitress returns with the wine and pours a little for Ingrid. Ingrid buries her nose in the glass, closes her eyes, and inhales; then she takes a slow sip, swishes the wine around her mouth, smacks her lips appreciatively, and says, "Perfect, Melody. You should pour yourself a little if you like."

As Melody fills our glasses, Ingrid says, "Of course I placed Danny Jr. on the waitlist for Tiny Geniuses Academy when we started trying to get pregnant, but they do not place children until they are three years old, and Danny's an August baby, just turned two. I wanted him to have something to prep him for Tiny Geniuses Academy. I just hope the other children at Mountain View do not drag him down. He is very precocious."

"Darling." Danforth sounds exasperated. How many times must I tell you? You can't call our son 'precocious' so long as he craps in a diaper."

Ingrid laughs, and a moment later, my tote bag vibrates.

I check my phone. Luke texted. I take a sip of my water and slide open the message.

She laughs like a dolphin.

I choke on the water and nearly spray it all over the table, but Ingrid is too busy talking about the advantages of the pre-college curriculum at Tiny Geniuses Academy to notice.

I surreptitiously text Luke.

Should we fake an emergency?

He immediately replies:

Are you kidding? And miss this train wreck?

Ingrid continues her monologue until the waitress arrives with the charcuterie. She orders a second bottle of wine and a few more appetizers and then tries to order entrees for the entire table, but Danforth places a restraining hand on her arm and says, in a warning voice, "Sweetheart."

"I have a sixth sense for what people should order, but Dan is right. People need to order for themselves. But Elodie, you will love the lamb and Luke, the short ribs are a dream."

Damnit. I wanted to order the lamb, but I order the scallops to spite Ingrid. Luke orders the short ribs. He always orders the short ribs if they are on the menu, but I still text him an angry emoji face.

Ingrid chatters about their home renovations, the irregularity of Danforth Jr.'s bowel movements, and the trip they are taking to Hawaii for Christmas. Luke and I exchange texts, and I actually enjoy myself. Then Danforth Sr. ditches his phone and draws Luke into a conversation about fantasy football, and I am left alone with Ingrid's self-important prattle.

Ingrid's phone, resting on the table near her wine glass, buzzes. "It's Becky! There is so much important board business."

I sit awkwardly as Ingrid sends a flurry of texts about "important board business" and Luke and Danforth Sr. jabber about fantasy football during what was supposed to be a romantic dinner with my husband. Instead, Ingrid hijacked us into a double date. Since I am being ignored, I check my phone. No texts. I can't even text my best friend—

Hold everything. Zoe might be off the grid in Alaska, but her mother-in-law is keeping her phone safe. I can send my best friend all the texts that I want and then she will have something to read when, desperate for gossip and connection, she emerges from the wilderness. My fingers fly:

You will not believe who I am having dinner with!

INGRID.

She has a son.

He is in Madison's preschool class.

Save me!

I keep texting Zoe until Melody arrives with our entrees. As I cut a scallop in half, Ingrid returns to the subject of preschool. "Elodie, I cannot believe you let that Charlotte woman be room mom instead of you."

Luke perks up. "Elodie was going to be room mom?"

My mouth is too full with scallop to protest.

"We needed someone to volunteer to be room mom, and I thought Elodie should do it," Ingrid says. "I think it's so important to be involved with your child's education."

"I want to be involved, but I'm too inexperienced. Besides, I'm too busy. I have to finish unpacking."

"We're nearly done," Luke says.

I kick his ankle under the table.

"I didn't go to preschool." I drag a scallop aggressively through the lemon garlic sauce drizzled artfully around the plate. "Let me be a regular mom this year."

"Nonsense," Ingrid says. "If you can juggle nine eggs blindfolded, you can handle anything, which reminds me, Elodie, you simply must tell Becky about all your circus talents so she can use you at school events."

"That's a great idea," Luke says.

I shake my head vehemently. "Absolutely not. I want to blend in."

"Life is too short to blend in," Ingrid quips.

"Says the woman with a completely normal childhood. Everyone thought I was a freak in college."

"No one—" Ingrid protests.

"Remember how you made me make balloon animals at Felix's Halloween party?"

"I suggested—"

"Remember all the frat boys harassing me to make balloon penises?" I hiss.

Both husbands choke on their wine.

"I've never heard this story," Luke says.

"Everyone was mocking me." My chest tightens. "I was amusing because I had grown up in the circus."

"You were interesting," Ingrid insists. "Intriguing. Mysterious."

"Freakish." I spat out the word. "I'm not passing that legacy on to my daughter. She won't be the weird kid with circus relatives."

"You—" Ingrid protests again, but this time, Danforth silences her with a hand on her shoulder.

"Please, Ingrid, I don't want anyone to know I grew up with the circus. I don't want them to know I can juggle or make balloon animals. Can we please keep my past in the past?"

"Okay fine," Ingrid moans. "If you want to keep all your amazing skills secret, I'll honor your wish."

"Promise?" I say, perhaps a bit petulantly.

"Promise."

Ingrid wants to say something more, but she restrains herself and we eat in silence for the next minute. Before the silence becomes too awkward, she says, "It will be such a relief when Danny goes to Tiny Geniuses Academy next year. At least they don't have thieves."

"What?" I ask. "Thieves?"

"I thought you knew. Everyone was talking about it after our session with Miss Lucy."

"I thought orientation was over after Miss Lucy finished." My voice trails away. I sprinted for the car with Madison when the session with Miss Lucy ended because she was teetering on the brink of Toddler Meltdown Mode.

"Officially, yes." Ingrid smiles and cuts her lamb expertly. "But lots of parents stayed to chat and about twenty of us ended up at a bar in Sierra Madre."

My cheeks flush hot. I am right back in the first weeks of my freshman year of college, hiding in our dorm room, living off potato chips and Lucky Charms, while Ingrid went to room parties, snuck into frat basements, and had a dazzling social life. She had her entire college life planned, from her major to her study abroad program to the subject of her senior thesis, and I lost my schedule and was twenty minutes late to my first class. But that was when I was eighteen. Some informal post-orientation socializing should not trigger me now, even if Ingrid bonded with other parents at a bar while I scrubbed green marker stains from Madison's tutu. I'm a grown ass woman, with a husband, child, and mortgage!

Ingrid savors a bite of her lamb and moans in ecstasy. "Next time we come here, Elodie, you must get the lamb."

Would Ingrid press charges if I lunged across the table right now and throttled her?

"What's up with thieves at preschool? Danforth Sr. asks.

"What? Oh, that." Ingrid waves a dismissive hand and takes a slow sip of the wine. "A few wallets went missing during Orientation. Monica — she's the co-op VP — says nothing like this has happened since her eldest start preschool ten years ago."

My chest tightens. Ingrid is already on a first name basis with the co-op's president and vice president; she is the new fundraising director; she even knows what family donated the playground. Meanwhile, I will have to spend the weekend memorizing the Parent Handbook so I do not wreck my daughter's shot at a normal childhood.

Zoe may be off the grid, but I know what she would

advise: I should limit my contact with Ingrid or she will ruin Madison's first year of preschool, just like she ruined my freshman year of college. I, however, have an idea that is either really stupid or absolutely brilliant.

"Here," I thrust my phone at Ingrid. "Send me a text. Then I can add you to my contacts."

Ingrid beams. "Great idea! We'll keep each other in the loop about preschool gossip."

Exactly.

4

"Smile! Say cheese! Look at me!"

Ingrid shifts her camera from the vertical to horizontal position while crouching on the pavement, angling the lens for the one photo that will perfectly capture this moment.

"Let's try the crayon frame again," Ingrid says. She whisks away the oversized novelty pencils that Madison and Danforth Jr. were clutching and hands them a frame she made from poster board and actual crayons. Ingrid fusses over Danforth Jr.'s hair, adjusts the collar of his Burberry shirt, and then returns to snapping photos.

"Danny, hold your side up a little higher. No, not that high. Okay, a little higher, stop! That's perfect! Big smile!"

Parents and children stream past us as they promenade into preschool. More than a few moms gape at Ingrid's elaborate set-up, and I cringe. I should have resisted when Ingrid texted last night and told me to meet her outside preschool a half hour before the official start of school for "a few quick photos." I spent every free moment yesterday studying the Parent Handbook so I could blend in, and now I stand out like a clown at a funeral.

This is what I get for giving Ingrid my phone number.

"Shout hooray!" Ingrid says.

"Daddy!" Madison drops her end of the frame and bolts toward Luke.

Luke scoops her up. "Is my big girl ready for her first day of preschool?"

"Yay!"

I shrug apologetically, but do not drag Madison back to the photo shoot. Madison wriggles out of Luke's arms, and the three of us pass beneath the arch of bougainvillea. Miss Blaire greets us at the entrance gate. "Madison!" Miss Blaire says, as if they are old friends. "I adore your pink tutu. Can I borrow it?"

Madison giggles. I tried to convince her to leave her tutu at home this morning, explaining the hazards of glue, glitter and paint, but Madison was deaf to my reasoning. At least I wriggled it off Madison last night after she fell asleep and scrubbed away the green marker stains, some crusty bits of oatmeal, and a brown blob that I desperately hope was play dough.

"Is that tutu good for spinning?"

Madison obliges with a spin and elaborate curtsy, and Miss Blaire claps. She is wearing a green apron decorated with enamel pins of a bluebird, a smiling sun, and a box of crayons. On her chin, a tiny smudge of pink paint adds to her radiance, and her shoes are silver glittery Toms. If Central Casting needs a preschool teacher, I have their woman.

Luke and I each take one of Madison's hands and we walk into the courtyard. "Up!" Madison says. We swing her arms and on the count of three, hoist her into the air. Nothing could ruin this magical moment.

"Good morning, Miss Blaire!" Ingrid says in a voice that projects across the entire courtyard. "I got you a little something to celebrate your engagement. Congratulations!"

The magic is gone.

"Thank you!" Miss Blaire squeals. Did I miss the memo about Miss Blaire's engagement? I am struggling to keep the teachers' names straight while Ingrid celebrates their romantic milestones.

Danforth Sr., wearing shorts, a ratty t-shirt, and flip-flops, and carrying a skateboard, slouches into the court-yard. "Luke! Did you see the end of the Patriots game?"

"Absolutely ridiculous," Luke says.

"You won't believe how our Commish just screwed the Taco again."

The men wander away, immersed in a conversation about fantasy football or Mexican cuisine or maybe both.

Ingrid and Danforth Jr. hurry over to Madison and me. Ingrid's camera is slung over one shoulder and she is wearing a wrap dress and heels. There is a long line for the outdoor sink, but Ingrid still poses Madison and Danforth Jr. and makes them wash their hands three times before she believes she has captured the moment. Then she makes them hold hands and meander to Miss Lucy's room while she walks backwards and snaps even more photos.

When we finally reach Miss Lucy's classroom, Ingrid will not let the children simply enter. She has a vision and is not afraid to execute it. She summons Miss Lucy, who gamely poses in the doorway to greet Danforth Jr. and Madison, waving as Ingrid encourages the children to smile. I suppose I will be grateful for Ingrid's shamelessness in twenty or thirty years when I am poring over old photos, but right now, I might die.

Ingrid photographs Danforth Jr. and Madison inspecting their cubbies and pressing their noses against an impressive saltwater aquarium. Luke and Danforth Sr. trail our progress around the room, quibbling over fantasy football tactics. Other parents and children explore the room and socialize. A mom with dark brown skin is wearing a mustard yellow fedora and chatting with a mom sporting pigtail buns, while a dad with a handlebar mustache shows something on his phone to a dad in sweatpants. A pregnant mom kneads play dough with her child while laughing at something Mr. Joe just said. People are connecting and establishing friendships while I am stuck in Ingrid's shadow.

"Ell-oo-dee," Ingrid whines. "Could you make the kids do something spontaneous? I need more candids."

"Doesn't that defeat the whole meaning of 'candid'?"

Ingrid shrieks her dolphin laugh. Parents stare. I make a mental note to never be funny in Ingrid's company again.

Danforth Jr. wriggles away from Ingrid and plops down at a table of railroad tracks. Madison takes an empty seat at the play dough table and squishes the dough, looking perfectly at home. My heart swells with a mixture of joy and sadness. Damn, motherhood is complicated.

"Good morning, Madison." Miss Lucy crouches down by the play dough table. "Would you like to make a name tag for your cubby?"

Madison does not answer, but follows her teacher to a low rectangular table. Miss Lucy fans out a rainbow of construction paper and Madison jabs her finger at a pink sheet. Miss Lucy writes "Madison" in sharpie on the bottom of the sheet while spelling her name out loud. Madison watches intently. "Would you like to decorate your name tag?" Miss Lucy gestures to a pile of stickers. Madison nods solemnly.

I take an empty seat next to Madison and gesture furiously at Luke. He rolls his eyes but joins us. "Can we help, sweetie?"

"No!" Madison peels off a cat sticker and adds it to her name tag. "Bye, Daddy! Bye, Mommy!" Then she reaches her hand into my rib cage, rips out my beating heart, and throws it in the trash can. At least, it feels that way.

Luke laughs and pecks Madison on the cheek. I stagger to my feet. We talked about this moment all weekend. We read picture books celebrating the first day of preschool and I promised I would always come back. I prepared myself for tears and tantrums. But this indifference? This callous disregard for my departure? What the hell?

I give Madison a kiss on the top of her head. Her brown curls do not even reach her shoulders yet. She peels off a zebra sticker and places it next to the cat. "Bye!" I say with false cheer, and wait for a crack in Madison's calm demeanor. My daughter contemplates a sheet of star stickers. A few feet away, a child clenches her mother's leg, huge tears rolling down her cheeks. My daughter drops the sheet of star stickers and returns to the animals. Madison wants me to leave. I am such a wretched mother that she craves our separation. She'll be applying to a boarding school for kindergarten.

"Madison feels securely attached to you," Miss Lucy whispers as I shuffle toward the door. "She knows her mama loves her and will always come back."

I try to say "thank you" but my throat chokes on the words. I blink back a few tears and duck outside before I am the mother wrapped around her child's leg, wailing and screaming a lament. Several parents stand outside the class-room. I should be friendly and say hello, but I lack the courage to interject myself into their conversations. These parents — especially the mom with the fedora — seem way out of my league.

Ingrid emerges from the classroom and accosts me with her camera. "How precious are they?" She scrolls through images on the preview screen and I must admit, her photos are pretty darn cute. Before I can answer, though, Ingrid spots Becky the co-op president on the other side of the courtyard and says, "Sorry, Elodie, got to dash! Board busi-ness!" She sprints across the sandbox, a flash of red on the bottom of her heels. Ingrid knows this is preschool, not an episode of *Sex and The City*, right?

I cast another forlorn glance at the parents chatting outside Miss Lucy's door before hurrying toward Luke. He is waiting for me ten feet away, frowning at his phone, but reaches an arm around my shoulder and gives me a squeeze before we walk back to the parking lot. Well, I may not have sowed the seeds for any new friendships, but at least I can enjoy a large iced coffee at Target without my toddler side-kick. Heck, I can go to a fancy coffee shop with long lines before Target. My heart thumps wildly. I do not need to rush into any Pasadena friendships. I should relish my alone time—

"Leaving so soon?" A woman clutching a stack of clip-boards steps into my path. For a moment, I assume the woman is an administrator, but then memory slides into place and I realize it is Miss Lucy's room mom Charlotte.

"Here you go," Charlotte continues, not bothering to wait for a response. She thrusts a clipboard into my hands.

"What is this?" I thumb through a stack of forms.

"Paperwork, so the parents in Miss Lucy's class can know

each other better." Charlotte leans toward me and flicks through the pages. "Background about your child, family, where you live, interests, blood type—"

"Blood type?" I laugh, appreciating Charlotte's sense of humor. "Is that in case a parent is a vampire and prefers O negative?"

Charlotte's upper lip curls. "If a child needs a blood transfusion, this will help us locate a donor."

Behind Charlotte, Luke grimaces. I stifle a laugh and focus on Charlotte. "When do you need these finished?"

"Before you leave."

I thumb through the pages. These are more detailed than the paperwork I filled out to enroll Madison at Mountain View. Thank goodness I did not volunteer to be room mom. It would never have occurred to me to ask parents about their blood type.

My eyes dart toward Miss Lucy's classroom, where several parents hold similar clipboards. I scan the courtyard. None of the other parents are filling out forms for their room mom. I look at Luke for help, but he is looking at his phone again.

"I don't have a pen."

Charlotte unzips her fanny pack and whips out a ballpoint pen.

Somewhere behind me, Mr. Joe says, "Michael, no, we do not climb on tables."

Charlotte's nostrils flare. "Mr. Joe," she says, already hurrying away, "we do not use negative language with Michael. It damages his ego."

Luke sidles over. "Do you need help with this?"

"No," I sigh. "Go to work while you can."

"I love you." H kisses my cheek and flees the courtyard.

I join the other parents with clipboards. The dad with

the handlebar mustache mutters, "Potty training questionnaire?"

The mom with the fedora says, "This is our third year at Mountain View and I've never had to fill out extra paperwork for a room mom. I don't even remember my blood type."

The woman with pigtail buns says, "There's a contract!"

I flip ahead and find the contract. My jaw drops open. "The contract prohibits using words like 'no' around the children."

I would never have asked the parents to identify their blood type and sign contracts. Regret swells inside my chest, but alas, it is too late now. I had my chance to be room mom, but I let my fears get the best of me and now a lunatic room mom reigns over Miss Lucy's class.

"Who is Braxton Hicks?" Handlebar Mustache Dad rubs his chin.

I bite my lower lip. I cannot laugh at a dad on the first day of preschool. But Fedora Mom sniggers, Pigtail Buns giggles, I chortle, and then everyone laughs, and soon I am laughing so hard that I gasp for air. I feel reborn.

Miss Lucy steps outside to investigate the commotion. Her eyes laser in on the clipboards. "Genevieve, do you mind?" Miss Lucy gestures toward Fedora Mom, who happily hands over her clipboard. Miss Lucy scans the forms, maintaining a poker face. She needs to move to Vegas if the preschool gig doesn't work out. "This is innovative," she says diplomatically, "but Dr. Konig needs to look at these before we let parents fill them out."

Miss Lucy has a room mom, but who will be the room mom's handler?

5

"When will the doctor see me?"

"I don't know," the receptionist says. "The doctor is a very busy man."

I sit on an itchy chair and scowl at a framed sign on the waiting room wall.

DR. DANKWORTH REQUIRES ALL PATIENTS TO STAY IN THE WAITING ROOM UNTIL CALLED, OR THEY LOSE THEIR APPOINTMENT. PATIENTS MUST PAY FULL PRICE FOR ALL MISSED APPOINTMENTS UNLESS CANCELLED A WEEK IN ADVANCE.

Wonderful. I scheduled a 9 a.m appointment so I would be on time for preschool pickup, and now I am might be late — Miss Lucy will think I'm a negligent, uncaring mother.

I open the novel I brought and try to read. It's impossible. A television blasts a nature program about mountain goats that no one is watching, which is impressive given the number of patients crammed into this room. Someone occupies every available seat plus three adults stand by the reception desk while a woman plays with her baby on the floor. Also, the room stinks of cigarette smoke.

I put the novel back in my tote bag and take out my phone. I have not texted Zoe since my accidental double date with Ingrid. She needs updates!

> Ingrid's son was wearing Dolce & Gabbana sneakers this morning at drop-off.

I hit send as Dr. Dankworth enters the waiting room. He has wild eyebrows, a bulbous nose, and an orange tan that reminds me of Donald Trump. Dr. Dankworth gestures toward me, and I stand. Then the doctor says in a gravelly voice, "How's my favorite patient?" and the gentleman to my right stands, and the two men exchange fist bumps. I have been here for two hours, and that man arrived eight minutes ago. Am I being hazed?

I send Zoe more texts to distract myself from the time:

> Then Ingrid warned her son to stay out of the sandbox so he does not ruin his new shoes.

> WTF? Her poor kid.

> She keeps telling people we were freshmen roommates and doesn't understand how we fell out of touch after graduation.

A gravelly voice shouts, "Where's the Ramirez file? Why is it so hard to find decent help?" The receptionist springs from her seat and dashes to parts unknown.

A few minutes later, the doctor's favorite patient waltzes through the waiting room. If Dr. Dankworth summons me now, I can stay for my appointment, but the doctor does not appear. From the office's innards, something clangs and someone grunts, reminding me of the cacophony some men make while lifting weights at the gym.

I check my phone, but Zoe has not replied. Obviously. She is churning butter in the woods of Alaska. I sigh and google "places to take my preschooler in the Pasadena area" and start a list including the zoo, the Arboretum, and a local children's museum. Maybe, if I fill my social media feed with photos of my amazing life in Pasadena, Zoe will persuade Paul to move to Pasadena when they return to the grid.

A comment on a blog post called "The Pasadena Mom Scene" catches my eye.

```
Where can I see Centerfold Mama in the
wild? Huge fan, coming to Pasadena for
the Rose Parade.
```

Dozens of responses follow this comment. My favorites include:

```
She hates Pasadena. Try Beverly Hills
and Malibu.
```

```
Why on earth would anyone want to meet
Centerfold Mama? She was in my
prenatal yoga class and made the
teacher cry.
```

```
I found out the Prince is going to my
daughter's preschool. We loved that
preschool, but I transferred my
daughter.
```

I am intrigued. Google tells me that *Centerfold Mama* is a

swimsuit model with a son about the same age as Madison and a podcast that features an endless series of cruel, often vicious rants about motherhood. Moms debate whether *Centerfold Mama* (no one knows her name) is an actress stirring up drama for fun or if she is just an awful human being, but both sides confess they cannot stop listening to her show.

Say no more. I open my podcast app and search for *Centerfold Mama*. It pops right up along with a picture of a woman with a lot of blonde hair wearing a string bikini while balancing a baby on one hip. I subscribe and check the time again. That's it. I'm leaving. I'll find a more reliable psychiatrist before I run out of Zoloft. I stand just as the doctor appears.

"Jones? Elodie Jones?"

"That's me."

"What? Were you leaving? Scared I might have some insights into your psychosis?"

"Um." Is he allowed to say that?

"This way." Dr. Dankworth, now sweaty and out of breath, heads down a carpeted corridor, and I spy several large weight machines and a shelf of barbels as the doctor leads me, not to his office, but to a narrow and doorless kitchen.

"Wow, you have a lot of freckles." Dr. Dankworth opens a cabinet, pulls out a tiny mug and saucer, and places them next to a silver espresso machine with several knobs and levers. A handwritten note taped to the side of the espresso machine reads, "For Dr. Dankworth's Use Only — No Staff."

Dr. Dankworth pours coffee beans into the espresso machine, hits a button, and over the sound of grinding beans, shouts, "I can assess a patient's deepest psychiatric complaints just from their physical appearance. Your freckles tell me your parents subjected you to severe child neglect by never giving you sunblock."

I bristle. "My parents did not neglect me. They gave me more sunblock than my siblings."

"Ah," Dr. Dankworth gloats and tamps down the freshly ground beans. "So they made you self-conscious about your freckles."

I am speechless.

Dr. Dankworth fiddles with the espresso machine and a few moments later, fresh coffee pours into the waiting miniature mug. "If it's not your freckles, what brings you to my care?"

"I just moved here from New York—"

"The Big Apple?"

"Brooklyn."

"That's a little better. Everyone in Manhattan has psychiatric issues."

I titter nervously.

"Well, you found the best psychiatrist in Pasadena. I am the best. You take Zoloft. Tell me about that."

Office staff buzzes nearby. The waiting room shares a wall with this kitchen. Dr. Dankworth raises his eyebrows expectantly, so I whisper, "Well, I did—"

"What?! I can't hear you!"

"I'd rather speak privately about this."

A last drop of espresso splutters into the mug. "Fine." Dr. Dankworth impatiently motions for me to exit the kitchen, saunters down the hall and pushes open the door to his office.

Dr. Dankworth sits on a leather swivel chair behind an enormous mahogany desk. The only other seating in the office is a couch covered with doilies and at least ten throw pillows. Sitting down, I discover it is even itchier than the furniture in the waiting room. I'd kill for a folding chair.

To my right, a large window affords a spectacular view of the San Gabriel Mountains, a range of rolling peaks north of Pasadena. From the preschool parking lot, you can glimpse the mountains peeking over the tops of nearby apartment buildings, but the view is nothing like this. I want to take photos with my phone.

I tear my gaze away from the window and study the office. Diplomas and certificates hang on the walls, and on the desk, there is a framed photograph of the doctor, his wife, and five children. Everywhere else, chaos reigns. Empty takeout containers, mugs, and a half dozen ashtrays filled with cigarette butts litter the desk and floor while cardboard boxes filled with books compete with stacks of patient files for floor space. The office reeks.

Dr. Dankworth slurps his espresso and gestures for me to speak.

"I had postpartum depression after my daughter was born."

"When was that?"

"2013."

He stares at me.

"I had insomnia, anxiety, and some OCD rituals, like checking the locks at night. I worked with a therapist and took Zoloft. My old psychiatrist thought I was ready to wean off Zoloft."

"I'll be the judge of that." Slurp. "Aside from Zoloft, what do you do to take care of your mental health?"

"I take walks."

"Good."

"I-"

A phone rings, and the doctor pulls out a phone from

his pocket. "Hello? Oh hey... No, I'm not busy. I was just thinking about you... Let me check my calendar... Is that movie with the werewolf out yet? No? Okay, next time... No, no, don't let me keep you. Bye!"

Dr. Dankworth glares at me, and when I do not speak, he snaps, "How was your childhood?"

"Um..." I stall, debating how much I want to divulge during our first appointment.

"Parents divorced?"

"No, they are happily married."

"Were you ever in a plane crash?"

"No."

"Ever abducted by a stranger?"

"No." I am struggling to keep the impatience from my voice.

"So you had a standard childhood?"

"I guess so."

Mental health professionals would drool over my childhood, but I don't have time to be a case study when the doctor runs two hours late and I need to leave immediately, if not sooner, to pick up my daughter from preschool. As far as Dr. Dankworth is concerned, I had a standard childhood, thank you very much.

Dr. Dankworth continues the Inquisition. "Do you have friends in Pasadena?"

"Not yet," I say, "but I'm hoping to make some friends at preschool."

"My wife met all her friends in baby classes."

The doilies itch through my leggings. "I considered being room mom to have an excuse to meet everyone."

The doctor makes a rude sound, leans back in his chair, puts his feet on top of the desk, and picks up a nearby chart.

"You shouldn't be room mom. It says here," he jabs the chart, "that you used to be a lawyer."

I nod.

"Go back to being a lawyer. Then you'll be ready to wean off Zoloft. Being a room mom will just prolong your suffering."

My eyes flick over to the clock on the doctor's desk.

"Am I keeping you from something more important than this?" His brow furrows and with his orange-adjacent complexion, he looks like a cranky Jack-o'-lantern.

"I have to pick my daughter up from preschool at 11:30."

The doctor types something on his laptop and says, "It's your brain, not mine. If you don't want to invest time in your wellbeing..." his voice trails away meaningfully.

"I take my mental health seriously. I made my appointment for 9 a.m. so I could do this and pick my daughter up from preschool."

"I'm a busy man, and I do my best to honor appointment times, but I expect my patients to be flexible. Fine." He drums his fingers on the desk. "We will keep you on the same dose of Zoloft, and I will see you next month."

"Next month?"

"Unless you would rather come back sooner?"

"No, it's just—" I heave myself off the couch and scramble to scoop up several pillows that tumbled to the floor. "I saw my old psychiatrist every three or four months."

Dr. Dankworth takes a long slurp of espresso. "I'm not just here to sign off on your next Zoloft fix. Do you want to make progress?"

"I do." My face flushes with heat.

"Then I'll see you next month for your entire appointment."

6

"I screwed up. I should have picked a different preschool."

"What?" Luke pours coffee into his travel mug. "Madison loves the place."

"I know," I say, fidgeting with my ponytail, "but I picked a co-op, so I have to volunteer in the classroom."

"Isn't that why you picked Mountain View?"

"Yes, but it's my first volunteer day and I don't know what I'm doing. I waited for the second week of school so I could learn the ropes, but I'm still clueless. What if I traumatize a child? Am I supposed to offer to pay for their therapy? What if I have to make Madison do something she hates, and she feels betrayed?"

"Elodie, my love, you're 'swirling the drain.'"

"Swirling the drain" is code for "freaking out over very unlikely scenarios." I could hit him. Then again, the man has a point.

"What if I screw this up?"

"Then we'll sell everything and start a pumpkin farm in

Arizona," Luke says as he fills another travel mug with coffee.

"You're crazy," I laugh.

"Nope, you're the crazy one for even worrying about this." Luke's eyes twinkle as he pours a splash of cream into my coffee, just the way I like it.

An hour later, I am seated in a circle with Miss Lucy, Miss Blaire, Mr. Joe, the kids, my fellow volunteers and our room mom Charlotte. I'm wearing an official yellow apron, so the kids know I am here to help, but Charlotte is not wearing an apron. She gave me a withering look when I asked if she was volunteering today. For those keeping score, that's Elodie 0, Elodie's Cluelessness 1.

As we finish singing *The Itsy Bitsy Spider*, Charlotte's son Michael jumps up, steps on a child's hand, knocks my shoulder with his butt, pushes his way out of the circle, and throws a wooden toy car at my back. I yelp.

"Michael," Miss Lucy says, "We do not throw—"

Charlotte clears her throat.

Miss Lucy's face tightens. "Michael, please join us for circle time. You can play with the cars later."

Michael throws another car that lands between my shoulder blades.

Miss Lucy and Mr. Joe exchange a meaningful glance, and Mr. Joe rises to handle the Michael situation. Miss Lucy nods at Miss Blaire, and Miss Blaire, who is sitting criss-cross-apple-sauce with two adoring girls on either side, strums her pink ukulele. A very impressive engagement ring sparkles on her hand as she begins a rousing round of *The Wheels On The Bus*.

Mr. Joe whispers, "No, Michael—"

Charlotte coughs.

"Michael," Mr. Joe says, "stop—"

Charlotte hisses, "That's on the list of damaging words. Didn't you read the handouts I gave you?"

Michael picks up a block and throws it at the aquarium. Mr. Joe lunges and catches it, so Michael kicks Mr. Joe and bolts toward the door. Mr. Joe limps after him, saying, "Michael, it's Circle Time. Please sit—"

"If he wants to go outside, let him go outside." Charlotte jumps to her feet. Poor Miss Blaire soldiers on and keeps strumming her ukulele, but no one is singing. The Michael Show is far too exciting.

Charlotte opens the door, Michael dashes outside and with a subtle eyebrow lift, Miss Lucy tells Mr. Joe to close the door and let Charlotte supervise her kid. We finish *The Wheels of the Bus* and the rest of circle time is blissfully uneventful.

"Could you man the manipulatives table?" Miss Lucy asks me as the children scatter. "It's right outside the classroom."

"Sure!" I say cheerfully, though I have no idea what the "manipulatives table" is. As I head for my post, I stop by the aquarium where Madison is watching a starfish creep along the pebbles. "I'm going outside, sweetie pie. Do you want to come with me?"

Madison ignores my question and asks, "Why does the starfish have so many legs?"

"Um, that's a good question—" but Madison hurries away to the play kitchen before I answer.

I step outside and spot a table covered with Duplos. An index card taped to the top says "Manipulatives Table." Victory! A few children click pieces together, and I hover over them, wondering if I am supposed to supervise or if I should crouch down and build something. I crouch and become engrossed in helping a child build a rocket-house-dog.

"Is that precious child over there in your class?"

I look up and see Monica, the co-op vice president. I stand and we watch together as Michael jumps on the playground's suspension bridge and shouts "Shit!" on endless repeat. Charlotte's ban on negative language apparently does not extend to obscenities.

"Yes," I sigh. "Poor Mr. Joe."

Poor Mr. Joe asks Michael to stop jumping on the suspension bridge — I'm not sure the ancient structure can take much more of Michael's abuse — but Charlotte shouts, "Do whatever you want, Michael! Listen to your heart! Don't let Mr. Joe crush your spirit!"

"She has a unique parenting style," Monica says. "I heard about her extra paperwork."

I lower my voice. "Is Charlotte allowed to stay all day and let her child—" I struggle for words.

"Run amok, tyrannize the teachers and endanger all the other children?"

Michael jumps off the suspension bridge, crashes on top of two children, and runs toward the outdoor sink.

"You took the words right out of my mouth."

"This situation..." Monica frowns. "It's unique. I've been at Mountain View for ten years, and I've seen some crazy moms, but wow, this is a special brand of crazy."

"I have not had enough caffeine for this drama," I say, as Michael knocks over an easel.

"I can't handle preschool without coffee."

"I left mine on the kitchen counter," I groan. "My husband made it special for my first volunteer day..."

"There's a coffee machine in the office."

"Can I use it?" My mind recalls a memory of the note taped to Dr. Dankworth's espresso machine.

"Of course. The official school policy is that parents are not supposed to drink soda or coffee during their volunteer day because," Monica makes sarcastic air quotes, "it 'corrupts the kids.' But the unofficial policy is that everyone brings the caffeine poison of their choice, and we just make sure the hot beverages stay out of the kids' reach."

"I'm supposed to watch the manipulatives table."

"I'll cover for you. Miss Lucy supports a parent's need for caffeine. Now Miss Carol," Monica pauses. "Miss Carol can be erratic."

"Really?" My ears perk up.

"Get your coffee, and I'll give you the lowdown."

Oh my god! I am about to get insider information before Ingrid!

I hurry toward the office and duck inside. Orchids are everywhere. There are orchids on the window ledges, orchids on the tops of every bookcase and shelf, and orchids on the white L-shaped reception desk. Several more orchids crowd around one of two computers. Amidst the orchids, a name plate reads "Dr. Konig, Mountain View Preschool Co-op Director." I make a mental note to give her an orchid for Christmas.

No one else is here, so I scan the room for the coffee machine. I spot it on a bookcase alongside a "living room corner" created by two couches, one love seat, three chairs — all shabby, all sporting distinct patterns — and a coffee table with a basket of random toys. Preschool families must have donated their living room rejects. I walk behind a striped couch, reach my hand toward a rotating tower of coffee pods, and —

"Can I help you?" a sweet voice chirps from behind me.

"Ahh!" I shout and knock over the tower of coffee pods.

"Sorry, sorry," and a woman with hair dyed purple and wearing a striped shirt tucked into a floral skirt crawls out from under the L-shaped desk. "I have to reboot the internet at least once a day," Purple Hair says as she collapses on an office chair customized with yellow faux fur.

"Monica said I could get coffee," I stammer.

Purple Hair nods. "That's what it's there for."

I fix the toppled tower of coffee pods and select caramel vanilla. Too late, I remember my manners and say, "I'm Elodie, Madison's mom."

Purple Hair reaches to shake my hand and says, "I'm Meredith, the preschool's receptionist, office manager, and plumber."

I press the button to brew coffee, and steaming brown liquid streams into my waiting paper cup. With caffeine in hand, volunteering today will be a breeze.

"Where is the director?" Charlotte storms into the office. The air around her cackles. Through the open door, I glimpse Miss Blaire and several parents peering inside.

"Can I help you?" Meredith folds her hands in her lap, nonplussed by Charlotte's apparent rage.

"I need the director."

The coffeemaker is dispensing my coffee in slow motion. I need my caffeine fix, but I also need to get as far away from Charlotte's wrath as possible.

"Dr. Konig is not in the office at the moment," Meredith says. "Can I help?"

"The teacher is harassing my son. I need the director!"

The coffeemaker sends its last splutter of coffee into my cup, and I pour in cream, slap on the lid, and bolt from the room.

Michael has returned to the playground and is climbing

up the broken slide. Midway up, he turns and jumps, pushes over a little girl, stomps on a sandcastle, and kicks sand into the faces of nearby children. Mr. Joe steers Michael away from the carnage while another teacher soothes the victims.

"There! You see!" Charlotte stomps out of the office and points at her son.

Michael lunges away from Mr. Joe and runs screaming toward a random classroom. A moment later, he emerges and waves something in the air. I squint. Scissors. In both hands! Oh my god, a two-year-old is on a rampage with scissors. They must be blunt, but my heart seizes with terror.

Meredith runs after Charlotte and shouts, "Dr. Konig!"

Dr. Konig, a tall woman wearing sensible beige pumps and a navy pencil skirt, appears from a classroom a moment before Michael throws a pair of scissors at Mr. Joe's face. She strides toward Michael while Charlotte shrieks something incoherent and rushes toward her beleaguered son. Michael, meanwhile, throws the other pair of scissors at Mr. Joe; Mr. Joe catches the scissors before they strike an innocent bystander; and Michael dashes toward the play structure.

I scan the courtyard for Madison's pink tutu and my knees wobble. She is on the playground! I drop my coffee and run into the sandbox. A natural disaster is unfolding, and I have to rescue my daughter before Hurricane Michael makes landfall.

Madison, oblivious to the rampaging Michael, jumps off the lowest platform and giggles as I scoop her up. I run for Miss Lucy's classroom. Madison laughs. I grab the hand of a boy I recognize from our class and drag him out of harm's way right before Michael tramples him. Mr. Joe acts as a human shield between Michael and the other children as Miss Blaire gathers up a few more children, and all over the courtyard, parents in yellow aprons scramble to locate and shelter their babies. Charlotte shouts at Dr. Konig about "abusive discipline" and "crushing her son's spirit." I reach the classroom and duck inside.

The atmosphere shifts immediately from "riot at a prison for severely deranged criminals" to "meditation retreat at a secluded nature sanctuary". Two little boys gaze at the fish, and several little girls twirl on the circle time rug while singing *Let It Go*. Madison wiggles out of my arms and joins the Elsa squad.

"What is going on?" Miss Lucy asks, the picture of serenity. She sits cross-legged on the floor by the play kitchen while a boy serves her a plate of plastic pizza and sushi.

"I'm not sure, but I think our room mom activated self-destruct mode."

Miss Lucy nods as she pretends to nibble the plastic sushi.

I do a quick headcount. All the children, minus Michael, are inside. I peek out the door and see Charlotte brandishing a broom like a sword and shouting obscenities at Dr. Konig. The Parent Handbook does not address this situation.

I turn toward Miss Lucy and say, "I'll be back. They could use some reinforcements."

7

"He's two years old! Stop treating him like a convicted felon!"

"Take a deep breath and imagine a tropical beach," Dr. Konig suggests with the composure of a seasoned police negotiator handling a hostage situation.

"I don't want to take a deep breath!" Charlotte waves her broom at the preschool director. "Stop trying to calm me down! I have a right to be upset! You're abusing my son!"

Meredith cowers in the office doorway, clutching a toilet plunger, and Michael rampages in the sandbox while Mr. Joe tracks him at a safe distance. I do not know how to help, but I trot toward the office to provide moral support. Halfway there, grit hits my face, and I am blinded. I lean over and blink as tears fill my eyes.

"Michael," Mr. Joe says in a level but stern tone, "we do not throw sand."

Michael throws a metal truck at Mr. Joe and hits his knee.

Someone needs to call the police, but as I pull my phone

from my apron pocket, I hesitate. Charlotte has gone berserk, but she doesn't need to be arrested.

I open a random classroom door and peek inside but do not recognize anyone. I open the next door, and this time, I spot Monica, who sits on the floor, surrounded by traumatized children.

"I'll come help," Monica says, peeling a child off her leg.

"Do you have Becky's number?"

"Yes, good idea," and Monica pulls her phone from her apron as I close the door.

I trot toward the office. Charlotte brandishes the broom, her hair in a tangled mess, and her posture conjures some wild, primal place from humanity's distant ancestral past. Dr. Konig remains very calm despite Charlotte's efforts to bludgeon her with a broom, and Meredith watches the scene from the office door with her plunger. I suppose any sane administrator would trade a plumbing crisis for Charlotte's descent into darkness.

"Why don't we continue this discussion in the parking lot?" Dr. Konig says.

"Oh! I see!" Charlotte screams. "You're worried about all the other children while you have no problem torturing my child!"

"How did anyone torture Michael?"

"Mr. Joe used the word 'no' with my son! Do you have any idea how toxic that word is? I won't let you crush his spirit!"

I give Charlotte a wide berth and reach the relative safety of the office. Meredith draws closer to me, and I whisper, "Has anyone called Charlotte's husband?

Meredith drags one distracted hand through her purple hair and clutches the plunger's handle with the other. "I suppose I could. I'm not sure."

"If you have his number on file," I mutter out of the side of my mouth, "I'll make the call."

Less than a minute later, Meredith hands me a sticky note with a phone number scrawled on it, and I make the call, bracing myself for what promises to be an awkward conversation.

"Hello?" a baritone voice answers.

"Hi, is this Charlotte's husband, Mark?"

"Yes?"

"A teacher used the word 'no' with your son today, and Charlotte got a little agitated."

Mark groans.

"She's been screaming at the director for at least five minutes—"

"I'll be right there!"

Charlotte jabs the broom toward Dr. Konig, and Michael runs away from Mr. Joe and slams into his mom's legs. She drops the broom, scoops him up and smothers him with kisses. I snatch the broom, and Dr. Konig smiles at me while Mr. Joe watches the reunited mother and son warily from the edge of the playground. The crisis is over.

Michael wiggles out of his mom's arms, runs over to Mr. Joe and punches him in the crotch. It is a feeble punch, but Mr. Joe winces and says, "Michael, no, we do not—"

For the next few seconds, everything happens in slow motion. Charlotte makes a guttural sound of pure rage as she scrambles off the ground and lunges toward Mr. Joe. Michael howls like a banshee and stomps on Mr. Joe's foot. Mr. Joe looks at Michael as Charlotte raises her knee in the air, grabs him by the shoulders and knees him in the crotch.

Mr. Joe is not having a good morning.

A man runs into the courtyard and heads straight for Charlotte. Michael shouts, "Daddy!" and I breathe a sigh of relief. Charlotte's husband was near preschool when I called, so that's one thing that has gone right today.

Mr. Joe clutches his man bits and moans from the ground. I hurry over and ask if he can stand.

Mr. Joe moans something incoherent about preschoolers, exorcisms and desk jobs while writhing in pain.

"Here," I offer my arm, "let's get you inside."

Mr. Joe staggers to his feet and limps to the office as Monica emerges from a nearby classroom. Together, we settle Mr. Joe on a couch.

"On a scale of one to ten, how bad is the pain?" I ask.

"It was a forty-two, but now it's like a sixteen," Mr. Joe groans.

Ingrid bursts into the office. She is wearing a green wrap dress and three-inch heels and carrying a quilted black Chanel purse. Her red hair cascades over her shoulders. "I got here as quickly as possible and Becky is on her way so we can have an emergency board meeting."

Dr. Konig strides into the office. "Thank you, Elodie, for calling Charlotte's husband. Mr. Joe," Dr. Konig pauses, searching for the right words. "Joe, do I dare ask how you are?"

"I don't think I'm going to die." Mr. Joe closes his eyes and hesitates as he takes stock of his injuries. "At least, not from this." He tries to stand. "I can head back to the classroom."

"Nonsense," Dr. Konig says. "Go home, and if you need more time tomorrow, I understand."

Becky whirls into the office. "What did I miss? Who got hurt? I was at the gym. Where's Monica? Which mom freaked out?"

"I'm right here," Monica says. "It was Charlotte from Miss Lucy's class."

"Charlotte was the room mom with the extra paper-work," Dr. Konig observes. "I do not think she is the ideal candidate for room parent."

Talk about the understatement of the preschool year.

"I don't think her family is the right fit for Mountain View," Becky says.

"When should we have the emergency meeting?" Ingrid asks. "Now? Tonight?"

"ASAP," Becky says, "so long as we have enough board members to vote on our course of action."

"We will," Monica says and then rattles off the names of several board members on their way to school.

I feel the urge to do something else, but my work here is done. The board will handle the appropriate response to Charlotte's ravings, whatever that may be, and they do not need my two cents. I should return to Miss Lucy's room.

"Monica," Becky's voice booms, "Miss Lucy needs another room mom."

A surge of adrenaline fizzes through me, and I under-stand my nagging feeling that there is something else I need to do. I take a deep breath. "Excuse me?"

Everyone turns and looks at me.

"I'd like to be Miss Lucy's new room mom."

8

"Password!" A girl twice Madison's size glares at me.

"Please," I smile indulgently.

"No!"

"Hamburger?"

"No!"

As a newly minted room mom, I can now climb the Forbidden Stairs. Gaps separate the steep wooden steps, and the structure looks one earthquake away from collapse. A high fence and child-proofed gate restricts access to the Forbidden Stairs, and a sign proclaims:

NO CHILDREN ALLOWED.

I missed this sign during orientation, but now that I see the stairs in the light of day, I am happy to comply with its edict. Unfortunately, the child leaning against the gate is not.

I say, in my most wheedling voice, "Pretty please with ice cream on top?"

"No!"

"Do I need to get your teacher?" I'm losing my patience with this girl who reminds me of the Emerald City's gatekeeper.

The girl steps to the side. I lift the child-proofing latch, and the girl lunges toward me. I slam the gate and scan the area for help; but Miss Blaire is not at her usual post by the front, and I feel lame summoning Dr. Konig or Meredith from the office.

"I want to see what's upstairs," the girl whines.

"It's very boring grownup stuff."

"Vienna Vega, get away from that gate!" A mom, arms akimbo, stands on the landing. "You know the rule!"

Vienna Vega scowls and stomps away. I open the gate as little as possible and squeeze through.

As I climb, my heart bangs against my ribs, first from a rising panic over the start of my room mom career and then because I am out-of-shape and need to reevaluate my exercise routine. I pause on the landing, catch my breath, and cross the threshold to the inner sanctum.

Poor Vienna Vega. She would adore the Upstairs Room. An old sofa and several folding chairs are arranged in a ring, and a folding table is loaded with bagels and coffee. Toys dominate the rest of the room. Dolls crowd bookcases; farm and jungle sets balance on bins filled with plastic animals; and I count four play kitchens and five doll houses. It's the land of excess toys.

"Welcome!" Monica waves hello and pats an empty folding chair that I gratefully claim. "Everyone, this is Elodie. She's the room mom—"

"Room *parent*," a dad growls. I cannot tell if he is teasing or offended.

"Elodie is the room *parent*," Monica rolls her eyes, "for Miss Lucy's class."

Silence.

"Hi," I say while my internal organs cringe.

More silence. It feels awkward, but maybe that's just me. The silence extends another beat. Okay, maybe it wasn't awkward before, but now it most definitely is.

Before the silence passes from "excruciating" to "soul-shredding," a mom with a strong chin asks, "Did you know?"

"Know what?" I squeak.

"That your predecessor was crazy?"

"Oh," I laugh. "No, not at all." I pause and flashback to the first day of preschool. "Actually, on the first day of school, she had extra forms for us. Is that normal?"

A mom with large hoop earrings says, "Forms? What sort of forms?"

"She wanted to know our blood type."

Everyone gasps.

"And whether we had an epidural."

The room hangs on my every word as I describe the paperwork, Miss Lucy's intervention, and a play-by-play analysis of yesterday's excitement.

The room returns to a cheerful babble as parents share their favorite preschool stories. Monica tells me about a parent who hid in the broom closet for seven weeks to spy on his daughter. Somehow this leads to an intense conversation about *Game of Thrones* and whether Jon Snow is really dead, and I forget I'm here for a room parent meeting until Becky struts into the room, clears her throat and claps for attention.

"Let's start the meeting! I need to get to the gym." Becky hands the nearest mom a stack of folders to pass out and launches into a speech, blathering on for several minutes about room parents being the bridge between teachers and parents. While talking, she does squats.

No one appears confused by Becky's exercise routine, but then, no one is paying attention. Monica covers her mouth with a hand and whispers, "She's in love with the sound of her own voice." I bite my lower lip to smother a laugh.

Becky switches from squats to burpees and introduces Monica. "Thank you, Becky, for putting my Room Parents to sleep." I adore Monica. "My job is to make your job as painless as possible. If things ever seem difficult, shout for help and I'll be there. If things ever seem stressful, remember: this is preschool, not the United Nations."

Becky's eyes narrow to slits as the parents chuckle.

Monica explains that room parents organize potlucks, class gifts for the teachers, and the class page on a popular photo website. I jot a note in my bullet journal to handle the website tonight. If I had known the job was this easy, I would have signed up during orientation.

"I'll send reminders for everything," Monica says before introducing Evan Mumford, a balding dad with intense biceps.

"Hey. I'm the family activities director." Evan half-waves from the back. "I'm not sure how that happened."

"Your wife signed you up," Becky illuminates.

"Another reason we're getting divorced."

The lone room dad laughs. He stops when he realizes Evan is not joking.

"Anyway," Evan says flatly, "our first event will be Trunk-or-Treat." He squints at a crumpled sheet of paper. "Then a movie night or something and the pancake breakfast, I guess."

"I'm sorry I'm late!" Ingrid, wearing heels and a pink

tweed shift dress, strides into the room. "I was helping Dr. Konig with a little *situation* downstairs." She emphasizes the word "situation" as if it is something too confidential for mere mortal room parents.

Evan takes this as his cue to hunch his shoulders and shuffle out the exit.

Monica says, "That's okay, we were just finish—"

"I would like to talk about fundraising," Ingrid says. "After all, it's the board's most important work. Frankly, I was shocked to learn the fundraising position was vacant. I assumed a veteran parent would have claimed the job." Ingrid surveys the room judgmentally. "I am grateful to serve."

The lone room dad stands, stretches, yawns and walks right past Ingrid to the refreshments. This prompts a mass exodus and nearly all the parents, myself included, head for coffee.

Ingrid raises her voice. "The main fundraising event is the auction in the spring."

Outside, a siren wails.

"We can't wait until the spring for fundraising." Ingrid's voice gets even louder. "So we will kick off fundraising at Trunk-or-Treat. We'll sell pizza, chips and drinks and there will be a raffle with several prizes, including front row seats to the Christmas concert."

Monica leans closer to me and whispers, "That's brilliant. Everyone wants front row seats so you can take photos during the show."

"I've prepared some supplementary materials," Ingrid continues, "to detail ways room parents can support fundraising, so we have resources to install a new playground over winter break."

"Summer is more realistic," Becky interjects.

"If we raise enough at Trunk-or-Treat, we could arrange a rush installation in December."

Several parents sit up straighter. The lone dad says, "I thought we raised enough money at the last auction to get a new playground this past summer."

Becky frowns. "We need to raise a little more money. The new playground should be installed next summer."

"I think we can get it done this winter," Ingrid says, "if everyone would take out their blue flyer."

I locate the flyer as Dr. Konig appears at the door. In her sensible beige pumps, she is almost as tall as Luke. "I'm sorry, but may I interrupt?"

A hush falls over the room. "Was anyone in the parking lot around 8:45 this morning?"

Parents shake their heads and mumble, "No." Dr. Konig nods and retreats.

Monica abandons the refreshments. "What was that about?" She peers out a window that overlooks the parking lot. "Is that a police car?"

Everyone crowds around the window. A police officer dusts a minivan for fingerprints while a mom wearing a yellow apron watches, rocking back and forth on her heels.

"That's the 'situation' I mentioned earlier," Ingrid says. Now she has everyone's complete and undivided attention. "Emmy forgot her phone in her car and went back to get it after circle time. She couldn't find her phone or wallet. Mary Mumford helped her search the car three times. Emmy's phone and wallet are gone."

"The thief strikes again," Monica says and pivots toward Becky. "That's three stolen wallets in two weeks. What now, El Capitan?"

9

During pickup, Miss Lucy announces, "We were very busy today. The kids might take extra long naps." The parents make appreciative comments, and Genevieve high-fives Ingrid. As we make our way to the parking lot (also a recent crime scene), I overhear parents begging their children to stay awake during the car ride home.

I cannot relate.

Madison has always been a high-octane child. I agonized over her sleep schedule during her first year of life because she was awake more than Zoe's son, Cosmo. As newborns, Cosmo snoozed twenty out of every twenty-four hours. Madison slept fourteen hours, tops. When Madison dropped her nap shortly after her second birthday, I was horrified, but now I'm over it. Instead, I endeavor to fill our days with activities and outings to wear my child down. Back in Brooklyn, we had a robust schedule of Mommy and Me classes, but when we moved to Pasadena, I assumed preschool would fill that void. I was wrong. Now I am hustling to fill our schedule , starting today with a Parent and Me swim lesson.

I carefully planned the entire afternoon: lunch at home; a long snuggle with picture books; then we change into our swimsuits and have a magical first lesson. Both lunch and the snuggle go according to plan. Things unravel when it is time to change into our swimsuits.

"No!" Madison glares at her suit, as if it were a medieval torture device.

"But it's pink and has a tutu." I lift the swimsuit's ruffle up and down enticingly.

"I want my circus tutu." My sister Colette bought the tutu at Target during our summer visit, so Madison insists it is from the circus.

"You can't swim with your tutu."

"Why?"

"Because it will get wet."

"Why?"

"Because we swim in water."

"Why?"

I close my eyes, pray for patience, and decide on a new tactic. "You can wear your circus tutu until it's time to swim."

"No."

I pull into the swim school's parking lot five minutes before our lesson. This gives us just enough time to get inside, remove the circus tutu and dip our toes in the water. I unbuckle Madison, set her down on a concrete path, grab our gear, and stride briskly toward the building. Madison tiptoes along a thin strip of concrete.

"Come on, Maddy! We're late!"

Madison ignores me and cautiously inches forward.

"Madison! Hurry!"

Madison pauses, gives me a look of pure contempt, and

says, "I'm walking the tightrope." Then she looks back at her feet and takes another step.

"Can't you walk the tightrope a little faster?"

"No, if I fall, I'll get eaten by the alligators."

I consider carrying her like a sack of potatoes, but the tantrum risk is too high. Finally, after several torturous minutes, Madison dismounts the concrete tightrope, and I usher her into an enormous room that reeks of chlorine. There are two pools: a deep one with swim lanes; and a shallow one filled with parents and children. In the latter, an instructor calls out names for the two o'clock Parent and Me lesson. We made it!

Almost.

"Okay, Madison, take off your circus tutu."

"No."

I kick off my flip-flops. "Sweetie, you can't wear your tutu in the pool."

"Why?"

My cheeks burn. All the other parents got their kids into the pool. Why am I such a failure? "If you wear the tutu in the pool, it will be too wet to wear for the rest of the day. It's like bath time."

I brace myself for further questions, but Madison simply raises her arms and mercifully lets me remove the tutu. I scoop her up, and we join a group of two moms, two dads, and four toddlers in various stages of distress, ranging from whimpers to full hysterics. Madison, who has never been in a proper pool, splashes the water experimentally, and I brace myself for her imminent meltdown.

It never happens.

Madison smiles and giggles as the other children wail and shriek. She eagerly dunks her head beneath the water and stays under so long, I worry she might drown. When the lesson is over, we play for another hour. The lifeguard observes she is the happiest kid he has seen all week.

The rest of our day is uneventful, and I forget my room mom responsibilities until bedtime. Then, in the middle of a lullaby, panic hits: I haven't made our class's web page!

I could do this tomorrow when I am fresh, but the other room parents probably put their class pages together last week when Charlotte was circulating questionaries about blood type. No, I have to do it tonight no matter how groggy I feel from today's pool antics. I grab my laptop and join Luke in the Womb Room.

Our house's prior owner painted every downstairs room a different shade of pink. The front room is cotton candy pink with a white ceiling and white trim; the kitchen is also cotton candy pink with dark pink appliances and a black and white tile floor; and the room we now occupy is dark pink everything: dark pink ceiling; dark pink walls; and even dark pink carpeting. During our first online tour of the house, Luke referred to it as the Womb Room, and the nickname stuck.

The furniture from our two-bedroom, one bathroom Brooklyn apartment does not fill half of our pink Pasadena house. That is why I furnished our front room with bins of toys, a squishy alphabet floor mat, and a beach chair and relegated our nice furniture to the Womb Room. I'd rather put our couch and television in the front room, but this room has the satellite hookup.

I add the contact information for every parent to our class page as Luke turns on a reality dating show. This takes much longer than it should, but nearly every aspect of motherhood happens in slow motion. Finally, I click the invite button and close my laptop.

"All done?" Luke asks.

"I think so."

Luke joins me on the brown leather couch, and I lay down and drape my legs over his lap. He picks up one of my feet and massages the heel.

"Did I miss anything exciting?" I gesture toward the reality dating show.

Luke does not answer. Instead, he abandons my feet and massages my calves. I sigh contentedly. His hands travel several inches north of my knees.

"This is not the way foot massages go at the nail salon," I murmur.

"I should say not." Luke drops the pretense of a foot massage and kisses my legs. A moment later, his chest presses against mine and we kiss. The reality show fades away and I forget my chores and concerns. Then, a large hairy mammal roars.

"What the hell?" Luke says.

"It's Chewbacca," I explain.

"I know it's Chewbacca."

The roar comes again as my phone vibrates on the coffee table.

"It's my new text alert. I thought it was funny. Do you want me to change it?" I tease.

"Later," Luke growls, and we continue where we left off for about thirty seconds until my phone roars again. And again. And again. My phone has turned into Chewbacca, throwing a tantrum about some broken part on the Millennium Falcon.

"I should probably silence that."

"You think?" Luke stays in place while I reach for my phone. I slide the alert button to silence mode but can't help noticing the messages. They are not, as I assumed, from Ingrid, but several unknown numbers.

"Hang on, let me check these." I open the first text as Luke huffs and sulks.

Do you know what happened today with the police? I
heard a child was hurt.

That must be from a preschool parent. I read the next message:

How many children got hit by the car?

Chewbacca announces more texts. I frantically scroll through the messages and determine that three parents are losing their minds over rumors that a car hit some children. I reach for my laptop to identify the panicked parents. Luke makes a disgruntled sound and stands.

"I'm sorry, I have a room mom crisis," I plead. "This will take two minutes."

"Chewbacca killed the mood."

"We can do CPR and save it!"

Luke frowns but sits on the armchair. He watches a base-ball game as I determine the frantic parents are Chloe, mother of Tristan, Maude, mother of Emma, and Clark, father to the twins Brianne and Brian. This takes a few minutes, but Luke is shouting at the ump, so I soldier on and text Chloe, Maude and Clark that no one was hit by a car. I close my laptop, determined to be done with my room mom duties for the night so I can spend some "quality time" with my husband and give Luke a "come hither" look, or at least, my best approximation of one. (I can never tell if my expressions convey sexiness or indigestion.) Luke reaches for the remote.

Chewbacca roars.

Luke sighs as I swipe open a message from Maude.

I was driving by preschool and saw the police. Ingrid
said a child got hit by a car.

I groan and turn to Luke. "Someone's wallet and phone
got stolen today at preschool and the police came. But
Ingrid told parents that a car hit a child."

"Sounds like this is outside your room mom
jurisdiction."

"It is! I'm supposed to organize potlucks, not squash
rumors."

"Put your phone on airplane mode and I'll distract you."

I am torn. On the one hand, I feel compelled to attend to
my room mom responsibilities. On the other hand, Luke is
undressing me with his sapphire blue eyes. But back to the
first hand, I am brand new to the room mom gig and do not
want to mess things up right away, but I have all day to be a
room mom. There is only a small window of time for
passion and romance.

My traitorous mind recalls a memory from orientation
of a mom bragging about her work as a swimsuit model. I've
spotted the swimsuit model a few times since, dressed
scantily and flirting with any nearby dads. Thank god her
child is not in Miss Lucy's class. My self-esteem could not
handle it. But I cannot help wondering what the swimsuit
model would do if we swapped places. Well, for starters, she
would not be slouching on the couch. She'd be giving her
husband a lap dance while wearing complicated red
lingerie, and she would never stoop to the indignity of being
a brunette with freckles, undergoing whatever treatments —
lasers, chemical peels, bleach, highlights, cryosurgery —
were necessary to maintain her beach siren vibes. My

husband must wish I would dial down the rumple and turn up the sex kitten.

"Let me text Ingrid and figure out what the hell is going on." A moment later, a text from the devil herself arrives:

Have you signed up for parking lot duty yet?

I reply:

Did a car hit a kid?!

Luke turns off the television and stands. I'm afraid he is stalking off to brood, but he massages my shoulders instead. I relax. He's right. I should switch my phone to airplane mode and ignore the preschool drama.

Chewbacca roars.

I did not want to tell anyone about the theft until Dr. Konig emailed the school. So I said some parents were worried about a child getting hit by a car. No need to cause unnecessary panic!

Ingrid might need a refresher course on the meaning of the word "panic." Luke's thumbs dig into my upper back and airplane mode beckons, but I am curious about her first message.

What did you mean about parking lot duty?

My phone rings. Luke tenses, and against my better judgment, I answer.

"The board voted to install security cameras in the parking lot," Ingrid says without preamble. "But they are not being installed for a few weeks. Until then, board members and room parents are taking turns patrolling the lot during preschool hours to make sure the thief does not strike. Some parents have already posted nasty online reviews about the thief and that is terrible publicity." Ingrid is talking so fast, I cannot get in a word. "Becky emailed a sign-up for parking lot duty. You need to sign up or you'll look bad."

"I'll sign up tomorrow." Luke takes me by the hand and leads me toward the stairs.

"Tomorrow will be too late," Ingrid insists. "The slots are nearly full. You're going to be the only room parent who doesn't take a shift. Is that the sort of impression you want to make the first month of school?"

"Hang up." Luke's voice walks a fine line between passion and simmering rage.

"I'll sign up now," I say and end the call. "I can't," I plead, "I need just a minute to sign up for parking lot duty."

Luke drops my hand. "I give up, I'm going to bed." He stalks away.

"No! I'm sorry! I just have to do this one more thing!"

Chewbacca roars (stupid Wookiee), and Luke says, "I have to get up early for court. Maybe some other time when you are less distracted." His tone of voice is accusatory, but I do not have time for his wounded feelings. I have to sign up for parking lot duty before I make a terrible impression on the powers-that-be at preschool.

10

"Excited for parking lot duty?"

"Yes, ma'am!" I strike a pose in my fluorescent orange crossing guard vest. The new security cameras are being installed after school, so today is the thief's last chance to prey upon unlocked vehicles.

Monica appraises my outfit. "It suits you. The orange brings out your cheekbones. By the way, I listened to podcasts during my shift. It helped pass the time."

"Is that allowed?"

Monica shrugs. "I didn't ask Becky, because I didn't want to know."

"Monica!" Becky shouts from an open window upstairs. "Hustle! And you! Room mom! More patrolling, less loitering!"

In a hushed voice, Monica confides, "No one wanted Becky to be president."

"Then why is she?"

"No one else volunteered."

I walk a lap around the parking lot, which is no straightforward task: a Prius nearly reverses into me; a minivan swerves into my path; and trunks fly open without warning. It's an insurance adjuster's nightmare.

A black Mercedes SUV honks and parks, and Ingrid, wearing a shift dress with a floral print and pink heels, hops out. "Good morning, Elodie Flimbizzle!"

"Jones," I hiss.

"Elodie," Ingrid sounds genuinely perplexed, "are you ashamed of your maiden name?"

"No!" but my flushed cheeks say otherwise. "I don't want to confuse the other parents. Or Madison. Or myself. You know, mama brain," I finish lamely.

Ingrid tips back her head and laughs at an inhuman infrequency, and I push away the image of a dolphin. "You worry too much." She lifts Danforth Jr., who's wearing a button down Burberry shirt, out of his seat and says, "The board is meeting with Miss Blaire's future father-in-law this morning."

"Why?"

"He owns Terrain de Jeux."

"Terrain de what?"

"Terrain de Jeux is an elite playground manufacturer that specializes in American craftsmanship and European whimsy."

"That's exciting," I say, and I'm not being sarcastic. Last week, a plank of wood cracked, and Becky repaired it with super glue.

Ingrid rattles on about price points and discounts while I tune her out and scan the parking lot for thieves, because I do not want Becky to catch me loitering again (she scares me).

"I hope we can work with Terrain de Jeux," Ingrid

concludes, transferring Danforth Jr. to her other hip. "The sensory stimulation on their units is unparalleled."

I snort.

"What?"

"I better keep patrolling. Enjoy the sensory stimulation."

The parking lot is far less perilous now that most parents have fled for coffee, yoga, and groceries. A red SUV hurtles into the lot as I finish my third lap, and the driver parks a few spaces away from my red SUV. In fact, our SUVs are twins: same model, same color, and probably the same year. A mom leaps out, sees me, and says, "I'm always late on my volunteer day!" She hauls a curly-haired boy from his car seat and dashes toward school.

I have the parking lot all to myself. For approximately the billionth time since moving here, I marvel at the Pasadena heat. Although it's the second Friday in October, the forecast predicts a high of ninety-nine degrees, and I swear, wiggly lines are already rising off the ground. I need a distraction.

Following Monica's advice, I open my podcast app and spot *Centerfold Mama*. Its cover art reminds me of someone, and the host supposedly lives in Pasadena, but I can't place the face.

I hit play on the most recent episode. My ears fill with dreamy electronic music and a few seconds later, a breathy voice reminiscent of Marilyn Monroe says, "While most women use motherhood as an excuse to let themselves go, I am a mom and swimsuit model. Are you desperate for ideas to keep your husband interested? Then you have come to the right place. This is *Centerfold Mama*." The electronic music reaches its crescendo and fades to silence. Then the woman with the Marilyn Monroe voice says:

Hello, listeners! It has been so hot in Pasadena.

Truth. I'm melting.

I am so sick of going to indoor playgrounds to escape the heat. You would not believe what happened yesterday. Our nanny cancelled on me last minute because her dad was sick. Like that's a reason to skip work. The Prince was so-o-o whiny and kept asking for the nanny — it's almost as if he likes her better than me. I gave him his iPad, but he wanted me to play. I turned on t.v. but he kept getting up and asking for hugs. So I took him to an indoor playground to get him to stop pestering me, but they did not even have a valet. I had to park my Ferrari next to a Prius. And you will not believe it. A mom came up to me and told me that the Prince was being wild on the moon bounce and needed more supervision.

I can't decide if "the Prince" is a loving nickname or not.

What nerve! Who does she think she is, telling me how to parent my child? Then another mom asked if I could take my phone call off speaker. What the hell? Everyone knows you have to use speakerphone or you'll get nasty acne.

After a long pause, Centerfold Mama sighs and continues her rant.

Can I talk about fat moms? Last week, I took the Prince to the beach because I needed some fresh pics for social media. The other moms were so fat. They should not

wear swimsuits in public. I get it if you have to gain
twenty pounds during pregnancy, but a baby is not an
excuse to let your looks go to hell.

I laugh out loud and listen as Centerfold Mama complains about moms who do not wear makeup, moms who always put their hair in a ponytail, and moms who wear cheap jeans. (Guilty on all three charges!) She brags about being the "smoking hot mom" the dads covet and ranks the dads at the Prince's preschool.

As Centerfold Mama complains about Pasadena's lack of high-end fashion boutiques, a person walks into the parking lot for the first time in over an hour.

"Hi, Miss Blaire." I wave as I remove my earbuds.

"Oh! Hi!" Miss Blaire startles. Her skin is extra radiant today despite the heat. "I didn't realize anyone was out here. Aren't the board members upstairs for the meeting with my fiancé's dad?"

"I'm not on the board. Room parents could also volunteer for parking lot duty."

Miss Blaire walks to a pink Volvo station wagon, and I follow to be friendly.

"It's my sister's car. Mine's in the shop." Miss Blaire opens the passenger door and retrieves a thermos. "I'm drinking a lot of smoothies, because I need to get in shape for my wedding!"

I nod, although there is not an extra ounce of fat on Miss Blaire. "When's the big day?"

"The last Saturday of April. I wanted a summer wedding, but April works better for my fiancé, and," Miss Blaire blushes, "my parents need to keep costs down."

"Weddings are ridiculously expensive."

"I'm blogging about ways to have a lavish but frugal

wedding and with a little luck, my blog will earn enough money for a few splurges, like wedding photos at the Arboretum."

A red Ferrari whizzes into the parking lot and takes the handicapped spot. A mom with a lot of blonde hair emerges and sprints into preschool, which is very impressive as she is wearing stiletto sandals.

"I should get back to the kids, but," Miss Blaire hesitates, "are your cheeks always this pink?"

I touch my face and groan. "I forgot sunblock."

"I have some in my locker."

"Thanks, but I have some in my car." I can practically feel baby freckles appearing as I rush to my SUV and yank open the door. A wave of vertigo hits. I know I have mama brain, but has my car always had leather interior? That's not my bag on the passenger seat. Who left a can of Le Croix in my cup holder?

"Arlo! Hurry! We're late!"

Two things occur to me simultaneously: (1) that voice is familiar, and (2) this is not my car.

I slam the door shut and head toward the other cherry red SUV in the parking lot.

"Excuse me?" A breathy voice says. "What the hell are you doing in Tricia's car?"

A woman with intensely red lipstick, a lot of blonde hair, and resting bitch face stares at me. She holds the hand of a boy with blonde hair styled in an upward swoop. We have never met, yet her voice is so familiar.

"I have the same type of car. I thought it was mine, and I needed sunblock and—" my blood fizzes with adrenaline.

"Arlo, get in." The woman puts her fists on her hips as her son clambers into the Ferrari. "It looks like I caught the preschool thief red-handed." Then, still sounding breathy, she screams, "Help! Help! I need help!"

"I'm not stealing, I swear. This is a big misunderstanding."

"Help! Help!" A sultry breeze wafts through the woman's blonde hair and, with her stiletto sandals, perfect posture and enormous breasts, she could be a model — just like the host of *Centerfold Mama*.

Who lives in Pasadena.

Drives a Ferrari.

Has a son in preschool.

And sounds exactly like this woman.

The entire board, plus Dr. Konig, swarm into the parking lot, expecting to find a violent crime in progress, and maybe I'm imagining things, but they seem a little disappointed that I am alive and well.

"She's the thief!" Centerfold Mama points at me.

"She's not the thief," Becky says. "She volunteered to patrol the parking lot today."

"But she was rooting around Tricia's car!"

"I wasn't." My voice trembles. "I opened the door to this car because I wanted to get my sunblock, but then I realized it's not my car. *That's* my car." I point and several board members "ahh," in understanding.

"That is Elodie's car." Ingrid steps forward, confirming my story.

"Why doesn't someone get Tricia?" Dr. Konig says crisply. She is impeccable, as always, in her navy pencil skirt and sensible beige pumps. "She can check if anything is missing."

A few minutes later, the late mom, now wearing a yellow apron, jogs into the parking lot and searches her car. The wait is torture. Tricia even crawls under the chassis to confirm the magnetic box that stores an extra set of keys is still there. "Nothing is missing," Tricia at last announces.

My shoulders relax.

"Are you sure?" Centerfold Mama sneers. It is a very attractive sneer. I suppose this is something swimsuit models practice in the mirror.

"Yes, Debbie," Tricia says, "I'm sure."

So Centerfold Mama has a name.

"I believe this is all a big misunderstanding," Dr. Konig says.

"Or I caught the thief before she stole anything," Debbie says, playing with her necklace. On a heavy silver chain, tiny clear diamonds surround a huge blue gem. It resembles the necklace in *Titanic* that old Rose throws back into the ocean. I am no jewelry expert, but Debbie's necklace looks expensive. Very expensive.

"That's a dangerous assumption to make," Dr. Konig says. "Just yesterday, I was at the grocery store and tried to open the wrong car because it looked like mine."

I love Dr. Konig so much.

"It's a bit unsettling that Elodie volunteered for parking lot duty right before the security cameras are being installed," Becky says.

I do not love Becky.

"She volunteered because she is a devoted room mom who cares about Mountain View," Ingrid says.

Damnit. Now I have to love Ingrid.

"Shall we return to our meeting?" Dr. Konig says, "and let's not discuss this misunderstanding with other parents. We all know how malicious gossip can be."

"Amen," Ingrid says. The board members nod their approval, and I resist the urge to dance a celebratory jig in the parking lot.

"Morons," Debbie huffs.

A wave of nausea dispels my urge to dance as Debbie drives away in her Ferrari without so much as a farewell. Something tells me that being on Centerfold Mama's radar can only lead to trouble.

11

"What makes you miserable?"

I blink, startled by the question. "Umm..."

I am back in Dr. Dankworth's office, seated on the itchy, doily infested sofa with far too many pillows. This was not my intention. My intention was to ditch this boar and find a new psychiatrist before my Zoloft prescription ran out, but every time I put "find new psychiatrist" on my to-do list, there was always another box to unpack, another load of laundry to fold or another booboo to kiss — motherhood might be full of difficulties, but at least it offers endless excuses for procrastination.

"Hello? Anyone home?" Dr. Dankworth assumes a mocking tone of voice that I never expected to hear from a psychiatrist, or any doctor for that matter. "What makes you miserable? Nothing? Is your life perfect?"

"It's not perfect," I grumble.

"Elodie, you need to open up and answer me honestly or you'll make no progress. So tell me: what makes you miserable?"

"Nothing." (Except I could use a different psychiatrist; and I'm terrified my freshman roommate is going to let my circus history slip and I will be the mockery of preschool; and my entire house is pink; but otherwise, my life is misery-free.)

"What? Hello? You're in a psychiatrist's office!" Dr. Dankworth lights a new cigarette with the one he is already smoking, crushes the dying cigarette against a patient file, and says, "Everyone is miserable."

"Well, I'm a little nervous about organizing the Halloween potluck for my daughter's preschool class." My fingers meanwhile are busy making a phantom balloon iguana, so I clench them together before my psychiatrist notices. Growing up in the circus, I preferred the study of balloon animal anatomy over the rigors of acrobatic training. I tolerated somersaults and cartwheels and mastered various flips, but abhorred aerial stunts, especially anything involving the trapeze. My parents did not force me to perform any tricks, but my siblings often recruited me to catch, hold and throw the trapeze bar as they practiced their one knee hangs, straddle whips, and shooting stars. In between tricks, my fingers flew through the motions of making elaborate balloon creations to distract me from the fact that I was standing on a small platform twenty-five feet off the ground. When I ran away from the circus, the nervous tic followed me into college lecture halls, law school exams, meetings with cranky partners, and now the doily infested couch of Dr. Dankworth. If Dr. Dankworth ever observes my tic, I'm doomed. I'll have to either tell him the truth about my circus childhood, including my fear of heights, or lie, but lying to one's psychiatrist does not strike me as the path to inner enlightenment.

"Why are you organizing a potluck?" Dr. Dankworth growls, too busy blowing smoke rings to notice my fingers.

"I'm room mom." I smile. It feels great to say that.

"You're room mom?" Dr. Dankworth looks at me as if I just admitted I have several dead bodies in my basement.

I nod.

"You did not mention that at our last session."

"I became room mom after that session. I volunteered to take over after the original room mom left."

Dr. Dankworth shakes his head. "The director thinks you are competent for this job? Does she know you are on Zoloft?"

My cheeks burn with shame and fury. "The preschool director does not need to know I had postpartum depression."

"Do *you* think you are competent for this job?"

My sweat glands activate. I did not have a conventional childhood and have been faking motherhood since the moment the nurse first laid Madison in my arms. If being room mom required a formal application, Dr. Konig, Becky and Monica would have laughed in my face.

"I think so." I dry the palms of my hands on my leggings.

Dr. Dankworth smirks. "Wow, you sound like you believe that. You know what you have?"

I swallow loudly.

"Imposter syndrome."

"Imposter what?"

"Imposter syndrome. It's when a patient has all the skills to do something, but doesn't think she's good enough."

I force my face to remain neutral as my brain throws a tantrum that would impress my preschooler. Dr. Dankworth is wrong. I can't have imposter syndrome, because I am actually an imposter.

Dr. Dankworth taps a finger against his left cheek, which is extra orange today. "You are using fake responsibilities to avoid working on your mental health and should go back to being a lawyer, not a room mom."

He thinks that being a room mom detracts from my mental health, but he wants me to go back to a career that made me miserable? Where did this man attend medical school? My eyes dart to the degrees framed on the wall. Harvard? I slump against the couch's heap of pillows and wonder if I should listen to my psychiatrist, update my resume and rejoin the legal workforce.

"So, what else makes you miserable?" Dr. Dankworth demands.

I shift my position on the doilies and scramble to think of an answer. My sessions with my old psychiatrist in New York were not like this. She asked how I was doing, and then we had a pleasant conversation for ten minutes, as if we were friends meeting for coffee. Sessions with Dr. Dankworth feel like a game of speed chess with arbitrary rules that change depending on his mood. If I do not figure out the rules of his game, he might change my diagnosis and force some new medication on me even though I know I am doing better and ready to wean off Zoloft. Dr. Dankworth huffs, and I say the first thing that pops into my mind.

"I was patrolling the parking lot last week at preschool and went to get sunblock from my car but accidentally opened the wrong SUV. Another mom saw. I explained it was an accident because the car I opened looks exactly like mine, but she accused me of being the preschool thief. She has a podcast and devoted an entire episode to me and said nasty things." Debbie published the episode the same day that we had our pleasant encounter in the parking lot, and although it's been a few days since the episode dropped, I have not spoken about it to anyone. Okay, I texted Zoe, but that doesn't count. My long chain of unread text messages is more secret diary than actual correspondence.

"What's the name of the podcast?"

"*Centerfold Mama.*"

Dr. Dankworth picks up his phone — it's on top of a styrofoam takeout container and beneath an ashtray — and taps the screen. I fidget with a doily. "There it is!" Seeing the cover art, he asks, "Is she an actress?"

"A swimsuit model."

"I'll say. Ah, Episode 127: The Preschool Thief."

He jabs at his phone and the intro music plays. My god, this is really happening.

Hello, listeners. You will not believe what happened today: I caught our preschool thief! As you know, someone has been stealing wallets and phones right out of parents' cars. I mean, seriously, how low can you get? Anyway, I had to take the Prince home early because we had a photo shoot for a magazine article. I know my life is more amazing than yours, but motherhood is not an excuse to become a train wreck. Follow my example. Dress better; wear makeup; and stop wearing the mom jeans.

"Excellent points," Dr. Dankworth says. My blood boils.

Okay, where was I? Right, I was taking the Prince home early and was walking to my car and I saw a woman opening a car that does not belong to her. It's a crappy SUV that belongs to Dough Face, remember her? The mom who looks like the Pillsbury Doughboy? Dough Face makes my skin crawl, but that does not mean some other mom can steal from her. What if the thief tries to steal from me next? I have some amazing jewelry and always keep a few pieces in the console of my car because I'm an influencer and need to keep my social media posts fresh. I also carry around a ton of cash. Like, if I meet the man of my dreams, and we decide to run away, I need enough money to buy a plane ticket to Tahiti without The Hubs knowing. Not that I would leave the Prince! He is the cutest fashion accessory I own. It takes a lot of effort to style his hair, but it is worth it.

Dr. Dankworth nods approvingly. I wish I could tune Debbie out, but I cannot stop listening despite having listened to this episode four times already. Have I mentioned I am a glutton for punishment?

So yeah, I would be DEVASTATED if the preschool thief broke into my car and got some of my jewelry or my Tahiti fund — ladies, if you don't have a Tahiti fund, you are just plain irresponsible — and there she was! The preschool thief! Wearing these tragic mom leggings and Birks that would have been cute, except her polish was the grossest shade of pink—

Dr. Dankworth half-stands to check my feet.

—and she was rooting around the passenger seat of Dough Face's car! I caught her red-handed! The preschool thief! Go, me!
I shouted for help and the entire board came running. I thought they would call the police and kick the thief's kid out of school, but did they? No, of course not. Dough Face checked her car and said nothing was missing, but Dough

Face is so stupid, she probably wouldn't know if the thief took her wallet! Or I stopped the thief before she took anything.

"Good point," Dr. Dankworth says, and my cheeks flush hot. Is my psychiatrist taking Debbie's side?

God, I can't stand the parents at the Prince's preschool. Dough Face and Needs Lipo and Saggy Buns. I don't belong in Pasadena. I'm a model, and I belong in Malibu, but the Hubs wants to be close to his parents.

"She belongs in Malibu," Dr. Dankworth says. He is definitely taking Debbie's side.

I am going to keep a close eye on The Thief. In the meantime, I hope she uses the money she has been stealing to get a facial. Her pores are tragic and seriously, she needs a pedicure and a personal trainer to target her flabby bits. She has a lot of flabby bits. Ew, her arms are basically bat wings.

"That's it!" Dr. Dankworth shouts and jumps to his feet, knocking an espresso mug to the floor. Brown liquid spills all over a stack of patient files as he strides over to the couch and looms over me. "You need to befriend Debbie!"

I'm too stunned to speak.

"Look at you." Dr. Dankworth grabs my right arm, holds it over my head, and gives it a little shake. "You have bat wings!"

My mouth drops open. I won't be entering any body-building competitions this year (or ever), but I wouldn't say I have bat wings.

"Do you belong to a gym?"

"No."

"Join a gym!" Dr. Dankworth finally releases my arm. "Befriend Debbie. Tell her you listened to her podcast and would like some advice. She might recommend a personal trainer."

"But she thinks I'm the thief!"

"Are you?"

"No!" I am so frustrated, I struggle to defend myself. "Not at all. I just opened the wrong car because it looks like mine. Same color, same model. She parked her SUV near mine. I was not stealing."

"Have you ever shoplifted?"

"Why would you ask that?"

"You're the one who brought it up." Dr. Dankworth paces his office while checking something on his phone. "It's your mental health, not mine. If you don't want to open up about being a thief and want to be stuck on Zoloft for the rest of your life, be my guest."

"I think I'm ready to wean off Zoloft."

Dr. Dankworth makes a rude sound. "You are obviously not ready for that. We can talk about that after your mental health has been stable for at least a year."

My chest deflates. This man seems like a total charlatan, but he went to Harvard, and he has the medical degree, not me. I should trust his medical opinion.

Dr. Dankworth escorts me to the front desk. "Befriend Debbie and work on your flabby bits, and stop obsessing over weaning off Zoloft."

I would scream, but then Dr. Dankworth might have me committed.

12

"What's that?" Genevieve examines the paper I just placed in between the saltwater aquarium and sign-in sheet. She's wearing a peacock blue fedora and looks fabulous.

"The Halloween potluck sign-up." I hope she does not notice the tremor in my voice. This is my first true test as a room mom, and I am petrified I will fail.

"Shit." Genevieve clamps a hand over her mouth. "I forgot. Halloween is in two weeks. All the good costumes will be gone by now."

"I bought Danforth's costume in June," Ingrid gloats, writing her name with a flourish in one of the entrée slots.

"What's he going to be?" I ask.

"Well, I'd like to be Joan from *Mad Men*, so I found the perfect Don Draper suit for Dan-Dan. Isn't that the cutest?" Ingrid, with her stunning red hair, likes to dress as famous red heads for Halloween. Freshman year of college, she was Jessica Rabbit. In subsequent years, she was Glinda the Good Witch, Ariel the Little Mermaid, and Peg Bundy. "But Dan-Dan wants to be a skeleton, so I got him the cutest suit to be Jack from *Nightmare Before Christmas*, which is perfect, because I was Sally five years ago." Ingrid concludes her speech with a piercing dolphin laugh.

"All good options," I say blandly, hoping to escape, but Ingrid grabs my arm and frowns at the potluck sign-up sheet.

"Elodie, are you sure you're happy with this?"

I scan the sheet but do not spot any typos or misspellings. "That's the one Monica circulated."

"It's just so vague. Instead of 'entrée,' wouldn't it be better to specify so we don't end up with three trays of mac and cheese?"

I had not thought of that. Ingrid makes a valid point.

Genevieve rolls her eyes and says, "I've done a dozen potlucks by now, and the sign-up sheet never specifies the dishes."

Ingrid lowers her voice. "But do you think we can trust these parents to bring appropriate dishes for our first potluck? Do you know what Josh brought for a snack on Monday?"

Josh is our token stay-at-home dad. He has a penchant for wearing stained sweatpants and flip-flops with socks and is currently on his hands and knees, searching for his car keys while revealing an uncomfortable amount of butt crack.

"One pack of bologna that was green, a mini snack box of raisins and a bag of peanuts. We are a nut-free campus!" Ingrid shakes her head. "What sort of idiot brings peanuts for snack?"

"Oh god," I say and reach for the potluck sheet. Ingrid is right. I have to be more specific.

Before I can reclaim the sheet, though, a mom named Ashley hip bumps me out of the way and writes her name in all caps in an entrée slot. A camaraderie has been slowly but surely building amongst the parents. We exchange tired smiles during drop-off and chat three hours later while waiting for Mr. Joe to open the door for pickup. Ashley, however, spends as little time as possible mingling. In the morning, she cuts the line at the outdoor sink to wash hands, exclaiming, "I'm late for pilates!" and during afternoon pickup, she waits outside a classroom on the other side of the courtyard, whispering with Debbie a.k.a. Centerfold Mama.

"Hang on, Ashley," Ingrid says, "I think Elodie is going to update the sign-up sheet and bring it back this afternoon. She needs to specify the entrées."

Ashley looks at us as if she has discovered something disgusting on the bottom of her shoe and says huskily, "I'm bringing my meatballs. They are legendary." Then she flounces away before anyone can reply.

Genevieve hooks her arm through mine and pulls me outside. Two children on tricycles scream as they race past us and narrowly avoid colliding with a cluster of children playing with a dollhouse. "Ignore Ingrid. It's a preschool potluck, not a royal banquet. Do you want the other parents to think you're micromanaging?"

Genevieve also makes an excellent point. If I am too specific with the sign-up sheet, parents will hate me; but if I am vague and the potluck is a disaster, the parents will think I'm incompetent and also hate me. I can't win.

"Hey, do you like yoga?" Genevieve interrupts my train of panicked thoughts. "I'm trying the nine a.m. class at a new studio. It's free this week."

Free yoga sounds like the perfect tonic for my frazzled room mom soul, but alas, I need to go home and figure out this potluck business.

"Danforth Junior, how many times do I have to tell you?" Ingrid drags poor Dan-Dan away from the playground. "We do not go into the sand when we are wearing Burberry."

A pool of liquid forms around Dan-Dan's feet. Someone is having a potty training regression.

"Ingrid!" I warn, but too late. The pee has already reached her Blahniks.

Ingrid's face turns a shade of red that matches her hair, and she stomps her heels, now wet with urine, against the concrete.

"Yoga?" Genevieve asks again.

"Hell yes."

For the next few days, I check the potluck sheet every time I sign Madison in and out of school. Parents claim the slots, and my head dances with fantasies of a Pinterest-worthy potluck, with orange and black bunting strung overhead and children nibbling meatballs while parents talk about how cute they look in their costumes.

One week before the potluck, I am folding laundry in the Womb Room when the first whiff of drama arrives via a text from Chloe.

Can I bring the paper goods? I already bought them.

Why on earth did Chloe buy the paper goods if someone else signed up for that job? Even I know this is an egregious violation of potluck etiquette, and I grew up in the circus. I take a deep breath and type a quick response.

Genevieve is bringing paper goods. Do you mind bringing juice boxes instead?

Before I can finish folding one of the three pink t-shirts that Madison wears with her ubiquitous tutu, my phone buzzes.

I'm so sorry to be a pain. I had the pen in my hand and was about to sign up for paper goods for Miss Lucy's potluck but Ingrid distracted me. She wanted to talk about the auction. Total mom fail by me.

Now I feel like a monster. Chloe's daughter is in the Pre-K class; her son Tristan is in Miss Lucy's class; and she is pregnant with Baby No. 3. I can barely manage one preschooler, yet I'm judging a mom with two preschoolers and one expanding uterus. I text Genevieve.

Hey, sorry to ask, but can you bring something else for the potluck? Chloe wants to bring the paper goods.

Genevieve responds before I finish sorting the socks.

I was super organized and bought the paper goods today during my Target run. I know, who am I? But I can return them and bring something else.

Bloody hell, I assumed Genevieve would buy the paper goods at the eleventh hour, but if she already secured them, I won't give her an extra chore. We're going back to yoga next week, and yoga could lead to friendship, and friendship is far more important than staging the perfect potluck. I text Genevieve:

No worries! Bring the paper goods.

Then I text Chloe:

> Genevieve already bought paper goods but bring yours, too. We can use the leftovers for the next potluck.

Come Thanksgiving, I will scream if anyone complains about Halloween-themed paper goods, but right now I am grinning because this is something I actually know how to do. Motherhood constantly presents me with tasks — from burping my newborn to managing Madison's pink tutu obsession — that are unlike anything I have ever done, making me feel inept and clueless, but as a lawyer, I juggled calls and emails from senior partners, opposing counsel, and clients almost daily. Juggling texts from preschool parents is a cakewalk by comparison. Just don't ask me to juggle eggs. I have not done that in years and my fellow preschool parents can learn about my juggling talents approximately never.

My next potluck crisis arrives a few hours later. This time, it is Maude.

> Help! I wanted to bring fruit, but Josh says he's bringing apple slices and won't switch. Help! I'm a lousy cook! You guys don't want to eat anything I make! I'll give everyone food poisoning!

Calmly and reasonably, I decide to ignore Maude's text until morning. It's late, Luke and I are watching television in the Womb Room, and I do not feel like texting about potlucks anymore today.

Maude does not approve of my strategy. My phone chimes three times in a row. Not cool, Maude, not cool.

"Good thing I wasn't putting the moves on you," Luke teases.

I laugh and turn off text notifications, and we continue watching *The Big Bang Theory*.

My phone rings.

Luke's head jerks back. "Who calls at ten at night?"

I grab my phone, intending to silence it, but accidentally answer. (Sometimes I despise technology.)

"Elodie! Thank god! I've been texting you for the past fifteen minutes!"

It's Maude, but I'm sure you guessed that already.

"I'm watching t.v." I play dumb. "Can we talk tomorrow?" The partners at my old law firm never called this late, but if they had, at least it would have been about something more urgent than the potluck fruit platter.

"Josh is bringing fruit to the potluck and I can't do something that involves cooking."

"Maude-"

"I'm freaking out!"

That's one way of putting it.

"I can't cook! I wanted to bring a fruit plate! They make those at Vons. It's so easy. I can't cook!"

"You don't have to cook."

"I can't cook! I'll give everyone food poisoning!"

"You don't have to cook!"

"I once brought a casserole to a family potluck and everyone got sick and my Aunt Irma was in the hospital and everyone said it was Cousin Greg's seafood dish but I know, just know, it was my casserole."

"Maude—"

"I didn't want to have kids because I'm such a terrible cook. I told Sven I will give them food poisoning every week."

Maude rants about her cooking phobia for ten minutes. Every time I try to calm her down, her voice goes up an octave and she talks faster, as if she is racing a timer and a comet will annihilate humanity if she does not convince me she is a horrible cook before the timer dings. When Luke joins me on the couch and leans close to listen, I whisper an apology. "Don't worry," he whispers back. "This is better than t.v."

After ten minutes of ranting, Maude pauses to breathe, and I seize the opportunity to say, "Maude, I have to go to bed. We will figure this out tomorrow, and I promise you will not have to cook. Bye!" I hang up the phone and set it to airplane mode before she can call me back. Once again, my years of dealing with obnoxious attorneys are paying off.

The next morning, I reluctantly take my phone off airplane mode. Forty-seven text messages from Maude appear. She also left three voicemails. I consider letting Madison play hooky from preschool so I do not have to deal with Maude at drop-off, but then I imagine Dr. Dankworth making a snide remark about my "crumbling mental health" and decide to tough it out.

Maude stands near the broken slide with a parent I don't know as I enter the courtyard with Madison. My entire body tenses. Maude waves cheerfully in my direction. She is luring me into a false sense of security. I hurry toward the outdoor sink. Maude runs toward us. Crap! I tug at Madison's arm, but before we take two steps, Maude blocks our path.

"Good news!" Maude announces. Her ponytail is so tight, I feel sorry for her hair follicles. "There was still a slot available for adult drinks. No cooking for me, hallelujah! Have a good day!"

"You too," I say as Maude practically skips back to the

parking lot. It's not even 9 a.m., and I feel like I have already experienced the emotional equivalent of three menstrual cycles. I expected a hysterical woman! In front of the entire preschool! And there goes Maude, oblivious to how depleted I feel. I am not her therapist. We are not even friends, and yet she took her toxic emotional waste and dumped it all over me.

Monica joins me and asks, "Interesting morning?"

"You could say that. I didn't know that room moms moonlight as therapists."

Monica laughs wryly. "That means they like you."

"Maybe they should like me a little less."

The night before the potluck, I email the class a reminder of what they signed up to bring: Ingrid is bringing mac and cheese, Genevieve and Chloe are covering paper goods, Maude is in charge of adult beverages, Josh will ruin the apple slices, assorted parents are bringing baked goods and side dishes, and of course, Ashley is bringing her legendary meatballs.

An hour later, Ashley texts.

What? I didn't sign up for meatballs. I signed up for
paper goods.

My mood goes from "cheerful and a little ebullient" to "irritated and nearly homicidal" in 0.02 seconds. I have already handled the paper goods drama. Ashley told me she was bringing meatballs. I text back:

Sorry, you signed up for the entrée.

Ashley does not reply. Crisis adverted. My room mom confidence returns.

The next morning at drop-off, Ashley confronts me, arms akimbo, when she sees the paper goods that Genevieve and Chloe brought. "But I brought the paper goods!"

Monica did not cover this at the room parent meeting. What am I supposed to do when a mom, aligned with forces of impenetrable darkness, tries to gaslight me about a potluck dish?

Ingrid, also arms akimbo, steps to my side and says, "Don't lie, Ashley. We both signed up to bring an entrée. Remember, you said you were bringing meatballs."

God bless Ingrid and her need to micromanage.

Ashley turns to me and says huskily, "But I told you last night that I was bringing the plates and napkins."

"What? At midnight?" Seriously, I am over this potluck drama. "Did you expect me to wave my wand and turn your paper goods into meatballs? The sign-up list is next to the aquarium. You signed up for an entrée."

Tears brim in Ashley's eyes, but I am not impressed. Last week, I overheard her bragging to Debbie that she can cry on command.

"Don't use fake tears on me," I snap. I feel like I have a grown a foot taller.

Ashley stamps her foot on the floor. Her tears evaporate. "Well! We are now an entrée short for our potluck!"

"Not a crisis," I say. "It's a preschool potluck, not a royal banquet."

Genevieve nods approvingly.

Ashley makes a Neanderthal sound, clenches her fists and storms out of the classroom. Ingrid, Genevieve and I exchange fist bumps and take a walk to get coffee before the

Halloween parade. We admire the kids' costumes and then set up the potluck. As we spread out a plastic tablecloth, Ashley adds a stack of entrées from Wholefoods to the buffet. She makes a point of not looking in my direction.

I make a point of not caring.

13

After all the drama over the Halloween potluck, I intend to enjoy a relaxed and fun evening at preschool's Trunk-or-Treat. Luke is leaving work early and meeting us at preschool; we will enjoy this fun family event together; and I'll treasure these memories forever. Unfortunately, the road to hell is paved with good intentions, and I am sabotaged by Ingrid before I don my witch hat.

"There you are!" Ingrid's nasally whine is almost as annoying as her laugh. This morning, she and Dan-Dan matched in their *Nightmare Before Christmas* costumes. Tonight, she rocks a green dress that the *Mad Men* costume department would covet. She is a miniature version of Joan, the sexy office manager. Yet another reason for me to loathe her very existence.

"Elle-o-dee, I need your help. Evan went AWOL. Becky and I have been setting up this event for him, and now the pizzas are late, so I have to pick them up. Evan was supposed to man the refreshments table, but he won't answer his phone. Can you do it?"

"Evan?" I ask.

"Our family activities director. He's in charge of Trunk-or-Treat. You were at the room parent meeting. Didn't you pay attention?"

I fight the urge to throttle Ingrid. Maybe she memorized the names of every board member, but I'm still working on the names of the children in Miss Lucy's class.

"Pleeeeeeease?" Ingrid pouts. "Pleeeeeeease?"

Luke, wearing a pink super hero cape that Madison picked, joins us just as Ingrid pushes her palms together in a fervent prayer pose.

"Do you mind starting Trunk-or-Treat without me?" I ask Luke. "Ingrid needs me to man the refreshments table."

"Not at all."

I expect Madison to protest and insist that mommy escort her to the Trunk-or-Treat vehicles, but the little traitor does not even say goodbye before running to the nearest car for candy.

Ingrid leads me to a humble folding table she transformed into an Instagram-worthy spread with an orange tablecloth and a floral centerpiece that involves chrysanthemums, dahlias and roses arranged inside a pumpkin. Individual chip bags are displayed in a large basket with a fancy bow on the handle, and a spool of orange raffle tickets leans against a clear acrylic box with a slit in the top and lock on the side.

Becky, wearing a tweed cape and cap, stands behind the table. When she sees me coming, she hisses at Ingrid, "Her? After what happened in the parking lot?"

My stomach lurches. The co-op president still thinks I might be the preschool thief.

"Of course," Ingrid says. "She was my freshman roommate in college. Elodie is not the thief."

Despite myself, I feel a rush of gratitude toward Ingrid.

An older woman with short grey hair stops at the refreshments table. "I'd like to make a donation." She waves a fifty-dollar bill in the air. "My granddaughter talks nonstop about preschool."

"Of course, thank you." Becky adds the fifty-dollar bill to a metal cash box hidden behind the potato chips basket.

"Becky! We're out of glue sticks!" A dad waves from the crafts zone in the middle of the parking lot where children decorate pumpkins. Becky hurries off, holding her cap down with one hand and brandishing an oversized novelty magnifying glass in the other.

Ingrid leans close and mutters, "She announced at the last board meeting that she was dressing up as Sherlock Holmes for Trunk-or-Treat so she could channel her 'sleuthing skills' and discover who the thief is."

I snort, enjoying Ingrid's company against my better judgment. Then she tips back her head and laughs like a dolphin, killing any sense of camaraderie. "I'll be back in a jiffy!"she cries and then dashes off to her car. I glimpse the red soles of her black heels and feel a surge of smugness: her dress might be all *Mad Men,* but the shoes are *Sex and the City.* I reach for my phone to text this observation to Zoe, but stop. Weirdly, it doesn't feel right to send snarky texts about Ingrid tonight. Maybe tomorrow.

For a few minutes, all I do is stand and smile as parents and children walk by. No one is interested in the sodas, juice boxes, chips, and raffle tickets I am peddling when there is free candy. Parents and teachers decorated at least forty car trunks for the occasion. Two Klingons stand next to a minivan with plastic orange pumpkins of candy. Mr. Joe wears a gorilla suit; the children give his jungle-themed sedan a wide berth. Becky has decorated the trunk of her minivan as a gym with actual free weights, a poster of young Arnold Schwarzenegger, and an open duffel bag filled with protein bars instead of candy.

I spy Madison accepting candy from an Elsa standing in front of a black Audi. It's Miss Blaire, and with her long blonde hair in a side braid, she plays the part perfectly. I assumed Madison would also want to be Elsa, but after our summer circus tour, she insisted on being a tightrope walker. She is wearing a bedazzled leotard, tights and ballet slippers, with the pink tutu that is the bane of my existence. She also has a shortened version of a tightrope walking pole I made her leave at home. Hopefully, no one asks too many questions about her costume or Madison might reveal my origin story. Luke and Ingrid know my retribution will be swift and furious if they says anything about The Flying Flimbizzles, but I cannot control the things my two-year-old says.

A car horn blasts and I am so surprised, I shriek out loud. Debbie parked her red Ferrari right next to the refreshments stand, and she is now honking her horn to get Ashley's attention. Debbie is wearing a French maid costume and call me puritanical, but she is baring an indecent amount of skin for a preschool event.

A mom stops at my table and requests a Diet Coke. A line forms, and I am busy handing out drinks, chips, and raffle ticket stubs when Ingrid arrives with the pizza. Then I am busy handing out slices of cheese and pepperoni while Ingrid runs to her car to get more chips and drinks. When Ingrid returns, the pizza line is so long, I stay to help. The line gets longer, so Monica, Miss Blaire, Mr. Joe, and several parents I do not know, including a mom with a dragon tattoo that starts at one wrist and ends at the other, come and plate slices.

After thirty busy minutes, business at the refreshments table slows down. Madison, running at full speed, crashes into my legs.

"Mama! Candy!" She proudly opens her bag and I'm hit by the scents of Halloween: sugar, chocolate, more sugar and a touch of plastic.

"Nice work." Mama will collect her candy tax after someone goes to bed.

"Craft table is under control," Becky announces, taking a pizza slice. She nods at the mom with the dragon tattoo. "Mary, you are a rockstar. Thanks for pitching in before your big move."

"It's the least I could do," the mom says meaningfully, hinting at a secret subtext.

"Mama! Circus!" Madison yanks my arm, and my blood goes cold. I should never have let her dress up as a tightrope walker. She does not talk much at school, but if she is feeling loquacious, she can certainly tell everyone that my parents and siblings are circus acrobats. And once that much is known, it does not take a rocket scientist to deduce that I grew up in the circus. And once that is deduced, it will be my freshman year of college all over again.

"She wants to show you the circus car." Monica points toward a minivan. I relax as Madison drags me past Luke, who is laughing with a cluster of dads, to a car decorated like the big top. Skeletons swing from a trapeze, a zombie walks the tightrope, and elephants balance on pumpkins.

"Did you make these?" I ask a mom dressed as a ringmaster.

"I did," she says. "I send my kids to preschool so I can make art at home alone." She beams down at Madison. "I think you love the circus more than any other kid at preschool."

Madison glares silently at the ringmaster mom. Have I mentioned how grateful I am that my daughter hates talking with preschool parents?

"Would you like a balloon animal?" A dad, dressed like a clown, pumps up a green balloon. "I can make anything you like so long as it's a snake."

"Yay, Madison, a snake!" I say while resisting the urge to transform the balloon into a bat, a ghost, a spider... but then I would be known as Elodie, the Lame AF Balloon Lady. This dad is out of his league, but that is not my problem. My balloon animal days are in the past and that is where they shall stay.

Madison and I do another circuit around the parking lot. I worry we are breaking some Trunk-or-Treat etiquette I do not know about, but the parents eagerly unload their excess candy. Then, fueled by a cocktail of sugar and exhaustion, Madison runs laps on the lawn. When the festivities dwindle, Luke carries our exhausted tightrope walker to his car and I help Ingrid clean up the refreshments table. Finally, when the last empty pizza box has been tossed into the trash, I open my car door but stop at the sound of an angry throat clearing.

"If you confess now, I might have mercy."

I spin around. Becky, nostrils flared and legs planted wide, is standing well within my personal space.

"Confess? Mercy?"

"There's a fifty-dollar bill missing from the cash box," Becky hisses. "A grandparent donated it right before you 'volunteered' to help with refreshments."

A French maid stomps over to my car. I am about to protest my innocence to Becky when Debbie points her feather duster at me and shouts, "That bitch stole my jewelry!"

"Excuse me?" My voice rises an octave higher than usual.

"What is going on here?" Dr. Konig, wearing a navy blue pencil skirt, sensible beige pumps and purple fairy wings, materializes as if out of thin air. "That sort of language is unacceptable at preschool."

"And stealing jewelry is?" Debbie waves the duster aggressively at me.

"Perhaps you could explain what happened without shouting," Dr. Konig suggests.

"I keep several pieces of jewelry in the console of my car. They are *very* expensive pieces of jewelry."

Anyone who listens to *Centerfold Mama* would already know that, but I doubt Dr. Konig would dirty herself with that show.

"I wanted to swap necklaces."

For a selfie, of course.

"So I opened my console and everything was gone. All my jewelry! Stolen! Including a priceless family heirloom. It's a necklace with a blue diamond surrounded by smaller clear diamonds on a silver chain."

I assumed that necklace's central gem was something other than a diamond, but if it is indeed a blue diamond, the necklace is even more expensive than I thought.

Dr. Konig turns toward Debbie's Ferrari where Arlo is playing with the steering wheel. "Is it possible that your son removed the jewelry?"

"Arlo would never do that!"

Arlo takes this opportunity to honk the horn several times and flash the headlights.

"Why do you think Elodie stole your jewelry?" Dr. Konig remains implacably calm.

"I saw her!"

I am too stunned to react.

"You saw Elodie remove the jewelry from your console?" Dr. Konig presses.

"No! But I saw her go into Tricia's car!"

Fortunately, most families left Trunk-or-Treat before Debbie screamed at me. Unfortunately, the families still here have wandered closer to witness the spectacle of a French maid shouting at a witch, and no one will leave until the show is over.

"That was a misunderstanding." Dr. Konig remains calm, but I detect a note of impatience in her voice.

"We thought it was a misunderstanding," Becky says, "but then Elodie worked the refreshments table tonight and a fifty-dollar bill donated by a grandparent disappeared. The evidence is incriminating."

"What? Seriously?" I should go into lawyer mode, but am too aghast to string together coherent thoughts and defend my innocence.

"All I saw was Elodie being helpful. Do we have any eyewitnesses?" Despite being dressed as a fairy, Dr. Konig commands all the dignity of a judge. Her talents are wasted on preschool.

"I suppose my jewelry got up and walked away on its own!" Debbie's chest heaves, and a nearby dad goggles her breasts.

"I did not say that." Dr. Konig's voice rises a notch. "Over a hundred parents came tonight."

"Yes," Becky retorts, "but Elodie was working the refreshments table and had access to the cash box and she was right next to Debbie's car."

Dr. Konig appears unimpressed with Becky's logic. "At least a dozen people worked at the refreshments table. Ingrid, Monica, Mary Mumford, Kelly Finkleberg, Wanda

Evans, Emily Talt, Alex Smith, Miss Blaire and Miss Ellen."

"Well, I know those parents and teachers," Becky huffs. "And I know they would not steal from preschool."

Dr. Konig's posture is perfect. "Miss Becky, just because you dressed like Sherlock Holmes does not mean you have his powers of detection. Perhaps *you* stole the fifty dollars and are now accusing Miss Elodie to divert attention from yourself."

Miss Blaire, radiant in her Elsa costume, steps forward. "Should someone call the police?"

14

I have texted Zoe fifty-nine times since Debbie accused me of stealing her jewelry. I know this because I reread and counted my texts before dawn today in a misguided attempt to fall back to sleep. Thus far, the Universe has ignored my prayers for Zoe to return to the grid and counsel me through this crisis. I hope her husband Paul falls off a glacier and gets eaten by wolves.

"Mama! You're not watching!"

I startle from my reverie and return my gaze to Madison, who is halfway across the balance beam obstacle course my father-in-law Ron installed in our backyard yesterday. Ron retired last year. At his retirement party, he was borderline euphoric about all the golf he was going to play. A week later, he sold his clubs on eBay, having discovered that he loathes the game. Then, during a routine trip to Home Depot, he stumbled upon his new passion: woodworking. He has already made Madison a dollhouse, a rocking chair, and at least a dozen pull toys, so of course, when he learned about her obsession with tightrope walkers, he asked if he could make her a balance beam. I agreed, assuming he meant a straight plank of wood raised a few inches off the ground. When I returned from running errands yesterday (gas, ATM, groceries), I was more than a little surprised to discover a ninja training zone in my backyard that includes planks of wood that zig zag, ladders, several salvaged stumps, and a section Ron calls "the wobbler."

Madison is now considering the best way to travel from the wobbler to a nearby stump.

"Do you want some help?" I offer a hand.

"No! I can do it myself!" Madison jumps, teeters, and falls to the grass below. She hurries back to the beginning.

"Madison, if you keep starting over, you won't make it to the end before preschool."

Madison ignores me. She's an early riser; we have been outside for an hour; and she has still not walked from one end of the "balance beam" to the other. How am I going to get her to school on time? The again, do I want to arrive on time and endure the stares and whispers of my fellow parents? Maybe Madison should practice her tightrope act indefinitely, and I can use this time to enroll her in a new preschool. The shock of switching schools mid-year will be less traumatizing than seeing me tarred and feathered during morning drop-off.

"Just one more try, Mama." Madison strides up a balance beam that rises at a steep angle.

"There's no rush, sweetie."

"Why?"

"It's okay to be late." (And miss a direct confrontation with gossipy parents.)

"Why?"

"Because." I take a long sip of coffee. "It is."

"I don't want to be late and miss circle time. I love circle time." She jumps to the grass and runs toward the house. "I love preschool!"

Damnit. I throw back my shoulders and follow Madison inside. Debbie's false accusations will not ruin my daughter's childhood.

Ten minutes later, I park and ignore my heart's wild thumping. Miss Blaire waits at the entrance gate as usual and swings it open as we approach. The future bride radiates beauty in her apron and glittery flats beneath the enormous pink bougainvillea that grows on the horseshoe archway. I look like a zombie after barely sleeping all weekend. My hair is a knotted mess, my eyes are puffy, and my freckles stand out against my wan skin.

Miss Blaire beams at Madison. "How was my favorite tightrope walker's Halloween?"

Madison plows past Miss Blaire, refusing to acknowledge the question. Two-year-olds can be dicks.

I follow Madison through the gate. Halloween was on a Saturday this year. Maybe parents and children have lingering candy-induced hangovers, and half the preschool families will sleep in and arrive late, and the other half will ditch school entirely. At most, there will be a few groggy parents in the courtyard. The villagers will not be waiting to chase me with pitchforks.

My heart seizes as I enter the courtyard. Every child must already be here with both parents. The din of chatting is deafening, but even worse, the din noticeably dips as I follow Madison to the outdoor sink. Someone stage whispers, "That's her." My adrenaline activates warp speed.

A woman with intense eyebrows and long, blood red fingernails steps into my path. "Hi, I'm Liz Huffenby." Her voice booms at the decibel level of a motorcycle engine. "My daughter Penelope is in Miss Cindy's class."

"Hi," I squeak.

"Are you Elodie Jones?"

"Yes," I squeak again.

"Are you the mom that Debbie said stole her jewelry? I heard Debbie's side of the story on her podcast. Did you know she has a podcast? It's called *Centerfold Mama*."

Debbie lost no time in recording an episode entitled "The Preschool Thief Stole My Jewelry At Trunk-Or-Treat!" She never used my actual name during the episode, but over a dozen parents witnessed her Trunk-or-Treat histrionics and could make the connection. Thanks to Liz Huffenby's booming voice, all the preschool parents are now in the loop.

"I feel like I am a horrible person for listening to Debbie's show," Liz continues, "but I can't stop."

I nod, speechless.

"So what happened?" Liz booms, flexing her fingers in a way that reminds me of bloody talons. Every parent and teacher must be listening. "Why does Debbie think you stole her jewelry? Did you?"

I swallow and open my mouth, but words will not come out. Help! My adrenaline hit the mute button!

"Miss Elodie didn't steal from Miss Debbie." I turn and behold my savior, Miss Blaire, who has abandoned her post at the front gate to defend my honor. Her silvery voice floats across the courtyard. "Miss Elodie emptied her purse and then let Miss Debbie search her car. Miss Debbie checked the glove compartment, the console, the trunk and all the seat pockets, and Miss Becky even looked under the mats and removed Madison's car seat."

"Really?" Liz purrs.

"I suggested we call the police, but Miss Debbie didn't want to. She said it was a hassle. But if someone stole her jewelry," Miss Blaire pauses for dramatic effect, "why wouldn't she want to summon the authorities?"

Liz Huffenby gasps. "You know, Debbie always talks about her jewelry on her podcast and complains that she needs more so she can change up her selfies. She knows we have a thief amongst us. I bet she assumed everyone would believe her if she said someone stole her jewelry from her car." Liz talks rapidly. "I bet she faked the whole thing so she can get the insurance payout and go on a shopping spree at Tiffany's."

I am suddenly very grateful for Liz Huffenby's booming voice.

"Poor Elodie!" Liz squeezes my upper arm. "I never believed a word Debbie said on her podcast."

"I knew Debbie was lying," a random mom says as she walks up to me. "She just wanted some attention. Did you see how she was acting at Trunk-or-Treat? Who dresses up as a sexy French maid for a preschool event?"

"I know," another mom chimes in. "She draped herself all over Barry for a selfie."

"The other moms in Miss Ellen's class are sick of Debbie," Liz Huffenby says.

"You have to ignore people like that," a mom with a mullet says.

I slip away as the moms recount Debbie's various crimes. It's all speculation and gossip, of course. No one has any proof that Debbie faked the jewelry theft, but whether or not someone stole her jewelry, I know I did not take it, and I do not want to be the prime suspect of The Great Trunk-or-Treat Jewelry Heist.

Outside our classroom, Ingrid forces a comb through Dan-Dan's curls. She beckons me over and murmurs, "I had Becky check the security footage from the cameras."

My heart soars.

"Unfortunately, the refreshments table and Debbie's car were both out of the camera's range."

Damn. That would have been such an easy way to clear my name.

"Miss Blaire just told me the craziest story." Genevieve adjusts her fedora as she joins us. "She said Debbie accused you of stealing her jewelry during Trunk-or-Treat."

"It's true." Then I quickly clarify, "It's true that Debbie accused me but I didn't take her jewelry."

"Of course not," Genevieve says. "Miss Blaire said Debbie faked the whole thing."

My inner lawyer winces, but again, I am more interested in my reputation than Debbie's. Let Debbie enroll her son at another preschool if she hates being the subject of rumor and speculation.

"I wish I had been there," Genevieve laments. "If anything like that ever happens again, please call me."

"And me," Ingrid says.

A pleasant feeling inflates my chest. For a moment, it does not matter that my best friend is somewhere in the woods of Alaska, churning butter or darning socks or whatever people living off the grid do.

"I forgot to tell you the good news!" Ingrid rubs her hands together. "It's official! The new playground is being installed over winter break."

"That's awesome!" Genevieve says. "How'd you manage that?"

"The board voted a couple of weeks ago on the maximum amount we can spend on new equipment. Last week, we received a bid we can afford. Becky is not happy, but she's outnumbered. We won't be getting anything from Terre de Jeux. Miss Blaire's future father-in-law couldn't give us a discount." Ingrid's smile falters, but she forces her lips upward again. "But yay! We are getting a new playground!"

"I'm sure anything will be an improvement over the current situation," I say. The playground groans in agreement. It's ready to go to the place in the big blue sky where playgrounds go when they leave this mortal plane.

Madison stomps over. "My sock is loose!"

"Here, sweetie." I hang my purse on a hook outside the classroom, crouch, and tug at Madison's sock. "Better?"

Madison runs away as thanks for my help. Like I said: two-year-olds can be dicks.

The teachers sing the circle time song. Miss Blaire approaches the classroom, towing a few reluctant children. The door closes, and I head for the parking lot. With my reputation restored, I can enjoy my morning at Target.

"Elodie!" A few moms talking outside the office wave me over. Their elected spokeswoman, a mom dressed in black, says, "We heard about the way you stood up for yourself at Trunk-or-Treat."

"Becky can be such a bully," a mom clutching a Starbucks travel mug says.

"Remember last year?" A mom with frizzy hair asks her friends. "How she accused me of leaving peanuts in the sandbox?"

"Or the time she said I stole clothes from the lost and found?"

"She probably miscounted the money."

After all the Debbie drama, I almost forgot that Becky accused me of pilfering money from the refreshments stand. While Debbie searched my car for her jewelry, Becky hunted through my wallet and purse for the missing money. She found a grand total of three dollars, because I had not been to the ATM in weeks. I finally went yesterday while Ron was installing the ninja course.

"You guys are so lucky to be in Miss Lucy's class," Frizzy Hair gushes.

"And Miss Blaire!" Starbucks Travel Mug says.

"How is Miss Blaire this year?" the mom in black asks. "Is she distracted by wedding plans?"

"Miss Blaire wouldn't let her wedding take away from her work at school," Starbucks Travel Mug protests. "After all, she's the preschool institution!"

As if summoned by our conversation, Miss Blaire herself walks by, holding my tote bag.

"Oh!" I step away from my new allies. "Miss Blaire! That's my bag!" I forgot I hung it outside the classroom when Madison complained about her loose sock.

Miss Blaire stops and hands me my tote. "I was taking it to the office," she explains. "Curious preschoolers and unattended bags do not mix."

Everyone chortles knowingly.

"Miss Blaire, can I see that ring again?" the mom in black asks.

Miss Blaire displays her hand for everyone to admire. As the other moms praise the diamond, my thoughts wander. The children are still inside the classroom for circle time. My bag was hanging on a hook outside. Why was Miss Blaire bringing my bag to the office now? Why didn't she wait until circle time was over?

"Have you picked a date yet?" Starbucks Travel Mug asks.

"April thirtieth! In Bulgaria!"

"Oh, how lovely!" "So romantic!" "Perfect!" the moms gush.

"My fiancé's grandparents are from Bulgaria, and we are

tying the knot in front of the ruins of a medieval church. I can't wait." Miss Blaire sighs dreamily.

"How's the blog?" I ask.

"Oh," Miss Blaire titters, "I decided against it. I was going to blog about having a lavish but frugal wedding," she explains to the gathered moms, "but being frugal is not my style. I'm using social media to raise money instead."

"That's so smart," Starbucks Travel Mug says.

"And of course," Miss Blaire rests her bejeweled hand against her chest, "we're inviting all the preschool parents."

"Oh!" "You are so sweet!" "How fun!" the moms chorus ecstatically.

Around the courtyard, doors swing open. Children emerge from their classrooms and surge toward the ancient wooden playground. I hurry off to my car.

At the Target Starbucks, as I open my wallet to extract my credit card, I notice the main pouch is empty, but I went to the ATM yesterday. There should be at least two hundred dollars. I check the main pouch again, then all the credit card pockets, and then my purse, but I already know the truth.

The preschool thief has struck again.

15

Cranberry sauce bubbles on the pink stovetop, two types of stuffing are already in the pink fridge, and three pies cool on the pink countertop. I check my list. It's time to knead the bread dough! But first, I check my phone.

Several frantic parents have texted. I smile indulgently and open a message from Josh, our token stay-at-home dad.

I forgot to buy dessert at the grocery store today! I'm sorry!

I shrug and text assurances that we have more than enough dessert. He would have brought something moldy, anyway.

The next text is from Chloe, who looks more pregnant every week:

I signed up to bring cornbread, but I'm too exhausted to bake. Can I bring drinks instead?

I baked two cornbread batches yesterday — simple mini muffins for the kids and ones spiked with jalapeños for the grownups — so there is no need for the pregnant mom to bake. I type:

More juice boxes would be great.

I open the last text from Debbie's minion Ashley. I wonder what stunt she will pull after the Halloween potluck.

FYI we are going to attend Miss Ellen's potluck tomorrow. I will bring my stuffing there.

I cackle out loud. Debbie's son Arlo is in Miss Ellen's class. Please, by all means, crash Miss Ellen's potluck so you can bond with the Centerfold Mama. Not sure how the parents in Miss Ellen's class will react, but that is beyond my jurisdiction. We do not need the stuffing Ashley signed up to bring. My stuffing is delicious.

You may think that I have taken on too much baking and cooking in order to avoid confrontation over the preschool Thanksgiving potluck. Let me assure you that is not the case. If Thanksgiving was a religion, I would be its high priestess. Thanksgiving with the circus was, shall we say, suboptimal. We usually had pizza and pumpkin-flavored cotton candy. (Yes, that is a thing. No, I don't think you should try it.) I spent my childhood Novembers daydreaming about cornucopias, crisped turkeys and pumpkin pies, and ever since I ran away from the circus, I have gone a little overboard on Thanksgiving to compensate. Alas, I can't this year. Luke's parents are going to Boston to visit his sister's family, and it's difficult to go overboard when you are cooking Thanksgiving for two adults and a preschooler who will insist on eating dinosaur-shaped chicken nuggets instead of turkey. The class potluck is my only opportunity to use the recipes I have been pinning all year.

I delete Ashley's text, sprinkle flour on the pink kitchen island, ease the bread dough out of the mixing bowl and knead enthusiastically. I may or may not be imagining that the dough is Debbie's resting bitch face as I punch and flop it over. Actually, it is much more satisfying to imagine the dough is the preschool thief, whoever he or she may be.

After discovering my cash had gone missing in the Target Starbucks line, I turned my house, car and wardrobe upside down, looking for the missing money. Buried in my tote bag, I found the ATM receipt confirming that I had indeed withdrawn three hundred dollars the day before. I should have reported the theft immediately to Dr. Konig, but the last person who handled my bag was Miss Blaire. If I cast suspicion on the preschool institution, a mob of angry parents would torch my house. Instead, to process my feelings about the stolen money, I texted a rant to Zoe involving a stream of obscenities so exquisite, I will not repeat them here.

I divide the dough into twenty balls. Other than Zoe, I have told no one, not even Luke, about the stolen money, and at this point, it has to remain my little secret. I place the rolls on baking sheets and check the sweet potato casserole. The smell of browning marshmallows wafts toward me and I relax.

"Mama! I'm home!" Madison storms into the kitchen, followed by Luke's parents.

Grandpa Ron leans over a pecan pie and inhales deeply.

He frowns at Grandma Ruth. "Why are we going to Boston for Thanksgiving?"

Ruth swats Ron. "Because our daughter broke her leg and needs help."

"But our daughter-in-law is a much better cook."

"Believe me, I know. If Shelly only sprained her ankle, we wouldn't go."

Last week, one of my nephews climbed a tree, freaked out, and insisted he could not get down. My sister-in-law Shelly climbed up to rescue him and, long story short, my nephew is fine, but Shelly is not. My in-laws planned to celebrate Thanksgiving in Pasadena with us and go to Boston for Christmas, but have you ever tried parenting three boys, ages seven through twelve, with a broken leg while your husband travels constantly for work? Neither have I, but it sounds like an absolute nightmare. Luke's parents are heading to Boston tomorrow and staying through the New Year to keep Shelly from having a nervous breakdown on top of her broken leg. I understand why my in-laws have to decamp to Boston, but I am still disappointed our first Pasadena Thanksgiving will be such a low-key affair. It's a shame my family can't swing by for a proper holiday feast.

That gives me an idea.

"Madison!" I say, after Ron and Ruth have departed. "Should we Skype with our circus family?"

"Yeah!"

I text my siblings and five minutes later, Madison is sitting on my lap at our kitchen table. I have placed my laptop at an angle that affords a few glimpses of my culinary magic.

The laptop screen fills with the faces of my parents and siblings. "We have a show soon, so we can't talk long," my dad says. Everyone is wearing red leotards that involve an unholy amount of sequins. Everyone, that is, except my younger brother Ferris.

"Uncle Clown!" Madison claps.

"Ferris," I can't help laughing. "Are you aware that you are wearing full clown makeup?" My brothers are not shy about wearing makeup for performances. They say that if their pores can breathe, they are not wearing enough. They do not, however, favor white skin and oversized lips.

Ferris runs his fingers through his hair. "I'm helping Chuckles."

"Boomer and Squeaks are on strike," my sister Collette says. "Heckles went home for Thanksgiving, Pumpkin has the flu, and Daniel will not get out of bed ever since the fire eater dumped him."

The clowns of the Sweeney Sisters' Dazzling Big Top Extravaganza are, shall we say, occasionally difficult. They really should have their own reality show.

"So Chuckles enlisted Ferris?" Ringmaster Sweeney, the great-grandson of one of the founding Sweeney Sisters, insists clowns have the hardest job of all.

"We've been practicing a few things," Ferris says, trying to sound nonchalant but failing miserably. "We have this routine that involves a lot of acrobatic tricks. Chuckles says I have potential. Maybe you could teach me some balloon animal tricks when you visit for Christmas."

Madison cocks her head to the side. "Oh," I say hurriedly, "I lost my balloon pump years ago. I can't remember the last time I made a balloon animal. I wouldn't remember how."

This is a series of blatant lies. One: I did not lose my balloon pump; I threw it out. Two: I remember clearly the last time I made a balloon animal (or rather, balloon penis).

And three: like riding a bicycle, I'll never forget how to make a balloon menagerie. But those days are over. I'd die from mortification if the preschool parents knew I can make a life-size kangaroo from balloons.

"Are you excited for Thanksgiving?" my mom asks Madison.

Madison shrugs. My feelings exactly.

"What's that on the counter?" my sister asks.

"Bread dough. I'm making homemade rolls for the preschool potluck tomorrow."

"Is that Louella's recipe?" Cormac asks. He is the second oldest of the four Flimbizzle siblings.

"No, but I am using Louella's pecan pie recipe." My mom's mother hates to be called by any nicknames that suggest she is old enough to be a grandmother, so everyone calls her Louella. I stand, lift my laptop and spin slowly to showcase my creations.

"Is that homemade cranberry sauce?" Cormac asks in a hushed tone as Madison slithers off my lap and wanders away. She loves her circus family, but has a very limited attention span for Skype.

"You should come," I say casually. "My cooking is better than anything you'll get for a circus Thanksgiving."

"We should," Ferris agrees.

My father shakes his head. "We have shows all next week."

"We should just go for the meal," Cormac says.

"We're in Florida!" my dad says in his most exasperated dad-voice. "We can't gallivant across the country for a meal."

"Maybe next year," I say, making sure I keep any trace of disappointment out of my voice. I knew they were in Florida this month and shouldn't have even suggested this ridiculous proposition.

"Or you can cook all of that again for Christmas," my sister says. The Sweeney Sisters' Dazzling Big Top Extravaganza will be in San Diego in December, so Luke, Madison and I will visit them for a week.

"No thanks, I'm not cooking a turkey in a RV," I say. My siblings protest until an off camera voice barks, "Oy! Flimbizzles!" and the call ends.

The next morning, Miss Lucy stops cutting feathers out of construction paper as I arrive with my collapsible wagon of potluck dishes. She says nothing, but quietly assesses my sanity. Genevieve and Ingrid help set up the tables for our potluck. Ashley stands on the other side of the courtyard with Debbie.

Miss Lucy decorated the classroom with the kids' November crafts: a flock of coffee filter turkeys festoon the windows; paper plate scarecrows fill an entire wall; and slices of pumpkin pie made from tissue paper and cotton balls hang overhead on a clothesline. There is even a ceramic turkey in the aquarium. The starfish appear indifferent.

"Ooh, what is Bear thankful for?" Genevieve examines a patch of construction paper pumpkins.

The children told the teachers what they were grateful for, and the teachers recorded their answers on pumpkins taped to the door. I read over Genevieve's shoulder.

"Aw, Bear is thankful for t.v. and ice cream." Genevieve pretends to wipe away tears of joy.

Ingrid joins us. "Where is Dan-Dan's?" She stands on tip-toe to read the pumpkins toward the top of the door. "Daddy?" she splutters.

"Don't feel bad." I give Ingrid a sideways hug. "That means Dan-Dan has to wake up Danforth the next time he has a nightmare."

Ingrid laughs, filling the classroom with her dolphin shrieks. Dan-Dan should be grateful he did not inherit his mom's laugh.

Maude's daughter Emma is grateful for preschool. Pregnant Chloe's son Tristan is grateful for robots and trains. Ashley's daughter Sophia is grateful for her parents. And my daughter? I scan the pumpkins.

"The circus?" Genevieve says, confusion evident in her voice. Ingrid, who has so far kept my childhood secrets, gasps loudly.

My cheeks burn, and my stomach twists with shame. I haven't done anything wrong. My parents were circus acrobats, not serial killers, and my childhood stories are very entertaining. But once the other parents know I can juggle, ride a unicycle, and make elaborate balloon animals, they will stop thinking of me as "Elodie, the somewhat competent room mom," and regard me instead as "Elodie, former member of The Flying Flimbizzles, certified circus freak, who should hire a nanny and go back to work if she wants to give her daughter a shot at normalcy."

Ingrid and I make eye contact, and she widens her eyes meaningfully, urging me to tell the truth. I ignore Ingrid, laugh, and say, "We went to the circus a few months ago. I guess it made quite the impression."

Genevieve nods. "No wonder she wanted to be a tightrope walker for Halloween."

Luke arrives in time for a classroom concert of songs about wobbly gobbly turkeys, and then it is feast time, and the parents swarm the spread and heap their plates as if today is the main Thanksgiving event.

"This is amazing," Genevieve says in between bites. She points to the multiple servings of stuffing on her plate. "Which one did you make?"

"Both." I am half-proud, half-embarrassed.

"I thought you made the sweet potato casserole?" Mr. Joe says.

"I did." My knees tremble. "I went a bit overboard."

"Thank you!" Genevieve says. "This is the only Thanksgiving I get this year. My parents are on a cruise in Europe, Mark's parents are going to Vegas, and I can't cook."

"I love cooking for Thanksgiving, but this year, it's just me, Luke and Madison, so I used the potluck as an excuse to try recipes. Maybe I'll skip the cooking next week."

"What?" Luke yelps, breaking away from a conversation with Danforth Sr.

"I can't justify baking three pies for three people," I say defensively.

"Yes, you can," Luke says.

"There will be way too many leftovers. Our kitchen is not big enough."

"I'll help you eat leftovers," Genevieve says.

A thought occurs to me, and before I can obsessively worry about it, I blurt, "Come to our house! Have Thanksgiving with us!"

Genevieve's face breaks into a huge grin. "Seriously? I'd love to!"

I look at Luke, belatedly realizing I should have consulted with him before inviting guests. I might be the high priestess of Thanksgiving, but there is probably something in our marital vows that covers the unexpected addition of near-strangers to holidays. Luke, however, is nodding his head enthusiastically. My husband prioritizes pie options and side dishes over intimate family gatherings.

"What's happening?" Ingrid appears at my side.

"Genevieve is going to celebrate Thanksgiving with

Elodie," Mr. Joe says. "You're so lucky, Genevieve. I have to go to my Aunt Jill's this year." He shudders involuntarily.

"Elodie is hosting Thanksgiving? I'd love to come!" Ingrid bounces up and down on her toes.

My mouth opens and closes, opens and closes, like a goldfish screaming inside its bowl.

"Are you really Elodie?" Pregnant Chloe asks. She has three slices of pie on her plate. "Do you mind another taga-long preschool family?"

It turns out that lots of preschool families do not have Thanksgiving plans. At least, as of Friday morning, they didn't. By the end of the preschool potluck, six families, Miss Blaire and Miss Blaire's fiancé are planning to cele-brate Thanksgiving with the Joneses.

16

M y cell phone rings as I am tying on my apron. I do not recognize the number, but telemarketers rarely call at 6:14 a.m. on a national holiday, so I answer.

"Are you feeling suicidal?"

"What?" I'm about to hang up, but the voice sounds familiar.

"Happy Thanksgiving! It's your favorite psychiatrist."

"Oh," I stammer, "Happy Thanksgiving."

"Do you have any plans to off yourself today?"

"No!" I frantically think back to our session last week. "I'm sorry if I said anything that gave that impression."

"Don't get your panties in a twist. I call all my patients on Thanksgiving. It's the beginning of suicide season."

That's a myth. Google it. Suicide rates do not increase during the holidays, but to be pleasant, I say, "Oh, that's interesting, but I need to get going. I have a lot to do." My voice brightens. "We're hosting Thanksgiving."

"*You* are hosting Thanksgiving? You never mentioned that."

"We are having some preschool families over. We made the plans last Friday. After our session."

"How many preschool families?"

"Six." Plus one ukulele-strumming teacher and her fiancé.

"Six families! Are you insane? Wait, don't answer that. But seriously, are you insane? Can you even name them all?"

"Of course I can."

"Name them."

"Genevieve, her husband Mark and their kids, Huck and Bear. Ingrid and Danforths Senior and Junior. Maude, Sven and their daughter Emma. Dave, Paula and their daughter Zelda." Named after the video game. "Chloe, John and their kids Maya and Tristan. And Stephanie and Clark and their twins, Brianne and Brian."

"And a partridge in a pear tree," Dr. Dankworth gruffly sings. "Sounds awful."

"I enjoy cooking and hosting Thanksgiving."

Dr. Dankworth makes a rude, dismissive sound. "You need to release your delusions of being the perfect mom. You do not have to be Martha Stewart for your kid."

A swarm of bees buzz in my chest. I am not striving to be Martha Stewart for my daughter. I am hosting this big Thanksgiving feast for myself, thank you very much. In a tight voice, I say, "Thanks for your concern."

"Call me if you have a breakdown," and he hangs up.

Luke staggers into the kitchen, yawning and stretching. "What's for breakfast?"

My jaw drops.

"Kidding, I'll go get bagels."

"Take Madison with you!"

Dr. Dankworth thinks I'm crazy, but I was born for this sort of insanity. Besides, the hard work is done. I have been prepping, cooking and baking since Saturday. Genevieve is handling place settings and decorations, and her husband Mark is bringing a case of his home-brew beer, which Genevieve insists is quite good. Pregnant Chloe is bringing kid drinks, wine and a ham, and Maude is organizing a craft project for the kids. Ingrid sent a cleaning crew yesterday, and my house is so immaculate, it looks like we were robbed.

Miss Blaire and her fiancé, Steve, arrive first. They smile tentatively, surprised that the inside of the house is as pink as the outside. Steve hands a bottle of wine to Luke, and Luke says, "Hitching Post? Is this from that restaurant in *Sideways*?"

"It is!" Steve beams. He must be a decade older than Miss Blaire. He has a full head of wavy brown hair, a strong jawline and even stronger shoulders. Miss Blaire found her perfect match at least as far as looks are concerned. Their babies will be gorgeous.

"I hear you're getting married in Bulgaria," I say as I tie on a fresh apron.

Steve shrugs and laughs. "That sounds about right."

"Can I help?" Miss Blaire says before I can ask any follow-up questions about Bulgaria.

I have tied on a fresh apron and am poised to smash the potatoes into oblivion. "Everything is under control." Except my psychiatrist, who was completely out of control this morning, but that is not the sort of thing I confide in my daughter's preschool teacher.

Madison tugs on Miss Blaire's hand and drags her upstairs to her bedroom. Miss Blaire exclaims over the pink staircase as I mash the red potatoes. The doorbell rings, and Luke welcomes the newest arrivals. Genevieve, carrying a box of dried corn and miniature pumpkins, gapes at the pink kitchen as she follows Luke through the house to our backyard. We are having a lunchtime feast to accommodate nap schedules, which means it is warm enough to dine outside for which I am eternally grateful, because the options for indoor dining are pink, pinker, and pinkest. The prior owner "pinkified" the backyard as well — pink fence, pink stones in the garden beds, and pink rose bushes border the lawn — but the blue sky and green grass reduce the risk of pink-induced migraines.

I stir the gravy as Luke discusses carving strategies with several dads, and outside, Miss Blaire strums her ukulele. Madison runs inside as I am arranging dishes on the kitchen island and holds aloft a pinecone with googly eyes and craft feathers. "Look at my turkey!" Glue oozes from the pinecone, but I set it on top of a paper towel amongst the dishes. This Thanksgiving exceeds my childhood fantasies.

An hour later, the kids gather in the Womb Room and Luke turns on *The Little Mermaid* so the adults can digest in peace.

Genevieve sighs. "Maybe the kids will fall asleep and take a three-hour nap."

Danforth Sr. snores from his folding chair. He is wearing a t-shirt and jeans while Ingrid is wearing a tweed knit dress and knee-high brown leather boots with heels, and Dan-Dan is wearing a three-piece burgundy velvet suit with a black tie. Madison is wearing her favorite Peppa Pig t-shirt, pink striped leggings, and the pink tutu, which is tattered, faded, and stained after four months of daily wear.

"This is so cozy," Ingrid says. "If Dan-Dan was at Tiny Geniuses Academy this year, we'd be dining in a mansion with a butler." She frowns as much as her Botox allows. "I think this might be better."

"What's for dessert?" Maude's husband Sven says, patting his tummy. Everyone groans.

A phone rings. Ingrid lunges for her purse, and seeing the Caller ID, clenches her jaw. "Becky," she hisses. "She keeps calling me about the preschool thief." She leans across the table for a wine bottle. Her speech is already a little slurred, so I am not surprised when she pours Merlot into her half-full glass of Chardonnay.

"Has the thief struck again?" Maude asks.

"Does Becky still think it's me?" I say, trying to sound casual.

"I know it wasn't you," Genevieve reaches across the table and pats my hand.

"Here, here!" Genevieve's husband Mark raises a glass. "When would you have time to steal? You obviously spent all year preparing this magnificent feast."

I blush as everyone heaps compliments on my cooking.

"It's not Elodie." Ingrid gesticulates with the same hand that is holding her glass. A generous splash of wine slops onto her dress, but Ingrid does not notice. "Becky thinks this will ruin preschool's reputation and there will be low enrollment next year because no one wants to send their child to a preschool with a thief."

"So who do we think it is?" Pregnant Chloe asks in a conspiratorial whisper.

"We know the thief was at preschool during orientation and the first day of school." Ingrid burps. "Also Trunk-or-Treat."

"And the day of the room parent meeting," I say.

"That's right," Ingrid hiccups. "Becky made a list of suspects. She put EVERYONE on the list. Parents, teachers, even Dr. Konig. Then she crossed out names. Ten families missed orientation, so we know it was not them. Two different families missed the first day of school because of travel plans, and several children were out sick on the day of the room parent meeting, but we still have over seventy sets of parents who could be the thief."

For the record, the men, congregated on one side of the table, are engrossed in a heated discussion about football.

"It could also be a teacher." Miss Blaire strums her ukulele.

"At least the thief has not struck since Halloween," Maude says. "Maybe they quit while they were ahead."

"I still wish I could clear my reputation," I mumble.

"Hey!" Genevieve sits up straighter. "Maude, you're a genius."

"I am?"

"Yes! The thief has not struck since Halloween." Genevieve's eyes sparkle. "The Mumfords must be the thieves."

"Who are the Mumfords?" The name is familiar, but I have met so many people since orientation and struggle to keep everyone straight.

"Evan Mumford was our family activities director," Ingrid says bitterly. "He was supposed to organize Trunk-or-Treat but went AWOL, and then he moved to Phoenix without bothering to tell anyone."

"Evan and Mary Mumford have a kid in Huck's class. Well, had," Genevieve says. "They moved to Phoenix the day after Trunk-or-Treat, so that's why the thief has not struck since Halloween. Because they moved to Phoenix!"

I am not convinced.

Genevieve continues in a hushed voice. "Can I tell you a secret?"

We lean closer together. Miss Blaire even stops strumming her ukulele.

"Mary told me that Evan has a gambling problem, and that's why their marriage is on the rocks."

Everyone gasps and makes exclamatory sounds of agreement. Now Genevieve's theory makes perfect sense.

"Gamblers have debts," Ingrid says in a knowing voice. "Oh! And Mary helped at the refreshments table during Trunk-or-Treat."

"She did?" I ask. "What does she look like?"

"Dragon tattoo," Ingrid says.

"You're right," I gasp. Not every mom in Pasadena sports a dragon tattoo that spans across both arms. "She definitely helped at the refreshments table. Becky thanked her for helping before her 'big move' and Mary said it was the least she could do." My brain swirls. "Evan talked during the room parents meeting, so he could have broken into cars before the meeting started."

"Mary Mumford helped Emmy search her car during the meeting," Ingrid adds darkly.

"Mary was complaining they needed to move to Phoenix for the lower cost of living because Evan went through their savings," Genevieve says.

That settles it. Evan's gambling problem put the Mumford family into serious debt, so Mary stole from her fellow preschool parents to have enough money to put food on the table. She started at orientation; then avoided suspicion by helping Emmy search for her phone and wallet during the room parent meeting; and stole the fifty-dollar donation as her last hurrah. Poor Mary. Thank god Luke does not have a gambling problem.

"I'm texting Becky." Ingrid stabs a finger at her iPhone. "Do you want her to apologize, Elodie?"

But I am not listening. I have a nagging sensation that I am forgetting something important.

"Elodie! Are you listening?"

"What?" I snap.

"Do you want Becky to apologize?"

I shake my head, my brain already back on my nagging feeling. Did I turn the oven off? Did Luke buy enough ice cream for the pies?

"What a relief," Miss Blaire plucks the ukulele strings again. "I hope the Mumfords are also the ones embezzling from preschool."

"What?" Ingrid shrieks, dropping her phone to the ground. "Someone is embezzling from preschool?"

This gets the men's attention. The table goes very silent. From the house, Sebastian croons the lyrics to *Kiss the Girl*.

"I assumed all the board members knew that already," Miss Blaire whispers. "Oh dear."

"Who would embezzle from a preschool?" Miss Blaire's fiancé Steve asks, sounding disgusted.

"There can't be that much money to embezzle," Danforth Sr. says, awake now and refreshed by his nap.

"How much? Where? How?" Ingrid splutters. "Who knows?"

"Yolanda told me. She was hysterical." Yolanda is the co-op treasurer. "I assumed she told Becky."

"Tell me everything," Ingrid says.

Miss Blaire twists a lock of hair around her finger and says. "Yolanda told me she was running the numbers before the board meeting, and she thinks thirty thousand dollars has gone missing."

"Thirty thousand dollars!" Ingrid drops her phone again, and Danforth Sr. plucks it away before she can do any more damage.

"How does thirty thousand dollars just go missing?" Genevieve says.

"Yolanda is not very good at math," Miss Blaire says. "There could be a surplus of thirty thousand dollars."

Ingrid wrestles her phone away from Danforth Sr. "I'm calling Becky!" she announces, tilting dangerously on her high-heeled boots as she marches across the lawn toward a pair of empty Adirondack chairs.

From the den, a child howls and then another child screams with pure rage.

"Who wants dessert?" I knock over a wax squirrel candle as I jump to my feet.

That's when I remember the thing I forgot: the Mumfords moved to Arizona on Halloween, but the money in my wallet disappeared the Monday *after* Trunk-or-Treat.

The thief must still be in Pasadena, and according to Miss Blaire's new information, Mountain View Co-op Preschool also has an embezzler.

17

The Monday after Thanksgiving, as I pass under the horseshoe arch covered in bougainvillea, I spot Ingrid sitting on the bottom of the broken slide and sobbing.

"Can you make sure Madison washes her hands?" I ask Maude, and without waiting for an answer, I hurry to the slide. "What's wrong? What happened?"

Ingrid sobs, hiccups, and continues sobbing.

I hover over my freshman roommate and place a hand on her shoulder. "Is Danforth okay?" I remember I have to clarify. "Junior? And Senior?"

"No!" Ingrid wails.

Oh my god. My mind goes to a dozen dark places.

"It's true," Ingrid hiccups. She takes a deep breath and wipes away the tears. "We have an embezzler."

"Thank God." I slump down into the sand with relief and kneel at Ingrid's feet.

"Thank God? Did you hear what I said? We have an embezzler!" A few parents look toward us and Ingrid lowers her voice. "Everyone with keys left town for Thanksgiving, so we didn't check the financial records until this morning. Miss Blaire was right. Thirty thousand dollars has disappeared from our checking account."

My jaw unhinges. For a corporation like Google or Microsoft, thirty thousand dollars means nothing, but for a co-op preschool, it is an obscene amount of money. "Will preschool close?"

"No, we have savings, but we can't get a new playground until after the auction."

"That's a relief."

"A relief?" Ingrid pounds her fist against the slide. It creaks warningly, and she springs up. "The auction isn't until the last day of April! This heap is on the verge of collapse."

"It just has character," I say. A few children jump on the bridge and the structure groans. "A lot of character."

"It's a pile of timber and rusty nails."

Several parents are now watching, so I link arms with Ingrid and steer her away from the center of the courtyard.

"I should never have enrolled Dan-Dan here!"

Liz Huffenby enters the courtyard. If she overhears Ingrid's complaints, the entire school will know about the embezzler before morning circle, so I hurry Ingrid up the Forbidden Stairs and close the door behind us. Ingrid collapses on an ancient couch. She looks awful. Her red hair is in a disheveled ponytail, and she is wearing sweatpants and a baggy t-shirt. Zoe would delight in the sight of my freshman roommate, sobbing on an ancient couch, but my heart aches for Ingrid.

"Becky was supposed to sign a contract for the new playground today," Ingrid wails. "It's not the deluxe playground I want, but it's affordable and the company promise to install it during winter break. Now Becky refuses to sign anything with an embezzler at large. We might never get a new playground! Do you know what sort of psychological toll this is taking on our children? Play is crucial to this developmental stage."

"And they are playing just fine on the old playground." I sit on the arm of the couch and stroke Ingrid's hair. My mind recalls a memory, long forgotten, of a similar moment during our first week of college when I came home and found Ingrid lying face down on the lower bunk, sobbing. Her hometown honey had dumped her by email, so I sat on the floor and stroked her hair until the storm of tears ended. I didn't start college despising Ingrid, and a decade and a half later, it's hard to remember how and why I came to loathe her so much.

Ingrid snuffles and the tears abate. She sits up and fixes her ponytail. "It's just so frustrating." She wipes tears off her face. "Who embezzles from a preschool? And why would Becky think it's you?"

"Me!" Now it's my turn to shriek and wail.

"Don't worry. No one else thinks it's you. Whoever it is has access to the school computers, and that's above your pay grade. I told the board our theory about Mary and Evan Mumford, and everyone agrees they must be the thieves."

Of course, I know the Mumfords are innocent, because the thief emptied my wallet after Halloween, but it's far too late for me to volunteer that information to anyone. Besides, the Mumfords moved to Phoenix — if an innocent party is going to be suspected better them than me. Still, I feel a traitorous pang of guilt for letting people believe the thief has left the state of California.

"The board put safeguards in place," Ingrid continues, "that should at least stop the embezzler."

"I wonder how we could catch them and make them return the money."

Ingrid sits up. "If we did, we could get the new playground installed." She sags backs against the couch. "But the preschool financial records are a mess. We can't even figure out where the money went."

"What if you hire an accountant?"

"Preschool can't afford that."

"How much did the embezzler take? Thirty thousand?"

Ingrid nods glumly.

"If any parents show up with a new car or fancy jewelry, they might be the culprit."

"I'm going to check the parking lot now!" Ingrid freezes. "Oh my god, what time is it?"

I check my phone. "8:42."

"Go! You'll be late!"

"My first appointment is at 10:30."

"But you have to enjoy the amenities!" Ingrid gifted me a spa day to thank me for hosting Thanksgiving. She arranged it with Luke, and his parents are picking up Madison so I can get pampered in style. "Hurry! Forget about the playground. Relax!"

Twenty minutes later, I am sitting in the far corner of a steam room, surrounded by billows and billows of hot, wet clouds. After the steam room, I will luxuriate in the jacuzzi with a cup of complimentary water flavored with cucumbers. Having Ingrid back in my life has its upsides.

A hissing sound fills the steam room, and fresh white clouds fill the air. The door opens, but the air is so thick with steam, the two women entering are not more than shadows. The newcomers sit on the marble bench by the door.

"I like the photos you posted this morning," a woman with a husky voice says.

"Thanks," says her friend, a woman with a breathy Marilyn Monroe voice. "They're from the photo shoot I did with Arlo on Tuesday."

Oh. My. God. I am in a steam room with Resting Bitch-face Debbie and her faithful sidekick Ashley.

"Where did you go?" Ashley says.

"Malibu of course."

My entire body is overheating. Sweat stings my eyes, my heart rate is up, and every fiber in my body is screaming at me to leave the sauna immediately, if not sooner, yet I also want to lurk and eavesdrop.

"Why did you pick Mountain View? Doesn't it interfere with your modeling schedule?"

"I didn't pick Mountain View." Debbie sounds disgusted at the very idea. "My old nanny did. Charles told me to find a preschool for Arlo because he needed 'socialization', so I told the nanny to visit some schools and pick the best one. The bitch picked a co-op. I wouldn't have signed the paper-work if I knew parents have to volunteer."

"Can't you just send the new nanny to volunteer? That's what I do."

"Charles said that if I do that, he'll dock my allowance. Not that I need the money," Debbie adds hastily, "but I like to keep a nest egg just in case."

"You're too good for Charles."

"I know."

The steam is thinning, and Debbie and Ashley look less like anonymous blobs and more like Debbie and Ashley. If they notice me, they might recognize me, but a fresh spurt of steam fills the room, and Debbie and Ashley return to shadowy blobs. This is my cue to escape. It's too steamy for them to recognize me even up close.

"I didn't recognize the necklace you were wearing in your post this morning," Ashley says.

"Charles got it for me in Singapore. He brought back several pieces to make up for the jewelry stolen during Trunk-or-Treat."

Damnit. Now I have to stay in case Debbie says something incriminating.

"Charles' aunt is super upset about the necklace. She keeps asking how I could lose a family heirloom." Debbie sighs petulantly. "How many times do I have to tell her it was stolen? Besides, it's insured."

"What about your earrings? And bracelet? Were they insured?"

"Of course. I'm going straight to Tiffany's when I get my insurance money. My sponsors also sent me some gifts."

"You're so amazing."

"I know." Debbie tosses her hair over her shoulder.

"Where do you think Elodie hid the jewelry?"

I clench my sweaty fists.

"Becky told me it was that mom with the dragon tattoo. She was stealing to cover for her husband's gambling debts."

Becky should not have told Debbie that. The board does not have any definitive proof of the Mumfords' guilt. Then again, I'm the mom still at preschool, not Mary, and I know I'm innocent.

Debbie stands, arches her back and reaches her arms overhead. I need to get out of here, but her naked body blocks the exit. I have to be strong.

"How long should we stay here?" Ashley asks. She sounds weary. My hopes rise.

"Ten more minutes at least. We need to flush out all the toxins."

I will be unconscious in ten minutes.

"Mmm," Debbie moans a little and goes into downward dog. "You know what I need? An affair. Charles is always leaving on business trips."

Ashley giggles. "An affair? With who?" She drums her feet against the marble floor. "Ooh, Roger plays poker with some bachelors. Do you want me to check if any of them are cute?"

"That's too easy. I want a challenge. I want a married man."

"Huh." Ashley considers this. "There are plenty of married doctors at the hospital. Roger could—"

"I want something challenging and scandalous." Debbie transitions into warrior pose.

Little black wiggly lines float around me. My freckles are melting. I resolve to duck behind my towel and scoot around Debbie when Debbie leans a hand against the door to balance herself and lifts a foot to her rump.

"I want an affair with a preschool dad," Debbie announces.

Ashley gasps. I throw up in my mouth.

"A preschool dad? Is there anyone divorced?"

"I told you," Debbie snaps, "I want a challenge. I'm not seducing a divorced dad. Where's the fun in that? I want to have an affair with a married preschool dad."

I want to scream, tell Debbie that she is a vile beast, and kick her in the crotch, but I am better than Debbie and will not stoop to her level. Besides, I don't have the energy to do any of those things right now.

"Come on," Debbie says, "let's go to the sauna." She pulls the door open and struts away as Ashley scurries after her. A little woozy, I stagger to my feet, walk to the door and pause. Through the steamy glass door, I see Debbie and Ashley take washcloths from a bowl of icy water. Debbie pats her ample bosom with the cloth, drops it on the floor and sashays into the sauna. Ashley follows, and I practically fall out of the stream room. With my back to the sauna, I crab walk away from Debbie and her schemes of seducing a married preschool dad.

Forget the preschool embezzler. I need to keep that woman as far away from Luke as I possibly can.

18

All around me, children emerge from cars decked in their holiday finest. Every child looks styled for the December cover of a parenting magazine — every child, that is, except my own. Madison insisted on wearing her favorite Peppa Pig shirt, faded rainbow leggings, and the pink tutu that will not die. She refused to wear the expensive holiday dress I bought at the mall even when I suggested wearing the tutu over the dress and offered several attractive bribes for her compliance. Next year, remind me to set fire to a small pile of money and save myself a trip to the mall.

As Madison and I walk to the outdoor sink, I am once again pulling my wagon, but instead of potluck dishes, it transports gifts for the teachers. Okay, I brought a few potluck dishes, but only cookies! I baked sugar cookies, shortbread, and gingerbread ninjas.

I don my apron and give myself a mental high five for mastering the co-op game. The Christmas concert starts at 9:30, followed by the potluck, followed by general mayhem.

If I am going to school for the concert and potluck, I might as well knock out a volunteer day while I'm at it.

At circle time, there is an unfamiliar face. Who is that little boy sitting next to Miss Lucy, with the blonde hair styled into a swoop? Is that? No, it can't be.

But it is.

As the children race outside to play, I saunter up to Miss Lucy and say as casually as possible, "A boy from another class accidentally attended our circle time. Does that happen often?"

"That was Arlo," Miss Lucy says in a neutral tone of voice. "He joined our class on Wednesday. Dr. Konig decided we are a better fit for Arlo's family."

I stifle the urge to spew expletives and head outside. Genevieve is volunteering for her older son Huck's class. I spot her guarding the broken playground slide and plow through the sand to reach her. "Did you hear we have a new kid in Miss Lucy's class?"

"At last." Genevieve steers a child away from the slide. "We've had an extra spot since Charlotte went berserk."

"It's Arlo."

"Not Arlo, as in Debbie's son Arlo?" Genevieve's smile does a sudden u-turn.

"The same," I moan.

"Any idea why we are receiving this Christmas blessing?"

"Miss Lucy said Dr. Konig decided our class is a 'better fit' for Arlo's family."

Genevieve scans preschool. A lot of parents lurk around the courtyard, waiting for the big concert. Genevieve waves at a woman with intense eyebrows and long red fingernails. "Liz!" Genevieve calls. Out of the corner of her mouth, she whispers, "Liz Huffenby knows all the gossip."

Oh, I know Liz. If she ever learns I grew up in the circus, everyone will know, and the parents will treat me like a monkey ready to perform tricks on command. I can still hear the echoes of the students living on my floor freshman year begging me to entertain them with juggling when they needed a study break.

"Genevieve!" Liz booms. "I miss having Huck in Daniel's class."

"I know, I miss Daniel, too," Genevieve says, laying on the charm. They exchange pleasantries, and Genevieve introduces me.

"Of course I know Elodie!" Liz crows. Translation: we talked once, and now she keeps close tabs on any rumors attached to me.

Genevieve continues, "We had a child transfer to our class this week. Have you ever heard of that happening?"

"Oh yes," Liz nods vigorously. "Let's see, Noah Adams switched classes because his mom thought the teacher played favorites. Albert P. switched classes because his dad thought Miss Heather was a communist. And Addy switched classes when her mom had a major falling out with another mom in that class and the hostilities were unbearable. There's usually a juicy scandal behind the transfer."

Genevieve cups an elbow with one hand and taps her other against her chin. "I wonder if there's a scandal behind our transfer?"

"Who is it?"

"Arlo, Debbie's son."

Liz Huffenby grins wickedly. "Oh yes, there has been drama. Debbie is awful. Did you know she has a podcast? She uses it to complain about the other kids and parents at Mountain View. In an episode last week, she ranked all the dads in Miss Ellen's class, and then she described, in graphic detail, how she would seduce each of them."

Shamefully, I already listened to that episode. I have listened to all the episodes.

"At a birthday party last weekend, she wore super revealing clothes and got caught kissing a dad behind the moon bounce." Liz runs a hand through her hair; her fingernails still remind me of bloody talons. "Naturally, there was an uproar and a bunch of moms in Miss Ellen's class threatened to pull their kids out of school if Dr. Konig did not expel Arlo. I guess Dr. Konig transferred the kid instead."

The playground groans. My thoughts exactly. Genevieve and Liz chat for a few more minutes, but I am not listening. My mind reels. I love this preschool, and Miss Lucy's class is at the center of that love. I have bonded with the parents during volunteer shifts, the morning ritual of washing hands, and the late morning conversations as we wait to pick up our kids. Nearly half the families came to my house for Thanksgiving. Now Debbie will ruin all our bonding with her toxic energy.

Miss Lucy rings a bell and we line the children up, an ordeal which takes several minutes. Several children push to be in the front. Bear keeps falling down on purpose. Madison and Maude's daughter Emma play tug-of-war over a baby doll. Once we have the children sorted into something resembling a line, several announce they must go to the bathroom, and Arlo sneezes, sending a gush of snot down his lips. Mr. Joe hurries the "need to pee" crew away while Miss Blaire dabs Arlo's face with a fistful of tissue.

I make a mental note to never be a preschool teacher.

As we wait for Mr. Joe and the kids to return, Miss Lucy distributes Santa hats. I hold my breath when she reaches Madison, but Madison dons the red and white hat while singing to herself. Miss Blaire gives the children jingle bell bracelets they made with pipe cleaners. The kids shake their arms vigorously, filling the courtyard with a cacophony of metal clinks. Part of me screams for Advil, but mostly I glow with the festive spirit. This is exactly the sort of rite of passage I craved for my daughter.

Madison holds my hand as we shuffle toward the church next door. Although Mountain View Co-op Preschool is secular, we neighbor a church that is also our landlord. Parents and grandparents have already crowded into the church, filling most of the pews. I curse silently. I am going to be stuck in the back, barely able to witness my daughter's first holiday concert.

Miss Lucy places a hand on my shoulder and murmurs, "Can you sit at the end of that row there with Madison?"

It's a Christmas miracle! Instead of being banished to the back corner of the church, I get to sit on the steps with the kids, where I can take close-up photos and videos of Madison while soaking up every moment of this precious experience. Madison and I sit down, surrounded by fidgety children. The church is decorated with poinsettias, a large wooden Nativity and a dozen fir trees that fill the air with the aromas of a Christmas tree lot. I point out Luke to Madison as he takes the last seat in a row of parents from Miss Lucy's class.

Dr. Konig stands in front of the children and waits for the audience to settle. Becky lurks a few feet away, holding a sheath of paper. Once the church quiets, Dr. Konig says, "Welcome everyone! Our performers can get a little antsy, so without further ado, let's enjoy our 2015 holiday concert!" Becky scowls but takes a seat in the front pew, and the children sing. Well, some children sing. At least half the children, including Madison, stare like deer in headlights at the parents, and more than a few sniffle and cry.

It does not matter. I am at my daughter's Christmas concert, and after this, we have a potluck that I organized. There was not a flutter of drama about the sign-ups. I also organized thoughtful gifts for the teachers (wine and Target gift cards), bought Dr. Konig a new orchid, and made fudge for Meredith, preschool's receptionist/plumber. I don't want to brag, but I am killing the motherhood game.

Midway through *Frosty the Snowman*, the church's front door bangs shut as a latecomer arrives. She is wearing a very short red dress trimmed with white fur. It is Debbie, and Sweet Baby Jesus, she dressed as Stripper Santa. Debbie says, "Hi, Arlo! Mommy's here!" Then she walks in front of the teachers leading the concert, stops in the middle aisle, and surveys the church for an empty seat. More than a few dads leer. I sigh with relief, because Luke is safe at the end of a full pew.

Debbie sashays down the middle aisle and stops right next to my husband. Bomb sirens blare in my head. Debbie says, her Marilyn Monroe voice echoing against the rafters, "Could you make room for one more?" The parents nudge together and Debbie squeezes in next to Luke.

The concert continues.

The children sing about Rudolph. Debbie whispers something in Luke's ear. The children shake their jingle bell bracelets. Debbie places a hand on Luke's thigh and asks him a question. He keeps his eyes on Madison and says something in response. Santa Debbie throws her head back and laughs.

Did you know that if you rearrange the letters of "Santa," you can spell "Satan"?

The concert drags on for an eternity. After the last song

is sung and the applause ends, I help Miss Lucy lead the children back to our classroom for the potluck while Debbie does who knows what with my husband. It probably involves dry humping. I settle the children into chairs for the potluck while screaming quietly in my head. Finally, Luke enters the class, deep in conversation with Genevieve's husband Mark. Santa Debbie enters right behind him with an effervescent Ashley by her side.

Debbie, strutting like a model on a catwalk, passes behind me on her way to the buffet. Several dads scramble to let her reach the Le Croix. In my leggings, aprons, and oversized black t-shirt, I feel like a nun.

"Can I do anything to help?" Luke leans over to peck my cheek.

Yes, I think urgently, *please leave and never return to preschool*.

"I think everything is under control," I say.

"Where's Ingrid?" Maude asks as we pile meatballs and mac and cheese on to red plates for the children.

"Hawaii." Ingrid might spontaneously combust when she hears about our new classmate.

My heart rate slows down to a manageable thump as everyone eats. The classroom is even more festive than the church with snowmen strung overhead, tissue paper dreidels taped to the windows, and Santa crafts tacked to every available surface. The aquarium is extra jolly with ceramic gingerbread houses and a gingerbread surfer dude. Luke huddles with two dads on the circle time rug, talking about fantasy football. Debbie stands on the other side of the room, flirting with Mr. Joe. Mr. Joe sends beseeching glances in Miss Lucy's general direction. Miss Lucy ignores Mr. Joe and assures Maude that Emma is on track for college.

Brooke, whose husband Josh brought the green bologna to school, crams cookies into her mouth.

"These are amazing, Elodie!" Brooke says, holding up the shortbread. "What's in this one?"

"Parmesan," I say. "I know, totally weird."

"But it works!" A shower of crumbs falls from Brooke's mouth to the floor. "And these sugar cookies are the best cookies I've ever had."

"Mmm," Pregnant Chloe says. Her belly is huge, but she insists she is not due until the spring. "What are these?"

"Dark chocolate peanut butter cookies," I say.

The room goes quiet.

"Oh god." My stomach heaves. "I completely forgot. Those are for Luke's secretary."

Miss Lucy is already yanking away any plates with the offending peanut butter cookies.

"Is anyone allergic?" Maude says. "Do we have any nut allergies? Oh my god, do we need an EpiPen?"

"We don't have any nut allergies in our class this year," Miss Lucy serenely says. "But better safe than sorry."

"I am so, so sorry." I dump the cookies in the trash. My heart races.

"It's okay, mistakes happen," Miss Lucy says. "No harm was done."

"I accidentally brought peanut butter sandwich crackers for snack Huck's first year." Genevieve hugs me from the side. "Don't beat yourself up. Now, tell me the truth: would it be totally weird if I rescue the cookies from the trash and take them home?"

I laugh. "Yes, unless you like your cookies with a side of glue and glitter."

The crisis is over, and I know this is going to sound weird, but I feel better than ever. I made a mistake with the peanut butter cookies, but no actual harm was done, and now Genevieve and I have an in-joke. I must be on Santa's nice list.

Madison runs over to Luke and drags him to the library corner. She climbs into his lap, and Luke reads a picture book about a duck's Christmas adventure. Then, from across the room, Debbie catches my eye and winks. My heart misses a beat.

Debbie saunters over to the carpet where Arlo plays with the wooden train set. She kneels down and reaches for the caboose, giving everyone a glimpse of the red thong "covering" her caboose. Then she sits and makes a big show of tucking her skirt to conceal her swimsuit model derriere. Luke studies the Christmas book, but I swear, his cheeks are flushed.

I am officially on Santa's naughty list this year.

19

I will not itch my vagina.

I will not itch my vagina.

I will not itch my vagina.

Wait a second: is my vagina itchy? Or is it my vulva? Damnit, I'm almost thirty-seven years old. Shouldn't I be able to keep the anatomical names for my lady bits straight by now? Well, whether it's my vagina, vulva or something else that starts with the letter V, it's itchy and over-the-counter remedies are NOT working.

I am sitting in the waiting room for a women's health medical group Ingrid recommended. I may not want a fancy purse, but for itchy vaginas and pap smears, I want the Coco Chanel of gynecologists. It's Madison's first day back at preschool after the winter break, and our holidays... well, they sucked. First, Madison got the flu, then Luke got the flu, and I played Florence Nightingale for two weeks. We had to cancel our trip to visit my family in San Diego. The Sweeney Sisters' Dazzling Big Top Extravaganza is in Alabama by now, and they will perform all winter in the South. Then they will work their way up the east coast before doing their usual summer circuit through New England. I missed my chance to visit them in an easy, civilized way, and if I want to visit, I'll have to fly cross-country solo with my preschooler and stay in a trailer or questionable roadside motel.

At least I didn't get the flu.

My appointment is in ten minutes. If this doctor operates on Dankworth Mean Time, I will be here for two more hours, but fortunately, this waiting room is civilized. Instead of a television blasting nature programs, there is a complementary K-cup brewer with pods for coffee and tea plus miniature creams and sugar packets. Also, unlike the seating in Dankworth's office, the chairs here are comfortable. What a refreshing novelty.

I have a novel in my tote bag but reach for my phone out of habit. According to my alerts, I have not received any new messages, but I still scroll down my one-sided text chain with Zoe. A thought occurs to me, so I type:

I'm in the waiting room of my new gynecologist.

Hooray for yeast infections!

What are you going to do if your lady bits get irritated in Alaska? I hope you smuggled in an emergency tube of Monistat.

I wait, but of course the dots signaling an incoming message do not appear.

Ingrid recommended my new gynecologist. You won't believe it, but she's not as awful as she was in college. Maybe she wasn't ever that awful. Maybe we were

young and stupid, you know? Yeah, her laugh is annoying, but it's not like she's the Antichrist.

I delete this message before I accidentally hit send. Zoe
truly believes that Ingrid is the Antichrist, and she has just
cause. Ingrid spiked Zoe's drink, and then Zoe danced
topless on a table, earning herself the nickname "Zoe the
Hoey" and then Ingrid stole Craig, Zoe's freshman crush. I
may be pathetic, desperate, and lonely, but I will not
embrace a friendship with Zoe's arch-nemesis.

I sigh and check email. The latest message announces
"Blaire and Steve's Wedding!" and includes a professional
portrait of the happy couple, details about the event,
including an address in Delchevo, Bulgaria, and links to five
different wedding registries. I add "decline Miss Blaire's
wedding invitation" and "buy Miss Blaire a wedding gift" to
my to-do list.

Next, I open an email from Monica:

**From: Monica Park Hillenbrand
<VP@MountainView.Com>
To: most-bitching-room-parents@moun-
tainview.com
Sent: Mon, 04 Jan 2016 09:04:19 (PST)
Subject: January Room Parent Business**

Dear Room Parents,

Happy New Year!

**Congratulations: you survived the
holiday gauntlet. You can sit back and
rest on your room parent laurels,**

**because we do not have any big events
in January or February. Valentine's
Day is low key. NO POTLUCK. The kids
just bring in cards, and there are no
room parent responsibilities.**

**I have some exciting news: we are
having a book fair in March! Our new
fundraising director Ingrid is spear-
heading the event, but she needs your
help. I'm attaching the link to sign
up for volunteer shifts at the book
fair.**

**Your faithful leader,
Monica**

Confession: I am disappointed that I will not get to organize anything for Valentine's Day, although the promise of
the book fair soothes my soul. I have never been to one, but
as the circus criss-crossed the country, book fair banners
affixed to school fences tormented me. Oh, how my young
heart ached to go to a book fair! I imagined it would be
something like the lovechild of a bookstore and Willy
Wonka's Chocolate Factory. Now that I am an adult, my
voice of reason insists a book fair cannot live up to my childhood expectations, but my inner child does not give a damn
about being reasonable and is doing cartwheels, backflips
and an Arabian double front. (Acrobats raised my inner
child.)

I click on the link as a pregnant woman on the other side
of the waiting room says, "Have you ever listened to this
podcast?"

"Oh yes, it's my favorite guilty pleasure. Did you know she lives in Pasadena?"

"That's the only reason I listen," Pregnant Woman No. 1 says. "She has expert advice about losing the pregnancy weight. I'm going to try her apple cider detox while breast-feeding."

It is rude to eavesdrop, but I listen anyway. I want to confirm they are talking about *Centerfold Mama*.

"I wonder what preschool her son goes to. I would never want to send my baby to a school with a thief."

Yep. They are talking about Debbie's podcast.

"It's Mountain View Co-op Preschool."

I take out my book and pretend to read.

Pregnant Woman No. 2 gasps. "I thought that was an excellent school."

"Not anymore," No. 1 gloats. "They don't even interview prospective parents. Can you imagine?"

My back teeth grind together.

"I prefer Tiny Geniuses Academy. I toured their campus last week and put this guy on the waitlist." No. 2 rubs her tummy lovingly.

I will not butt into their conversation.

"We put our baby on the waitlist when I quit the pill."

"Smart. Do you know if they ever caught the thief at Mountain View?"

"No, but according to *Centerfold Mama*, it's one of the room moms."

I stand and blurt, "That's not true!"

The pregnant women turn and stare at me.

"My daughter goes to Mountain View." My heart is trying to escape my rib cage. "The thief moved to Phoenix, and she was never a room mom." That's a lie, but it's the lie everyone believes at preschool, so it's good enough for these judgmental women.

No. 1 tilts her head. "What about the embezzler?"

No. 2 gasps. "There's an embezzler?"

"My friend Megan sends her children there, and she says there is an embezzler. Preschool has lost three hundred thousand dollars! Megan is planning to transfer her kids at the end of the year."

"It's only thirty thousands dollars," I mumble.

"Maybe the room mom is the embezzler," No. 2 speculates.

"The one who brought the peanut butter cookies to the Christmas potluck?"

"Debbie said she was laughing about it."

"Can you believe the nerve of some people?"

"Hello? Who forgets about the nut ban? She could have killed a kid."

"It's like they will let just anybody be a room mom these days."

"Totally incompetent."

The pregnant women gloat over my mistake as my cheeks burn with shame. I made dark chocolate peanut butter cookies for Luke's legal secretary, but I stacked all the cookies together on the kitchen counter and grabbed the peanut butter ones during the morning rush to get to preschool on time.

"I'm in that class," I interject. "The cookies were a mistake. She's a good room mom."

"She sounds like an absolute disaster," Pregnant Mom No. 1 declares. "Not everyone is cut out for motherhood."

"Elodie Jones?" A nurse in pink scrubs appears at the waiting room door.

"That's me." Before I walk away, I whisper, "I heard the teachers at Tiny Geniuses Academy let the kids watch television during snack time. Do you know what screen time does to a child's intellectual development?" Their mouths drop open. As I walk away, I add, "Good luck with labor and delivery!"

Yes, I'm evil, but my vagina is itchy, and they deserved it.

I follow the nurse past a scale, the resident phlebotomist, an examination room with stirrups (shudder), and a bathroom. The nurse stops at the end of the hall and gestures for me to enter a corner office that has a large walnut desk, shelves filled with books, and plush leather chairs for patients. The desk is tidy, free of ashtrays, empty takeout containers and stacks of patient files.

"I thought I had an appointment for an examination?"

"Dr. Shafaei likes to meet her new patients in her office first."

"It just seems more civilized," an older woman with grey hair says as she breezes into the room, offering me her hand. "I'm Dr. Shafaei. I like to chat before I ask you to get naked and put your feet in the stirrups." Dr. Shafaei sits behind the walnut desk and peruses my paperwork. "Postpartum depression," she smiles warmly at me. "I'm sorry you had to deal with that. It's very common, but people hate talking about it."

I silently thank Ingrid for hooking me up with this angel.

"Are you still taking Zoloft for the postpartum depression?"

"Yes." I play with the cuff of my sleeve, feeling unsettled by what the pregnant women said. Am I a disaster of a mom? Am I cut out for motherhood? Why wasn't I more careful about the peanut butter cookies? I swallow and focus my attention on the present moment. "I was ready to wean off Zoloft last year, but we moved from New York to Pasadena and my psychiatrist thought I should stay on Zoloft until I felt settled here."

"Oh goodness, yes. When did you move?"

"Last summer."

"How do you feel now?"

I pause and reflect. Right now, between my itchy vagina and the judgmental moms in the waiting room, I feel lousy. Overall, however, life is good. Ingrid has kept my secret, and I fit in with the other preschool moms. "I'm feeling great. I love Pasadena."

"Have you given any thought to weaning off Zoloft?"

"I have." My confidence whooshes away as I think of Dr. Dankworth. "My new psychiatrist says I'm not ready."

"If you don't mind my asking, who is your new psychiatrist?"

"Dr. Dankworth."

For a moment, Dr. Shafaei's face darkens, but then she smiles and says slowly, carefully choosing her words, "He is an interesting character."

"Yes, he is." I chew the inside of my lip.

Dr. Shafaei scrunches her face, debating how much she wants to say about Dr. Dankworth.

"He's awful!" I say. I have told no one about my appointments with Dr. Dankworth, and I can bear it no longer. "He smokes during our sessions and takes personal phone calls on his cell phone when I'm talking. He has weight machines in his office and lifts weights even if he is running over an hour late and has a dozen patients stuck waiting. At my first appointment, he wanted me to tell him about my mental health in the office kitchen while he was making a smoothie and lots of people were nearby."

I stop ranting, appalled with myself. I do not know Dr.

Shafaei. Maybe she takes phone calls while her patients have their feet in their stirrups. Backpedaling, I say, "I'm too sensitive. He is the doctor, after all, and went to Harvard."

"Oh, I don't think you are being sensitive," Dr. Shafaei hurries to say. "You are not alone in your experiences with Dr. Dankworth. Harvard produces its fair share of jerks."

I am not losing my mind. Dr. Dankworth *is* awful. A weight that I did not realize I was carrying leaves my shoulders. I could cry, hug this woman, and yodel.

"I could recommend my favorite psychiatrists."

"Yes!" I smile, but then a heaviness settles in my stomach. "It's just."

Dr. Shafaei smiles encouragingly.

"I have wanted to find another psychiatrist since our first appointment, but I'm worried about my Zoloft prescription. Sometimes it takes a while to get an appointment with a psychiatrist." My voice trails off as the weight settles back on my shoulders.

"I will write you a prescription for Zoloft, if that happens. Let me make a note of that in my file."

Twenty minutes later, I leave the office with a prescription for my yeast infection and a new lightness to my step. You can say I'm crazy, but I am actually grateful for my itchy vagina.

20

"Good morning!" Genevieve waves from across the street. Today's fedora is mustard yellow. "What a beautiful day for a party!"

I unbuckle Madison and say, "We did not get this sort of weather in January in New York." The grueling October heat was penance for the glory that is January in Pasadena, and if I ever see snow again, it will be too soon.

Ingrid parks behind Genevieve. "Good morning!" She opens the trunk of her car and pulls out an enormous gift bag. Danforth Sr., wearing jeans and a t-shirt with a picture of a yeti, emerges from the black Mercedes SUV with Danforth Jr., who is wearing a plaid blazer, button-down shirt, bow tie, and slacks.

I gesture between Danforth Sr. and Ingrid. "How are you two married?"

Ingrid throws back her head and laughs, and an image of Flipper leaps into my mind. I have to stop being funny around her.

"Where's your lesser half?" Danforth Sr. asks.

"Getting a haircut. He'll be here soon."

We walk down the block toward the house with balloons out front. This is the first preschool birthday party we have attended and I am taking mental notes for Madison's April bash.

"I've never been to this neighborhood," Genevieve says. "The houses are enormous."

"I never thought of the Rusts as living in a mansion," Ingrid says.

I hate to be judgmental, but I have to agree with Ingrid. Josh, a stay-at-home dad, wears ratty stained sweats which do not always cover his hairy butt crack; and the last time I saw Brooke, she was spewing cookie crumbs all over the floor during the Christmas potluck. Their son Gavin is a cute boy with chubby cheeks and a penchant for climbing on tables and smearing his boogers on the wall. On second thought, I guess he is not that cute after all.

We reach the house with balloons. "Hang on." I grab Madison by the arm. "Let me double check the address, baby girl." I take out my phone and pull up the invitation. This cannot be the right place.

It is the right place.

The Rusts do indeed live in a mansion, but their mansion is, shall we say, the black sheep of the neighborhood. Shutters hang at odd angles; the grey paint is peeling away; and two windows on the second story are broken. The "landscaping" is worse: dead lawn; dead bushes; a dead tree that has fallen over; and a decomposing couch.

We creep toward the front door. Something hisses, and Ingrid screams as an opossum emerges from the bowels of a nearby couch.

Josh's head appears from a window on the second floor. "That's Frank!" he hollers. "Give the couch a wide berth. He's a bit territorial."

"I can't go inside that house," Ingrid whispers.

Again, I have to agree with her. My every maternal instinct screams at me to fake a sudden emergency and ditch the party, but that would not be nice. I am the room mother. It's my moral obligation to attend this party and have a good time.

A shingle slides off the roof and shatters near the front door.

On second thought, I just remembered that I need to rearrange the junk drawer in the kitchen today.

"Come on, ladies, be brave." Danforth Sr. strides toward the party, and the children run after him. I guess we are doing this.

A vile smell assaults my nostrils as soon as I cross the threshold, and by the time I recover from the shock, Madison is halfway up a geometric climbing dome. I gape with a mixture of awe, disbelief, and horror. It seems ingenious to keep one of these structures inside, yet I cannot help seeing all the ways my child could die.

"Elodie! Thanks for coming!" Brooke shambles over and embraces me. She is wearing a helmet that holds two cans of beer and has tubes for drinking. "Welcome to our home. What do you think?"

"It's..." I search for something that will not sound rude. "It's so big!"

"Yes, it is." Brooke's face falls. "It's a bit too much for us. We can't keep up with the maintenance, but Josh inherited it from his uncle and we couldn't say no to a free place to live. Can I get you something to drink? Beer? Something stronger? Diet Coke?"

"Diet Coke would be great." I follow Brooke past the climbing structure, through a dining room with a crystal chandelier and broken folding table, and into the kitchen.

Brooke retrieves a glass from the sink and opens the freezer. I see things I can never unsee. There is a pile of hamburger meat on the bottom shelf, and that's it: no bag, no wrapping, no nothing. Next to the pile of unbagged meat, there is a bag of ears, snouts, and a curly tail. I shudder. At least the pig parts are in a bag. Brooke wipes her hand across her nose, grabs a fistful of ice from a bin and plunks them into a large red plastic cup.

I glance at the sink as Brooke pours my Diet Coke. Chunks of raw chicken surround the drain. I blink hard and look again. Yes, I saw correctly the first time: there are huge chunks of raw chicken splattered around the sink. Forget being nice. We have to leave this party before any food is served.

Soda foam overflows from the cup and Brooke slurps some off and hands it to me. I thank her. A tiny piece of my soul dies.

Madison is on the floor playing with some broken dinosaurs. The floor is carpeted with a thick orange shag matted with all sorts of filth that the pink tutu is absorbing into its tattered tulle. I am officially burning the tutu as soon as we get home. (Okay, I don't have the courage to do that, but I will scrub the scrap of fabric that was once a tutu until my hands bleed.)

"Let's go outside." I grab Madison's arm and haul her to her feet before she can protest. There are only a handful of guests outside, and I cannot fathom why so many parents would stay inside a house teeming with traces of the Bubonic plague.

"Doggy!" Madison runs away from me.

"No!" I tackle her on the cracked concrete ground as the "doggy" strains at the end of a chain.

Danforth Sr. edges toward me, keeping a firm grip on

Junior's arm. "What breed is that?" he says, sounding almost as terrified as me.

I gulp. "Can Rottweilers mate with mountain lions?"

The monstrosity snarls, and it sounds prehistoric. "Inside was better," I say, and we flee back into the cesspool.

I pass Genevieve at the back door. "I need fresh air," she says, then pales as she spots Cujo.

"No, you don't." I shove her in my haste to get my child to safety. Her orange fedora falls to the ground and we leave it behind. The fedora will have to fend for itself. We retreat to the living room not because it is a desirable destination, but because it is the least horrifying option. Debbie, wearing a slinky beige dress, steps through the front door with Arlo.

"What room is this?" Debbie sneers.

Brooke hurries over and takes the present that Debbie is holding. "Welcome! This is the living room."

"Oh god, you can't possibly do any living in here." Debbie gingerly steps over the mangled remains of a teddy bear.

I turn around and cover my mouth to stifle a laugh. I do not want to encourage Debbie, but for once, I welcome her cruelty.

"Arlo, don't touch a thing." Debbie scratches her arm. "Does this house have fleas? Arlo, we're leaving."

Debbie marches over to Arlo, who is playing with the recycling bin, and wrenches a crumpled beer can from her son. Madison shrieks, "Daddy!" and Luke enters the party.

"We have to leave," I whisper as Luke, holding Madison in his arms, swoops down to give me a kiss. My immune system groans as filth, vermin, and the stench of death overload it.

"What a delightful surprise," Debbie purrs. She has

abandoned Arlo to the recycling bin and is standing so close to Luke, her breasts graze his arm. Does this woman have any sort of moral compass? I want to tell her to back away from my man, but Luke does not seem to mind Debbie's attentions. If I say something snarky, I'll just draw attention to our differences and there's no winning against a swimsuit model.

"Daddy! There's a doggy! Come see!" Madison twists out of Luke's arms and drags him toward the back door.

"Oh, I love dogs!" Debbie says. "Arlo, come see the doggy!"

I follow, determined to chaperone my husband, but am waylaid by a hand on my shoulder. It's Ingrid.

"We have a crisis," she says.

"I know," I say, uncertain whether she is referring to Debbie or the backyard beast.

"The embezzler got past Becky's safeguards."

I drag my fingers through my hair as my brain processes this new information. "How much did they get?"

"Another five thousand!"

"What were the safeguards?"

"We changed the password on the computers."

"And?"

"That's it. What else could we do?"

Honestly, I have no idea.

Ingrid continues. "We can't keep hemorrhaging this sort of money! What if word gets out? And you know word will get out. We can forget about the new playground. We aren't even going to have enough money to keep preschool afloat next year."

I know, from my time in the gynecologist's waiting room, that word is already out and parents are loath to send their children to Mountain View Co-op Preschool. This, however, is not the time or the place to tell Ingrid that. This is the time and place to devise an excuse to leave the party immediately, if not sooner. We can worry about the embezzler once we have escaped Cujo, the Bubonic plague, and whatever is the source of that awful smell.

"Forget the embezzler," I whisper urgently. "There's raw chicken in the sink."

Ingrid's jaw unhinges.

I continue, "We need to leave before cake is served, but how can we do that without offending Brooke and Josh?" Despite my desire to leave this party, I still do not want to hurt the Rusts' feelings.

Ingrid says, "Let's—" and a gagging sound, followed by a commotion of babbling kids and shouting adults, interrupts. We rush toward the chaos.

The birthday boy is puking on the coffee table.

Ingrid and I flee Puke-A-Palooza. I find Luke outside with Madison, watching the beast. Arlo, bless his heart, is standing near the door, sobbing from sheer terror, and Debbie is consoling him instead of seducing my husband. "Don't ask questions," I say to Luke, "but we have to leave. Now."

"Trust me, I don't need an explanation."

I would like to make our escape without reentering the contamination zone, but alas, a six-foot pile of trash blocks one side of the house and a precarious heap of pallets barricades the other. "We go inside," I say, "and make a beeline for the front door, end of discussion."

I reenter the kitchen — so gross — and Luke follows with Madison. We walk past the broken folding table and ill-advised climbing structure. Freedom is close. We just have to sidestep the coffee table in the "living" room and we are home free.

I pause on the threshold of the living room. My god, it's the three-year-old version of a crime scene. A pool of vomit on the coffee table drips onto the orange shag carpet. Puke drips down the walls. I hold my breath before rushing for the front door.

"We have to sing! We have to sing!" Brooke wails as other parents make a desperate bid for freedom. "Please!" In a hysterical voice, she sings *Happy Birthday*. I would keep on course for the front door, but Brooke stands right in front of it, holding a lopsided cake. On cue, the kids sing, and the parents stand defeated, as if the *Happy Birthday* song has cast a dark magic spell and no one can leave the party until it is over. Even Debbie is standing at the edge of the living room, mumbling the words.

Josh lights the candles. One whizzes and shoots off sparks. I think it might be a firecracker. Brooke puts the lopsided dessert on the coffee table, and at the end of the song, Gavin leans over and vomits on the cake.

21

L uke finds me on the bathroom floor at 3 a.m. typing an email on my phone.

He crouches next to me. "What are you doing?"

"Trying not to die."

"Are you emailing?"

I drop my phone as a fresh surge of nausea hits. Whatever was ailing the birthday boy now ails me, but I am impressed that my immune system staved off the imminent collapse for this long. When I finish vomiting, I say, "I'm supposed to be the volunteer parent tomorrow. Today. In five hours. I need to find a sub."

"Don't worry about it." Luke rubs my back.

I puke a little more. Even in the throes of nausea, I have the energy to loathe our house's prior owner for installing a pink toilet in a bathroom with a pink tile floor and pink tile walls.

Luke offers me a paper cup of water, and I take a sip even though I am giving my stomach fresh ammunition. "I have to find a sub," I groan. "It says so in the parent manual."

"Can't I do it?"

"What?"

"I'm a parent. Don't dads ever volunteer?"

"Yes, but you have work."

"We settled that big annoying case last week. I can go to the office when Madison is done with preschool and take her with me. It'll be fun."

"Take Madison to the outside sink to wash hands when you arrive, and after you sign in, put on your apron, and—"

"I will figure it out. Just take care of yourself."

I want to protest, but my stomach lurches and I am too busy being sick to think about anything else.

I wake at nine and panic. We are late! It's my volunteer day! Then my stomach heaves and I remember: I have a stomach bug; Luke took Madison to school; he is the volunteer. I stagger down the pink staircase so I can watch television in the Womb Room. Maybe *The Price Is Right* will distract me from my misery, but alas, I cannot find my favorite game show, so I settle on an *Ally McBeal* rerun.

I check my phone, expecting a deluge of panicked texts from Luke, but there is only a single text from Luke, devoid of panic:

Everything under control. Feel better. Love you.

I am about to set my phone on the table when a text from Ingrid arrives:

Why would you let your husband volunteer with Debbie?

Mother.

Of.

God.

I get up to puke. Leaning over the downstairs toilet, I think about my husband, spending three hours with preschool's resident succubus. The last time Luke saw me, I was heaving my guts into a pink toilet, and now he is cavorting around preschool with a swimsuit model. She probably tied the apron in a way that accentuates her trim waist and enormous breasts.

When I finish puking, I text Ingrid.

I got sick from that godforsaken party.

Ingrid replies:

Six kids are out. Worst party ever.

I smile despite the agonizing pain in my stomach. Ingrid texts again:

Ew, Debbie is prancing around the sandbox.

An image of Debbie in a bikini pops into my head. I shove it away and type:

Why are you still at preschool? I thought you volunteered last week.

Ingrid sends several replies in rapid succession:

Emergency board meeting.

Embezzler crisis.

Also, the thief.

Nervously, I ask:

Has the thief struck again?

Ingrid replies:

Last Friday.

Without thinking (too! much! nausea!), I type:

Maybe the thief while strike when I am out sick, and then Becky will know it's not me.

Ingrid responds:

You are a genius!

I type:

???

Ingrid does not respond, and I return my attention to the television. It's a quarter past nine, so Luke must be outside, chasing kids around the playground while pretending to be a sand monster. Debbie will be standing as close to him as possible, touching his arm and giggling at half the things he says...

I wake up, sweaty and disoriented. On the television, the host is showing a pair of enthusiastic homeowners how to update their patio. It's 11:47 a.m., so preschool is over and Luke is far from Debbie's clutches. I have forty-seven new text messages: one from Luke, and the rest from Ingrid. I check Luke's message first:

> Preschool was fun. Taking Madison to lunch, then the
> office. Love you.

What sort of "fun" are we talking about? Does Luke mean, "Wow, I loved spending time with Madison" or "Debbie knows how to have a good time — would you consider an open marriage?"

I open Ingrid's stream of messages and learn she left the board meeting and hung her purse on a hook outside Miss Lucy's classroom, hoping to tempt the thief. Then she repositioned her chair at the meeting to monitor her purse from upstairs. A child put a glue stick inside it, and a mom volunteering for another class stood near the bag but did not look at it. Miss Blaire eventually noticed the purse and returned it to Ingrid for safekeeping.

At pickup time, Ingrid tried again, this time leaving her bag outside Miss Ellen's class. Then she "forgot" her bag and walked all the way to her car with Danforth Jr. before "remembering" and returning to fetch it. No one had disturbed its contents. Even the glue stick was still there. Ingrid plans to "set bait" for the thief on Friday if I am still sick.

A thought rises from the depths of my subconscious: *Zoe would never do this for me.* I stuff the traitorous thought down. The nausea must be addling my brain.

A new text arrives before I can respond to Luke or Ingrid. It's from an unknown number, so I open it, fearing the worst (husband and beloved daughter in a fiery wreck on the freeway, come to the morgue to identify their remains). The text reads:

> Thanks for sending your husband to preschool today.
> He's quite the catch!

Lovely. Debbie is taunting me by text. I create a new contact with the name "Satan" and then stagger to the trash can to puke. Please, if there is any goodness in this universe, let this be a twenty-four-hour bug. I have to get better and keep Luke away from that woman.

It is not a 24 hour virus, or a 72 hour virus, but the flu in all its violent glory. Luke stays home with Madison while I divide my time between the bed and couch. At some point during my convalescence, Luke brings me a medium-sized padded envelope with a return address in my brother Ferris' handwriting that says: The Flying Flimbizzles, The Circus, Somewhere In The Midwest. I squeeze the contents. Something inside is hard, but something else is squishy. Ferris often sends souvenirs from the circus's travels, but I have no idea what he could have sent this time.

"I can't even," I moan as a fresh wave of nausea grips my digestive system.

"Do you want me to open it?" Luke asks gingerly.

"Don't care."

"Okay, you can open it when you feel better."

Luke waits for a response. I do not respond.

"Where should I put it?"

"Don't care."

For a grown ass man with a grown ass job, my husband sometimes astonishes me with his capacity to require hand holding for the most basic of domestic tasks.

"I'll just put it in your purse so it doesn't get lost, okay?"

That's a terrible idea. My purse is where things go to die.

The last time I cleaned it, I found a newborn size diaper, a box of petrified raisins, and several socks from our trips to indoor playgrounds, but I am too busy lurching off the couch to puke to explain all this to Luke. By the time I finish my latest round of vomiting, I have forgotten all about the mystery package.

Debbie continues to torment me with a steady stream of texts.

> Your husband looked so yummy during drop-off.

> Luke is way too hot for you. I'd do something about those freckles.

Then, my favorite:

> Is Luke having an affair with a secretary at work?

I fall asleep and have a fever dream in which Luke asks me for an open marriage and then introduces me to a secretary at his office, who turns into Debbie, and Debbie grows tentacles out of her head and eats me alive.

The flu continues through the weekend and into the next week. Ingrid enlists Genevieve and they leave several unattended bags at different strategic points: hooks outside classroom doors; the adult's bathroom; the office; and even the supply closet. The thief does not strike despite the temptation of Ingrid's Chanel, Kate Spade and Louis Vuitton purses and Genevieve's vintage clutch, Trader Joe's tote bags, and Fjallraven backpack.

The first Monday of February, eight days after I succumbed to the flu, I feel mostly human. Luke takes Madison to school, reminding me to "take it easy" so I do not relapse. I follow his advice, stay in my pajamas, and settle into the Womb Room for a Netflix session. This lasts for eleven minutes. Then, feeling a surge of energy after eight days of mandatory repose, I get up and tell myself I will just wash the breakfast dishes before returning to "take it easy" status. The breakfast dishes turn into a load of laundry; the laundry turns into a little weeding outside; and by the time I'm rushing to preschool for pickup, I have removed an ugly shrub and plotted the layout for a vegetable patch.

So much for "taking it easy."

Gardening, however, was invigorating. So invigorating, in fact, that I feel unstoppable and have no desire to return to the confines of our pink house. When Madison runs to me, I scoop her up and say, "Should we go somewhere? We need a mommy-daughter date!"

"The zoo!"

The zoo it is.

In the not so distant past, I wished my daughter napped like other preschoolers, but today, I am grateful for my high-octane girl. If I had to rush her home for a long nap, I would spend the afternoon prowling the house like a caged animal. Instead, I get to admire caged animals while soaking up the fresh air and strengthening our mother-daughter bond.

We gush over meerkats, flamingos and gorillas. Then Madison climbs into her stroller for a snack break and I steer us into the Australian cul-de-sac. A kangaroo hops around its enclosure, and Madison claps with delight when a joey peeks out of its mama's pouch. At the next enclosure, we not only spot a koala, but the koala drops off its perch, scampers across the dirt, and climbs up another eucalyptus tree. From the look of pure rapture on Madison's face, her tightrope walker obsession might get some friendly competition from Australian wildlife.

Once the koala disappears into the canopy, Madison abandons her stroller and runs toward a raised cement border built around several plants. Never mind what I just said about her tightrope walker obsession. No matter how cute they may be, the marsupials have no chance of diminishing Madison's passion for walking along anything that resembles a tightrope.

"What's in there?" Madison, still on her makeshift tightrope, points at a building we have never visited.

"I don't know. Should we go see the Komodo dragon?"

"I want to go in there." Madison hurries toward the mystery building and opens the door before I can articulate a protest. I hurry after her; the door slams shut; and darkness envelops us.

"Take my hand," I say, my chest tightening.

"Why?"

"So I don't lose you."

"Why?"

"Because it's dark."

"Why?"

"Let's go find out."

Hand in hand, we walk down a hallway, turn a corner, and enter an enormous room that is almost entirely dark, but tiny floor lights save me from crashing into a pillar. As my eyes adjust, I see a habitat with a few scraggly trees and hollow logs. I lift Madison to see, but not much is happening.

"Where are the animals?"

"I don't know," I admit, my.eyes scanning the darkness.

"Mama?"

"Yes?"

"Why is it dark?"

"Whatever lives here must be nocturnal."

"Oh, so it's awake at night." Madison states this with total confidence, and I do not know who to thank: Miss Lucy or Peppa Pig?

I stroll around the habitat's perimeter, pausing at an illuminated sign. "There's supposed to be a wombat in here," I tell Madison.

"What's that?"

"It's like a tiny bear-pig. Sorry, baby girl, it's not out today. Maybe next time."

Then, just as I step toward the exit, something rustles, and a shadowy form emerges.

"It's the wombat!" Madison bounces in my arms.

"It is," and we watch, mesmerized, as the pudgy wombat waddles from one end of its cage to another and back again. Occasionally, startled by the sound of someone coughing or sneezing, it sprints to a log propped in the middle of its enclosure, but mostly, it waddles. We do not leave until the wombat disappears into an inner chamber we cannot see.

Two hours later, after visiting the giraffes, chimps, and our favorite baby hippo, Rosie, I push an exhausted Madison back to our red SUV. We listen to the *Frozen* soundtrack, and I don't mind when Madison begs me to play *Let It Go* for the fifth time in a row. My heart is so full from our magical afternoon, I can handle anything the universe throws my way.

My phone pings as I unlock our front door. It's Genevieve:

Whatever you do, don't listen to Debbie's latest podcast episode.

Madison heads upstairs, babbling something about her dollhouse. I mumble, "Have fun," while swiping to *Center-fold Mama* on my podcast app. There it is. The most recent episode: *My Plans To Seduce A Married Man*.

I will not listen to this filth while my daughter is upstairs playing with her dollhouse.

I press play.

> *Good evening, listeners. I am feeling super sexy tonight because I am on the verge of an affair.*

I drop my phone on the black and white tiled floor. The episode continues.

> *Late last year, I decided I deserved an affair, but I didn't want to run off with the next guy that flirted with me. That's too easy!*

Debbie laughs at her witty humor while I retrieve my phone. The floor is disgusting, so I grab the broom.

> *No, I want a challenge. I want an affair with a married man. And not just any married man: a married dad at the Prince's preschool.*

I sweep a week's worth of crumbs into the dustpan.

> *I had a list of several candidates.*

Debbie describes the candidates while Madison plays upstairs and I empty the dustpan into the trash. As I listen, I try to identify the dads: one sounds like Danforth, Sr.; another sounds like Josh, our token stay-at-home dad (an interesting choice); and a few sound like they might have kids in Miss Ellen's class. Then Debbie says:

I made my decision last week.

I stop sweeping.

Do you remember the woman who is the preschool thief?

That would be me.

Her husband is way out of her league. She keeps him away from preschool and does all the volunteer days and drop-offs and pickups. Smart move. She knows if he saw the other moms, he would realize he was due for an upgrade.

I clench the broom so tightly, my hands hurt.

Last week, the thief got the flu. Poor thing. Her hot husband volunteered at school, and guess what? It was my day to volunteer, so I spent the entire day flirting with him and using all my tricks. I laughed at everything he said, asked him questions about himself, pulled my shirt down as low as possible, and even went to the office and got him coffee.

I walk into the Womb Room.

Oh, and of course, I touched him whenever possible.

I beat the sofa with the broom until I collapse from sheer exhaustion.

22

"Emma's going to hate me," Maude says, her voice wobbling with the threat of tears. "I am such a horrible mother."

"You are not a horrible mother." I pass a pink gift bag filled with Disney Princess Valentines to Madison.

"I am, I am," Maude frets. "Emma told me a month ago that she wanted to give Black Widow cards at the Valentine's party."

"It's not a party," I say. "It's a 'card distribution event.'"

Valentine's Day is a low-key affair at Mountain View Co-op Preschool. The children deliver their Valentines into white paper bags decorated with stickers and then they go through their loot at home. Monica informed the room parents last month we do not have any Valentine-related responsibilities, and Miss Lucy assured me this was indeed the case. A humble "card distribution event" feels anticlimactic after all the hustling I did for Halloween, Thanksgiving and Christmas, but at least I can't screw anything up.

Madison is wearing pink socks, pink leggings, a pink shirt, a pink sweatshirt and, of course, the tutu that shall not be named. Said tutu might be faded and sporting several gaping holes, but my girl still owns this holiday. She will deliver her Disney Princess Valentines and homemade peanut-free cookies, and then I will kiss her goodbye and go to yoga with Genevieve. I hate to admit it, but I am feeling very smug about my competence.

"I went to fifteen different stores," Maude laments. "I couldn't find Black Widow anywhere! The best I could find was Superman." Maude shivers despite her puffy coat. "My child is going to have permanent psychological damage."

Miss Blaire, framed by the arch of bougainvillea, waves hello and opens the gate. She adorned her golden hair with glittery heart barrettes, and beneath her apron, she wears pink jeans and a heart-patterned blouse.

"It's okay, it's only Valentine's Day." I pat Maude's back. "Your child will not have permanent psychological damage."

And then I freeze.

Oh my god.

I am such a horrible mother.

My child is going to have permanent psychological damage.

Outside every classroom, parents are decorating doors. One mom covers the closest classroom door with doily hearts while another mom festoons the next door with pink love birds. The lone room dad is plastering an enormous sheet of white butcher paper decorated with purple hand-prints on a third door. An unseen hand squeezes my heart. The parents decorating classroom doors are all room parents.

Shit, shit, shit!

"They are decorating the doors," I whisper to Maude. "I didn't know I was supposed to do that."

"Yay," Maude says, "I'm not the only one ruining Valentine's Day."

I should never have volunteered to be a room parent. My earlier successes were dumb luck. I have been tricking everyone into thinking that I am a competent room mom and at last, I'm busted.

Monica strides toward the office, her grey shirt emblazoned with the words, "But First, Coffee." She stops when she notices my forlorn expression. "What's wrong?"

"I didn't know I was supposed to decorate our class door." I gesture toward the other classrooms helplessly.

Monica shrugs. "It's not my favorite tradition."

"It's a tradition?" My fingers move rapidly as I revert to my old tic of making phantom balloon animals during times of stress.

"It's a tradition, but the board does not sanction it," Monica says. "I'm not allowed to mention it to room parents."

"Why not?" The unseen hand squeezes my heart again as I teeter on the brink of a panic attack.

"There used to be a contest, and the class with the most festive Valentine's door won a box of donuts. Parents treated this as a matter of life or death, but my third year here," Monica furrows her brow, "or maybe it was my fourth? Anyway, things got dark. Someone vandalized the decorations at night."

"Vandalized?" Genevieve asks. I did not notice her arrival, but she stands beside me, sporting a pink fedora.

"They turned it into an art installation involving soiled diapers."

I can't believe there was ever a scandal bigger than the preschool thief, but I believe this is it.

"Why would anyone do that," I say, "at a preschool, of all places?"

"It's been awhile, but if memory serves, a helicopter mom was upset that her son had used scissors during an art project to change his haircut."

"So why are we still allowed to decorate the doors?"

"The board tried to ban it, but an enraged mom posted some negative online reviews, so the board chickened out and let parents keep decorating. Stupid preschool politics."

"Monica! We need to talk before the tour! I can't run late! I need to get to the gym!" Becky, arms akimbo, shouts from the top of the Forbidden Stairs. She is wearing ankle and wrist weights.

"Speaking of politics," Monica mutters, "I'm not supposed to tell you this, but don't leave valuables unattended. The preschool thief struck again last week."

Curses! I know I am at the top of Becky's list of suspects. If only the thief had succumbed to one of Ingrid's and Genevieve's traps and struck while I had the flu. The Valentine decorations, however, are the more urgent crisis.

"This is a crisis." I turn to Genevieve as Monica clomps up the stairs to join Becky.

"Hardly." Genevieve adjusts her fedora. "People just need to watch their wallets."

"Not the thief. I haven't decorated Miss Lucy's door for Valentine's Day!"

"Who cares? The kids won't notice, and it's a lame tradition."

"But all the other room parents are doing it. I look lazy and incompetent."

"Or, you look like you have a life beyond these preschool walls." Genevieve does not conceal her exasperation.

I wish I could channel Genevieve's relaxed attitude and

stop worrying about fitting in with the other parents. You know what? I will stop caring about what other parents think — tomorrow.

The play structure groans. It doesn't care what other people think.

The click-clicking of heels striking the courtyard floor alerts me to Ingrid's presence. "The decorations are amazing. Becky is starting a tour of prospective preschool parents." Ingrid lowers her voice to a conspiratorial whisper. "Enrollment is down for next year. Thanks to the thief and embezzler, our reputation is in the toilet. If this trend continues, I don't think there will be enough tuition to keep preschool afloat next year." Her face tightens with a flicker of concern, but then she throws her shoulders back and says, "I bet we can get a few parents on the tour to enroll thanks to all the Valentine decorations."

I sigh. "Tell Becky to steer clear of Miss Lucy's room."

Ingrid turns to look. "Elodie! Our door is naked!"

"I know," I moan. "I didn't know about the tradition. Monica never mentioned it."

"I heard about it last week at a board meeting and should have mentioned it to you. This is a crisis."

"It's not a crisis," Genevieve says in a sing-song voice. "It's just a preschool classroom door."

"What do I do?" My fingers frantically make ghost balloon creatures, so I grip my hands behind my back.

"Get red, pink and white construction paper and cut out hearts."

"That won't be very good." Our neighboring classroom has a balloon archway, felt banners, and is that a cupid topiary? Yes, it is a cupid topiary. "I wish I had more time to plan something."

"We will improvise." Ingrid pulls her red hair into a messy bun. "We will make it spectacular!"

I gather paper, tape and scissors and commandeer a table outside Miss Lucy's classroom. Maude, Pregnant Chloe, and several other parents drift toward our impromptu command center and join our efforts.

"How is this?" Genevieve holds her first "heart" aloft. I suppose one could describe it as a heart if one has a very active imagination.

I thrust a handful of hearts at Genevieve. "Tape these to the door."

"I'm going to run home," Ingrid says, but then her phone rings. "There you are!" she answers crisply, with the presence of a campaign manager. "I need the box... yes, now... at preschool, of course. Where else would I be?" She hangs up and takes the hearts from Genevieve. "I'm sorry, Genevieve, but I have a vision, and this is not it. I just emailed you a photo. Go to the office and print it."

The tour has started on the other side of the courtyard. There is still time to make our door spectacular.

"Calm down." Genevieve returns with a formal portrait of Miss Blaire and her fiancé that she hands to Ingrid.

"I know you don't think this is a crisis," I say to Genevieve as I attack a sheet of pink construction paper with scissors, "but I love Mountain View. Enrollment is down and I don't want to make a poor impression on prospective parents."

"I love this preschool, too, but everyone is helping." At least ten parents are cutting out construction paper hearts that Ingrid tapes into a rainbow shape. "A crisis," Genevieve continues, "would be something like an earthquake or flood. This is just a problem, and we are fixing it."

"I need more white hearts to make the clouds!" Ingrid

says, now sounding like an ER doctor working on a gunshot victim.

"I'll get more white paper!" Maude sprints to the supply closet.

Danforth Sr. arrives a few minutes later with a large cardboard box. Today he is wearing jeans, a ratty Stanford t-shirt, and flip-flops. Ingrid is wearing a Diane von Fursten-berg wrap dress and Manolo Blahnik heels.

"Here's your junk." Danforth drops the box at Ingrid's feet and bows with a flourish.

Ingrid shoots him a death glare as she pulls out a pink and gold garland and drapes it over the door. Danforth Sr. whispers something into her ear and she elbows him play-fully. Aw, it's sweet. My freshman roommate found her soulmate.

A few minutes later, Ingrid has transformed the entrance to Miss Lucy's classroom. Above the hooks for coats and umbrellas, she hung cardboard cutout decora-tions for a bridal shower: wedding bells, bouquets, the bride and groom, and several cupids. A border of paper hearts surrounds the black-and-white photograph of Miss Blaire and her fiancee. Above the drinking fountain, there is a wooden plaque with a chalkboard heart and painted words that say "Countdown To Our Wedding." Ingrid uses a piece of pink chalk to write the number "85" on the heart.

"You had all that on standby?" I say.

Ingrid blushes. "I was decluttering a closet yesterday and was taking Dan's old fishing gear to Goodwill."

"Against my wishes," Danforth Sr. growls.

"You haven't gone fishing in years!" Ingrid pauses. "But if you want to keep the gear, of course you can. And if I want to keep a box of bridal shower decorations—"

"Even though all your friends are happily married—"

"Then I will keep that box of bridal shower decorations," Ingrid concludes, swatting her husband.

"Thank you! You're my savior!" I throw myself into Ingrid's arms and give her an intense hug. The children won't be traumatized! Future Madison will have to find something else to complain about to her therapist. "Where did you get that countdown sign?"

"I ordered that on Etsy for our wedding. I never could let it go. It also doubles as a countdown to the auction."

"It does?"

"Yes, Miss Blaire is getting married on the same day. Such a shame that we won't be able to go."

"It's in Bulgaria," I say. "Not even Sofia, but some remote village."

"This classroom is for our youngest students," Becky booms. The tour group of prospective parents peers at us like we are meerkats at the zoo. "The children are having their Valentine parties today."

Not a party. A card distribution event.

"To show extra love to our wonderful teachers, the room parents decorated the courtyard for the holiday."

The board might not sanction these decorations, and there might not be a box of donuts at stake, but with zero notice, our door is still the best. Ingrid's bridal shower decorations even trump the cupid topiary. #Winning!

From the middle of the sand area, the playground groans ominously.

"How old is the play structure?" a prospective mom holding a toddler asks.

"I'm not sure," Becky says evasively, "but we have plans to replace it soon!"

Clarification: the board was on the verge of signing a

contract for a new playground when they learned about the embezzler, and now plans are in limbo.

"When?" the prospective mom presses.

"This summer," Becky lies.

"Or never," Ingrid mutters before disappearing into our classroom.

"What about the thief?" a dad asks.

"Excuse me?" Becky stalls.

"My wife heard two moms talking at an indoor playground about a thief at this preschool."

Becky puffs up her chest. "Someone outside the community was breaking into unlocked cars. We installed security cameras in the parking lot and resolved the problem."

Actually, the thief's shenanigans were not limited to the parking lot; the security cameras did not prevent further plundering of purses and wallets; the thief struck again last week; and the thief is most definitely a member of the preschool community. But other than that, everything Becky said was true.

The playground groans as if it cannot tolerate Becky's lies.

Miss Lucy appears at the threshold of the classroom and rings the bell for circle time. Shrieking children hop off the play structure and dash to their classrooms.

A mom wearing a business suit asks, "What about the embezzler? My friend says preschool might not have enough money to operate next year."

A grimace flashes across Becky's face. "I can assure you —" but she does not get to finish her sentence.

CRACK! A loud sound reverberates through the courtyard as one of the playground's wooden pillars snaps in half. The bridge collapses, another pillar tips and topples to the ground, and the broken slide follows suit. With a mighty crash, the playground caves in and collapses, sending up a cloud of sand. The parents touring preschool scream, grab their children, and run. Meredith bursts from the office with her plunger and drops it in shock. Classroom doors fly open as teachers and parents rush to see what happened. Becky faints.

Genevieve grabs my shoulder to steady herself.

"Is this a crisis?" I whisper.

"Yes," she says slowly. "This is a crisis."

23

"Give me your phone."

"What?" I pull my tote bag closer to my side and shrink into the doily strewn couch.

"Give me your phone." Dr. Dankworth towers over me, one hand holding a smoldering cigarette and the other extended and waiting. The orange shine of his fake tan is extra fluorescent today.

"Why?"

"Do you care about your mental health? I'll give it back." Dr. Dankworth snaps his fingers.

I open my bag and before I can process what is happening, Dr. Dankworth rips the entire bag from my hands and rushes back to his desk. I watch helplessly as he dumps my bag on a full ashtray and paws through its contents. "Tampons, wallet, keys, boring, diapers, wipes, where's your vibrator?"

I hate him. I really, really hate him. I want to walk out and never see him again, but I am out of Zoloft refills and the psychiatrist Dr. Shafaei recommended doesn't have openings for new patients until July. I claimed the first available appointment and wrote it on my calendar with a Sharpie, but in the meantime, I need a psychiatrist. Yes, I know, I know. Dr. Shafaei said she would keep me supplied with Zoloft, but what if she gets hit by a bus and the new psychiatrist moves to Iceland without notice? Dr. Dankworth might be difficult, but at least I am familiar with his brand of difficult. Until I meet the new psychiatrist, I will attend our monthly appointment, play the part of the obedient patient, and get my Zoloft refills.

"Ah!" Dr. Dankworth pulls a large padded envelope out of my purse. "What's this?" He studies the return address. "'The Flying Flimbizzles, The Circus, Somewhere In the Midwest.' What sort of kinky business are you into?"

"It's from my brother," I say defensively as my fingers knot tightly in my lap. I forgot about the envelope that Luke put it in my purse. It's been a few weeks since I recovered from the flu, but like I said, my bag is where things go to die.

"Your brother! I am all for kinkiness but not incest."

"That's disgusting."

Dr. Dankworth rips the envelope open. Tell me this is a violation. The Medical Board of California cannot possibly sanction this behavior.

He pulls out a note and reads it aloud in a mocking tone. "Dear Elodie, I was going to give this to you for Christmas in San Diego. I remember when I was little, I thought your pump was better than a magic wand. Make some magic for Madison. We all miss you. Love, Ferris." Dr. Dankworth looks back inside the envelope and his eyes widen. "Elodie, I am deeply concerned," he says as he tips the contents of the bag on to his desk. Tiny balloons and a red plastic pump tumble out. Dr. Dankworth picks up the balloon pump and says, "What the hell do you do with this? Do you insert it—"

"It's a balloon pump," I say before my psychiatrist utters

something that can never be unheard. "My family is in the circus. Hence, the return address. As a kid, I enjoyed making balloon animals, but I haven't done it in years. My brother thinks I should make some for Madison."

Dr. Dankworth slaps his desk with both hands, making several ashtrays rattle. "You grew up in the circus?"

"Yes."

"And you didn't think to mention that until now?"

"I'm here for postpartum depression. It didn't seem relevant."

"Didn't seem relevant?" His voice rises. "Didn't seem relevant? Of course it's relevant. Childhood is a huge part of our psyche, and your parents messed you up."

I bristle. It is one thing for me to feel like my circus childhood left me with a few issues, but it's quite another thing for my psychiatrist to insinuate that my unconventional upbringing caused yet-to-be-diagnosed mental disorders.

Dr. Dankworth continues. "Your parents neglected your upbringing."

"That's not true."

Dr. Dankworth shushes me. "This," he stabs the plastic balloon pump, "explains why you feel like an imposter. I see a lot of moms who have imposter syndrome because they have low self-esteem, but *you*," he points the balloon pump at me, "*you* don't have imposter syndrome. You feel like an imposter because you are one. You don't have the experience to be a stay-at-home soccer mom. Your kid is screwed."

On the outside, I stiffen while on the inside, an 8.7 earthquake shakes my internal organs, ligaments, and very soul. I want to scream, punch Dr. Dankworth, curl up into the fetal position, smash a chair through the window, and beg for mercy.

Dr. Dankworth walks over to the couch, drops a handful of balloons in my lap, thrusts the pump in my face, and says, "Show me."

"Show you?"

"Make me something."

"Something?"

"Why do I keep hearing an echo? Make me a balloon dog."

I stretch out a yellow balloon and snap it on the pump. If Dr. Dankworth wants me to make something, then I will make him something, but it won't be a dog. I inflate another yellow balloon and then several black balloons and twist them together, forgetting everything but the balloons. When I am done, I hold up my creation.

"You can make a bumblebee?"

I shrug. "That's easy."

"My eight-year-old is obsessed with squids."

Without speaking, I inflate several pink balloons and produce a squid.

"Jesus, Elodie, that's amazing. Why on earth did you leave the circus?"

"Because," I say, uncertain how to answer that question. I love my family, but the circus did not feel like home. Something inside of me was always screaming for something else, and I ached to put down roots. That, however, feels too mystical and amorphous to tell my psychiatrist. "I just didn't want to be in the circus," I mumble.

"But you lit up when you were working on the balloons. I've never seen you so alive."

Maybe that's because Dr. Dankworth's office is a pit of despair, but I don't say that out loud.

"You belong in the circus."

I half-stand and offer the balloon bee and squid to Dr.

Dankworth. As he studies them, I rescue my tote bag and retreat to the doily infested couch, tucking the pump and balloons back inside.

Dr. Dankworth thrums hairy fingers against his fluorescent orange cheeks and says, "You worry about being a stay-at-home mom because deep down, you know you are out of your league."

"I don't worry about being a stay-at-home mom."

"Yes, you do."

"I might have been a little insecure in the fall," I confess, "because we moved cross-country and my daughter was starting preschool, but I don't feel that way anymore."

"No." Dr. Dankworth stands. "You can't be a stay-at-home mom. You are right to worry." He snaps his fingers. "You should go back to the circus. That's where you belong."

"No, it's not. I belong right here. In Pasadena."

"You should have seen yourself when you were making this magnificent squid!" Dr. Dankworth picks up the squid and pops it in his excitement. "You, Elodie, are not a soccer mom. You belong in the circus."

My psychiatrist thinks I am a circus sideshow, but how much credit does his analysis deserve? Sure, he went to Harvard, but as my new gynecologist says, Harvard produces its fair share of jerks. Maybe, instead of revealing the secret depths of my soul, Dr. Dankworth is just being a dick. A surge of energy makes me sit up straighter.

"Absolutely not," I say defiantly. "I don't belong in the circus. I want to raise my daughter right here in Pasadena. You're making up issues I don't have."

"You're projecting on me. Go back to work. Hire a nanny. You can't be a stay-at-home mom."

"Of course I can," I splutter.

Dr. Dankworth ignores me and stands by the window,

contemplating the mountains, or rather, he gazes in the mountain's general direction. Stormy grey clouds obscure the view, and rain patters against the window. I was planning to take Madison to the Arboretum this afternoon — it's been on my Pasadena bucket list all year — but we will not be visiting any botanical gardens in this weather, thank you very much.

Dr. Dankworth spins back toward me. "Deep down, you don't even want to be a stay-at-home mom. That's why you got postpartum depression, and that's why you worry about messing up. You want to be a lawyer again."

"I don't want to be a lawyer. Being a stay-at-home mom is my work."

Dr. Dankworth smirks, exuding skepticism. "It's work, but it's not your vocation."

"It *is* my vocation. I'm good at it, and I love being room mom."

"You're an imposter and should let someone else be the room mom."

"I'm not an imposter. I'm a great mother and a fantastic room mom." My voice quivers.

Dr. Dankworth shakes his head. I want to punch him. No, I want to leave. No, I want to punch him and then leave.

"So maybe you are a great mom. Maybe you're a decent room mom, but it's not what you want."

"Yes, it is!" My voice is so loud, everyone in the waiting room must hear. I don't care.

"Why?"

"Why?" I stop and consider. "I don't know why, but I feel it in my bones. My days are messy and crazy, but they feel right and I'm kicking ass."

"Hell, yes!" Dr. Dankworth raises his hand in the air.

I shrink into the doilies.

"High five!" Dr. Dankworth moves his hand toward me. I raise my hand automatically and we high five.

"That was pathetic. Come on. HIGH FIVE! You know you want to be a stay-at-home mom!"

I reach back my right arm and this time, our hands slap together so forcefully, a jolt runs up my entire arm. I am exultant, like a goddess standing atop Mt. Olympus, casually sipping nectar while flaunting my immortality.

"Great work today, Elodie, great work." Dr. Dankworth leads me back to the waiting room. "See you next month!"

Maybe there is a method to his madness after all.

24

"We need more donuts!" Ingrid waves the moment I enter the book fair. "Man the register and I'll be back in a jiffy!"

It's a Monday morning in early March, and today is the first day of the preschool book fair. Our landlord, the neighboring church, let preschool commandeer their social hall for the week-long event. The social hall is a drab building behind the parking lot with flickering fluorescent lights, undecorated off-white walls, and snot green tile floor; but Ingrid transformed it into a pop-up bookstore. She draped turquoise tablecloths over folding tables, arranged enticing piles of books, and decorated the walls with posters of popular children's literature. Bunting criss-crosses overhead, and the entire room is ringed with shelves and shelves of books. A dozen rumpled parents wander the fair, and another dozen huddle around a circular table, pecking at the remains of Ingrid's free donuts.

Next to the cash register, there is an enormous empty jar labeled "Donations!" I drop a dollar bill inside.

A mom hands me a stack of books, and I hum to myself while scanning the first one.

"What are you doing working the cash register?" Becky scowls at me as she enters the fair. She steps behind the cash register and starts doing squats.

"Ingrid had to get more donuts and asked me to help." I scan a picture book about a yeti.

"Why didn't *you* get the donuts?" Becky drops to the floor into a plank.

"I don't know. I got here ten minutes ago and Ingrid asked me to man the register."

"Only board members work the cash register," Becky snarls from her plank position on the floor.

I do not like this woman. Have I mentioned that?

I offer the scanner to Becky. "I didn't know. Here you go!"

Becky leaps to her feet and grabs the scanner. She scans the same picture book three times, jabs the register at random, and adds a $4000 donation to the sale before shoving the scanner back at me and saying, "Fix it."

I fix it, suppress an evil smile, and finish the sale. Becky wanders away to look at the books, but really, she's watching me. I refuse to be intimidated. Even though it has been several days since my appointment with Dr. Dankworth, I am still elated by our session and my newfound confidence that I am living my best life, owning my right to be a stay-at-home mom, and nailing the room mom gig. Becky can glare all she wants. She will not make me doubt my right to be involved with preschool life.

Ingrid returns with donuts and coffee and resumes command of the cash register. I run to get the yeti picture book as Becky admonishes Ingrid for letting me work the cash register.

After school, I take Madison to the fair, and we leave

with a stack of picture books. On Wednesday, we visit again and I tell Madison she may pick one more book. We leave with another stack. I do not have a book problem. We just need more shelves.

Friday morning, I return for book fair's last hurrah. Luke is working from home and picking up Madison so I can be Ingrid's sidekick before and after school (while keeping a healthy distance from the register, thank you very much).

Ingrid is hanging a new sign as I arrive. It proclaims:

Last Day For Book Fair!
Get Your Raffle Tickets Here!

"Raffle tickets?" I pull out my wallet. "What for?"

"Unlimited drinks during the auction."

I return my wallet to my tote bag, because the last thing I need is unlimited alcohol at a preschool function.

"Becky and I had a bit of a showdown at last night's board meeting," Ingrid continues. "We need an off-site venue for the auction."

"Why?" I inspect a table of picture books.

"Because people want to spend money on a reputable school, not a dump with a crappy broken playground. If we have the auction here, we'll just inspire more families to register somewhere else."

"People are registering at different schools?" I look up from the picture books so quickly, my neck hurts.

"Absolutely. Enrollment for next year is way down. We were going over the school budget and it's depressing. If we lose any more families, we won't have enough revenue to keep school open next year."

"What?!"

"If we finalize plans for the new playground, I'm sure

more families would enroll." Ingrid sighs. "That's why I'm having this raffle."

My brow furrows. "I don't get it."

Ingrid massages her temples as if she is weary of managing so many clueless parents. "Becky keeps insisting I have already exceeded my budget for auction expenses, but I haven't. I'm using the same vendor that Mountain View has used for over a decade for all the auction rentals, and I've called in a dozen favors for decorating supplies, but Becky is president and she refuses to sign off on the expense of an off-site venue. I did, however, convince the board to let me use any proceeds I can raise from a raffle today to secure one."

I may not need unlimited alcoholic beverages, but I don't want preschool to collapse like the old playground. I pull out my wallet and buy five raffle tickets.

Outside, car doors slam as parents arrive and depart. Ingrid stands at the open doorway and watches, but no one comes to the book fair. I wonder if her red Manolos and black sheath dress scare away customers. She looks like she runs a fancy boutique in Beverly Hills, not a preschool book fair.

I say, "Maybe everyone is waiting until the afternoon," and Ingrid mutters something about balloons before hurrying away. I text Luke:

Do you want anything from Starbucks?

Seconds later, my phone rings. "Have you had breakfast?"

"I had a bite of Madison's soggy Cheerios."

"Want to try the new diner by the car wash?"

Ten minutes later, I am seated in a red booth, contemplating an oversized menu and debating whether I want an omelette or the French toast that is coated in corn flakes. After a cheerful waitress takes our order, Luke busts out our old Uno deck and shuffles the cards.

"We haven't done this in ages." I take and sort my cards by color.

"I can't remember the last time we went out for breakfast," Luke says as he plays the first card.

Before Madison was born, we went out to breakfast every weekend — usually twice. At first, we talked, held hands, and gazed adoringly into each other's eyes. (Just kidding about that last bit. Does anyone actually do that?) Then, during a long weekend in Vermont, we spotted a family playing cards while waiting for their food. Later that day, Luke invested in an Uno deck at a gas station and playing games while waiting for breakfast became one of our favorite rituals.

When I was pregnant with Madison, I assumed we would be one of those families that went everywhere with our newborn, but between postpartum depression, sleep deprivation, and all the stuff we needed to pack to leave the house, our breakfast outings became an ordeal that we quickly abandoned. We tried to revive the breakfast ritual once Madison turned one, but our precious daughter was an absolute terror, fussing, screaming and wrecking general havoc and chaos. Maybe we'll try again when she's eighteen.

I draw cards from the deck until I get something I can play. "The next time your parents take Maddy for a sleepover, let's go out for breakfast."

"Agree."

I lose the first game but win the second moments before our food arrives.

"Oh my god, this is the best French toast I've ever had." I saw off a large bite and place it on Luke's plate.

"Try this." Luke transfers a generous chunk of crab cakes to my dish. "So what is next on your room mom docket?"

"Easter." I refill my coffee from the pot our waitress thoughtfully left at our table. "There's a big egg hunt and class potluck."

"How many treats are you making?"

The man knows me well.

"Less than a dozen, more than one." I savor a bite of French toast. "The real question is what I should put in the Easter eggs. I hope the school hunt redeems last year's debacle."

Last year, Zoe insisted we celebrate Easter with her in-laws in Connecticut. She promised an idyllic affair that would make the Barefoot Contessa jealous. We got a drunk uncle wearing a bunny suit that looked like something from a horror movie; a buffet of leftover pizza, highly suspicious deviled eggs, and beef jerky; and an egg hunt organized by Zoe's prepubescent twins who hid the eggs in dangerous places — next to a broken bottle, floating in the pool, at the top of a ladder — and then jumped out and screamed at the two-year-olds whenever they found an egg.

Madison had night terrors for weeks and still hates rabbits.

Luke scoffs, "Madison doesn't remember last Easter."

"Tell that to her subconscious."

"So, what are you planning for the school hunt?"

I finish my bite of French toast and lean back in my chair. "Chocolate melts, so I got these tiny fuzzy chicks at the bookstore, but then I saw adorable bunny rings online. Madison won't like them, but the other kids will. And then I was thinking I'd organize surprise Easter baskets for the teachers. We could fill plastic eggs with a little treat from each kid. Why are you staring at me?"

Luke smiles. "You look extra cute when you get excited about room mom things."

I lower my voice. "Am I turning you on?"

"Kind of."

"Then I better not tell you my plans for the end-of-year potluck."

When I return to preschool, Ingrid is tying a gigantic bouquet of balloons to the social hall's front door.

"I thought we agreed no additional expenses for the book fair!" Becky storms across the parking lot, her ankle weights bouncing menacingly. She is not wearing wrist weights today but is carrying a set of barbels.

"I bought these for myself," Ingrid huffs. "I'm not charging them to preschool."

Becky scowls. "Book fair is costing us money." She squares her shoulders and begins a set of bicep curls.

"What are you talking about?" Ingrid throws an arm into the air. "I bought the donuts and coffee and used some decorations from home. The book fair company sent everything else. We earned rewards, and the teachers can pick new books this afternoon."

"Why has a hundred dollars gone missing from the till?"

"A hundred dollars?" Ingrid stiffens. "I've been bringing the cash to the office safe every day when the fair closes."

Becky switches to shoulder presses. "The money must have gone missing during the fair itself. Yolanda says we're a hundred dollars short. Who had access to the till yesterday?" Becky's eyes slide toward me.

Ingrid rattles off several names. "Monica, Yolanda, Dr.

Konig, Miss Ellen, Mr. Joe, Miss Blaire, and what's the maintenance director's name? Greg. And of course, you helped."

"And her?" Becky nods toward me.

I flush with indignation.

"Elodie helped with the register on Monday, but no one paid with cash then."

"Didn't she help Wednesday?"

Would it kill her to use my name?

I cross my arms across my chest. "I checked inventory on Wednesday, and Dr. Konig worked the register."

"Who stole the money?" The cords of Becky's neck tighten.

"It wasn't me," I protest.

"Maybe," Becky says grudgingly. Then her face brightens. "But you are no longer Miss Lucy's room parent."

"What?!" Ingrid and I yelp.

"The Browns are back. They are a lovely Mountain View family that had to go to London last August for a work thing. Now they are back in Pasadena and their youngest is joining Miss Lucy's class on Monday. Natasha Brown is a big fan of Miss Lucy and told me she was so bummed she missed being Miss Lucy's room mom again. Since you weren't the original room mom, I decided a change would be best for all."

I deflate like a popped balloon. I wanted to be the original room mom but was too scared and self-conscious to volunteer. It's too late to explain that now.

"Thanks for all your help," Becky says disingenuously, bending forward and pulling up her free weights for a backward row. "But what with Debbie's accusations and online reviews—"

"Online reviews?"

"She has written some nasty reviews about how we let thieves and embezzlers be room mom."

"But I'm not a thief!" I splutter. "You know I'm not the embezzler. I wouldn't know how to embezzle from preschool if my daughter's life depended on it."

"We don't have space for a new family in Miss Lucy's class," Ingrid says. "Arlo transferred to our class, remember?"

"Chloe asked to transfer Tristan to Miss Ellen's class after volunteering last week with Debbie. She was upset about a remark Debbie made about her pregnancy weight, so Tristan is switching to Miss Ellen, and Natasha's daughter Clementine will join Miss Lucy's class."

"You can't do this," Ingrid's voice rises an octave. "Elodie is an amazing room mom."

Becky straightens and shrugs. "A majority of the executive board decided this is for the best."

"Meaning you harassed Yolanda and Mei into submission and ignored Monica," Ingrid sneers.

Becky ignores Ingrid and turns back to the preschool office, but instead of walking like a normal person, she does a set of lunges across the parking lot.

I slump down on a folding chair outside the social hall. I am no longer Miss Lucy's room mom. The co-op president thinks I am the thief and embezzler, and Debbie will crow about this on her podcast. I can't go back inside the book fair. I might as well sit outside until the sun turns me into a pile of ash.

25

M aude parks and waves as she gets out of her car. "Any big plans for our Easter potluck?"

I shrug and slump further into my chair. I do not get to make big plans for the Easter potluck or any future potlucks because everyone thinks I am the preschool thief. We could switch preschools, but I would miss my friends and thanks to Debbie's podcast, half the moms in Pasadena will avoid me wherever we go.

Ingrid appears at the doorway and aims a megaphone at preschool. "Last day for book fair! Last day for book fair!" She waves eagerly at a few parents as they emerge from their cars, but the parents ignore her. Ingrid's body sags and she heads back inside the social hall to oversee book fair's nonexistent customers.

I swipe open my phone, the instinct to text Zoe still automatic after all these months. Her husband had to choose this year of all years to live off grid. I need her counsel and support, so I open my text diary, but what is the point? Shoving my phone back into my bag, my fingers bump against something I do not recognize. I grab the foreign object and bring it out to inspect. It's the padded envelope from Ferris, the one with the pump and balloons. I shove it back into my tote bag, pulse racing, but no one is looking toward the book fair. Besides, the parents are already gossiping about me thanks to Debbie's podcast and Becky's suspicions. I might as well add "circus freak" to my shredded reputation.

I pull out a few balloons and pump. I can't save preschool. Ingrid has already done everything possible to lure parents to the book fair. If they do not want to browse the books and buy raffle tickets, then the auction will have to languish alongside the termite-infested remains of our illustrious playground. I twist a pink balloon into petals and attach them to a green balloon stem. Ta-da! I add the balloon flower to Ingrid's balloon bouquet.

Synapses fire and produce an idea so crazy, I know I need to do it. I stand and get to work. Ingrid, sensing my burst of activity, comes to investigate and stumbles when she sees me. "What are you doing?"

"Improvising!"

"I thought you wanted to keep this sort of thing a secret," Ingrid whispers. "Maybe we should pack up the books—"

"I changed my mind. Ta-da!" I present Ingrid with several balloon flowers. The parking lot is filling up with cars, and Miss Blaire has assumed her post at the entrance gate. "Hurry!"

"Hurry?"

"Give these to Miss Blaire."

Ingrid stares as if I have officially lost my mind. Maybe I have.

"Have her hold the balloon flowers and tell the kids to go to book fair for a free balloon animal."

Ingrid's eyes light up and she hurries across the parking

lot while I set up a balloon station at the back of the social hall. By the time Ingrid returns, I am wearing a balloon crown and have placed a balloon dog, monkey, and pig next to the donation jar.

"Monica is here to help!" Ingrid announces, and Monica clicks her flip-flops together and does a mocking salute.

"Monica, man the cash register. Ingrid, stay here to help with raffle ticket sales." I act like the ringmaster, directing where everyone should perform. Becky would not approve, but what else can she do — kick my family out of preschool?

Ingrid and Monica man their respective stations, and just as Monica turns the cash register on, a trickle of parents and children arrives. They spot my station and head toward the crazy balloon lady. A shy girl with her hair in braids reaches me first.

"Would you like a balloon animal?" I ask.

She nods solemnly.

"What's your favorite animal?"

"Elephant," she whispers.

"Sophia, she can't make an elephant," her mom says. "That's too complicated."

"Elephants are easy!" Less than a minute later, I produce a pachyderm. "I hope you don't mind that I made an African elephant. The big ears are more fun."

The girl claps and takes her elephant, and Ingrid wastes no time in asking the mom if she would like to buy a ticket for the raffle.

"Of course." The mom takes out her wallet, and I turn to my next customer. At least ten children have formed a queue. Ingrid gives me an encouraging thumbs up, and I make in rapid succession a giraffe, another elephant, and a monkey. Dr. Konig arrives in sensible beige pumps and a

pleated blue skirt and assumes command of the line of children. Parents drift toward the tables and shelves, but I am
too busy making balloon animals to check if anyone is
buying books.

"Luke!" a Marilyn Monroe voice shrieks. "You are
wicked!"

I glance up from the flamingo I am making. Debbie,
wearing Daisy Dukes and a white tank top despite the chilly
March weather, has linked arms with my husband and is
whispering something in his ear. Her nipples are visible
from the other side of the room. I accidentally give the
balloon flamingo two necks and force myself to look away
from my husband and Mountain View's resident succubus.
With moms like Debbie, the best thing to do is ignore them.

"Can I pump balloons?"

Luke towers over me, our difference in height exaggerated because he is standing and I am crouched over a two-
headed balloon flamingo. He is extra sexy today, his grey
hair a little rumpled and blue eyes framed by the black
glasses he got last week. Debbie lurks at a nearby table,
monitoring our interaction, seeking any cracks in our
marriage that she can exploit.

"Sure," I say, "do you remember how?"

Luke drags over a chair and joins my balloon animal
station. "Worst case scenario, I pop a balloon in my face and
make the kids laugh."

Years ago, before we were engaged, Luke took me to
Boston for his oldest nephew's birthday party. When I
learned Luke's nephew was obsessed with the circus, I
volunteered to make balloon animals for the kids. Luke was
my sidekick, and we made a great team. He bantered with
the three-year-olds while pumping balloons, and I created a
full circus menagerie. Luke loved being my sidekick at his

nephew's party, but that was before pregnancy wrecked havoc on my complexion, hair, and waistline. I'm sure Luke would now rather wander the book fair with Debbie in her Daisy Dukes than associate with his dumpy wife.

Still, Luke and I slip back into our balloon animal schtick as if the circus birthday party was yesterday. The line of children waiting for balloons animals grows and grows under Madison's watchful eye, who stands next to me, watching to make sure none of the kids' put the moves on her mommy. Ingrid keeps tearing off raffle tickets, and Monica works nonstop at the register. The donation jar is crammed with bills, including multiple twenties.

A little boy reaches the front of the line. "Can I get exercise barbells? My mom won't let me play with hers." A moment later, Becky's shadow darkens the balloon in my hands.

"Let me see what I can do." I twist, ponder, untwist, twist some more and triumphantly produce a set of balloon ankle weights and barbels.

Becky studies me appraisingly and hands her son a ten-dollar bill for the donation jar. "Where have you been all year? We could have used you at Trunk-or-Treat."

Actually, they did use me at Trunk-or-Treat. Remember how I manned the refreshments table even though I wanted to walk around the parking lot with Luke and Madison? And how I kept working even after Ingrid returned with the pizzas? And then, after all my hard work, Becky accused me of stealing money from the preschool till? Yeah, I remember that too.

I do not, however, mention any of this to Becky. Instead, I smile pleasantly, make a balloon frog for my next customer, and silently curse the co-op president for stealing my room mom crown.

Arlo reaches the front of the line. "Could I have a yacht?"

"A yacht?" I frown. I suppose I could make a boat.

"Mommy wants a yacht but daddy won't get her one. This is for mommy," Arlo explains.

Debbie strides over laughing. "Oh, kids, they say the darnedest things." Debbie tosses her hair over her shoulders. "Arlo, of course daddy would buy me a yacht if I wanted one. He knows he has to keep mommy happy." Debbie laughs again. I accidentally vomit on her feet. (Just kidding. But wouldn't it be cool if I did?)

When I finish Arlo's yacht, Debbie gives him a dime to put in the donations jar. I am not judging her. She mentioned during a recent podcast episode that she wants to upgrade her engagement ring, because her three-carat diamond does not sparkle enough on Instagram, but she also needs SO MANY necklaces, so she has to be careful about how she spends her money. Debbie cannot donate more than a dime at the book fair when she needs more diamonds.

Okay, I lied. I am totally judging her resting bitch face.

Next up is a girl already holding a balloon lion. "Could I have a unicorn?" she asks boldly and loudly.

"I told her every kid only gets one," a gravelly voice booms behind me, and I immediately know who it is. Liz Huffenby continues loudly, "But after Penelope saw Norah's unicorn, she insisted she had to have one herself. Don't worry, I'll buy more raffle tickets!"

Ingrid beams. Someone is getting her off-site auction venue.

I set to work on the unicorn.

"Elodie Jones," Liz Huffenby asks, projecting her voice so everyone can hear, "where did you learn to do this?"

For a moment, time slows down. The babble of parents

and children dies away, and I feel as if I am standing at the edge of a precipice. Liz Huffenby lives for gossip. If I tell her I learned to make balloon animals while growing up in the circus, then I might as well hang a banner about it in the parking lot; but I am also tired of hiding from my friends.

"The circus." I choose a half-truth that will hopefully satisfy Liz Huffenby's curiosity.

"How fun! Was it like a weekend workshop?"

I present the unicorn to Liz Huffenby's daughter. "Not exactly a weekend workshop." I take a deep breath. "It was more like I grew up in the circus."

Parents turn and stare. I have the attention of every adult standing within earshot. An hour ago, I would have rather died than face such humiliation, but now I have leapt off the precipice and I am flying. My embarrassment over being a circus freak has evaporated. If Liz Huffenby wants to spread the news that Elodie Jones grew up in the circus and can make fantastical balloon creatures, she can be my guest.

"My parents are acrobats," I continue. "The Flying Flimbizzles of The Sweeney Sisters' Dazzling Big Top Extravaganza. My maiden name is Flimbizzle, and I was part of the act as a kid. My brothers and sister are still acrobats, but I went to law school. I'm the family black sheep."

Several parents laugh.

"Clowns get a bad rap, but our clowns were super cool. I was never interested in being one, but I loved making balloon animals."

Actually, I still love making balloon animals. The past hour has been the most enjoyable hour I've spent at preschool. I was so worried about fitting in and being the perfect room mom that I forgot to relax and enjoy my life. Now I am an ex-room mom flaunting her circus history, and I am sparkling. I thought I had to know all the ins and outs of school life in order to be a good mom, but I just need to be myself. I'm not an imposter. We are all improvising and making it up as we go.

When the last customer leaves, Monica practically skips to my station. "We sold five thousands dollars in books today!"

Ingrid sings, "And we sold over one hundred raffle tickets!"

Yolanda counts the money in the donation jar with Becky. "Six hundred and twenty-seven dollars and ten cents!"

"Thank god Debbie donated that dime!" I cackle. I know. I'm evil.

Everyone laughs, Ingrid's dolphin shriek the loudest. With Debbie, everyone is a little evil. Even Becky.

Ingrid pouts and puts her hands on her hips. "I can't believe you guys don't think Elodie should be room mom!"

Becky mumbles something, but I interrupt. "It's okay. I know Debbie is being difficult. I don't need to be room mom."

It's true. I don't need the title of room mom to ensure my daughter has a magical childhood. I can make magic happen at the motherhood circus, no matter what my title.

If only I knew a magic spell to reveal the preschool thief's identity. If I could fix my reputation, life would be pretty darn perfect.

26

"**I**s it true?" Maude whispers.

"Was that an early April Fool's joke?" Genevieve glowers from beneath her fedora.

"But you're such a great room mom!" Zelda's mom Paula says.

It's the Monday morning after book fair, and I am standing outside Miss Lucy's classroom, surrounded by a half dozen parents. Last night, I emailed our class about the new room mom:

From: Elodie Jones
<ElodieJones79@genericemail.com>
To: Miss-Lucy-Parents@mountainview.com
Sent: Sun, 13 Mar 2016 21:43:02 (PST)
Subject: Our New Room Mom!

Hi everyone,
I had a lot of fun being room mom, but
I am passing the torch to Natasha,

```
whose daughter Clementine is joining
our class on Monday. I know everyone
will join me in welcoming Natasha!
```

```
Elodie
```

I was very pleased with my missive. I did not lie, but I also did not reveal the details of my shameful dismissal. Being a lawyer taught me how to massage the truth.

"Elodie, why?" Maude whines. Her ponytail is so tight today, it is giving her a face lift. "I'm not good with change. I can't handle a new room mom this late in the year."

"Natasha was supposed to be room mom all along," I tell Maude and the nearby parents with false cheer. "I was the backup."

"That's right!" A petite brunette wearing baggy black harem pants and a long embroidered tunic appears at my side. She has thick bangs and some serious bracelet game. Several inches of bracelets of all types line both of her arms: metallic cuffs, beaded bangles, dainty circlets, leather bands and tangles of friendship bracelets. "Hi, everyone! I'm Natasha." She waves and her bracelets clink together.

"Hi, Natasha," a few parents grumble. This lifts my spirits, but I swear, from this moment on, I will do my best to like and support Natasha.

"I told Becky last spring I wanted to be Miss Lucy's room mom, but then we moved to London for my husband's job." Natasha emphasizes the word "London" as if we should all be jealous of her amazing life. "I'm so happy it worked out that I could finish the year as room mom. I'm sure Elodie did a fine job." Natasha runs her fingers through her hair, her bracelets jangling like wind chimes. "But now that I'm here, you'll get the full benefit of my experience. I'll email soon about some changes to the Easter festivities."

Let me amend my prior statement: I am going to do my best to support Natasha and be nice, but like her? That's asking too much.

"I know we have a thief amongst us." Natasha pauses and looks pointedly at me. "I don't want to name any names." Again, she looks at me. "But I hope, for the sake of preschool's reputation, the thief comes forward and confesses her crimes." Natasha pivots toward me. "Elodie, is there anything you want to share?"

The air cackles with tension. I want to share many things, but none are nice. "No, I'm good," I say through clenched teeth, and the other parents back away and disperse. Ingrid, however, lingers on the pretense of erasing the number on the "Countdown To Our Wedding" chalkboard.

"You know," Natasha places a hand on my shoulder. Ingrid writes "54" on the chalkboard, but her eyes stay on Natasha. "We should go get coffee now. You can tell me everything you did, so I know what to fix."

Ingrid swoops in and says, "I need to steal Elodie for auction business." She links our arms together and whisks me away before Natasha can react.

"Thanks," I mutter as we weave through clusters of chatting parents.

Arms still linked, Ingrid steers us toward the preschool parking lot. "No time to waste. We have a busy morning."

I check over my shoulder. "You can drop the act. Natasha isn't following."

Ingrid ignores me.

"Hey," I say, as we pass through the main gate and wave at Mr. Joe, "where's Miss Blaire?"

"Day off." Ingrid does not break stride. "She had to take care of wedding things today. I think she has a dress fitting."

Ingrid does not release my arm until we reach her black Mercedes SUV. I open my mouth to speak, but before I draw breath, Ingrid has opened the passenger door, pushed me inside, and closed the door in my confused face.

"Ingrid, what are you doing?" I ask as she turns on her car. "I have errands."

"Your errands can wait." Ingrid guns out of the preschool parking lot. "The raffle was a tremendous success, but preschool is still in danger of closing." Her voice takes on a somber tone. "Several parents already switched their kids to a new Montessori school near Old Town. They aren't even bothering to finish the school year."

"Because the playground collapsed?"

Ingrid changes lanes and speeds past a Prius. "And because we have a thief, and because there's an embezzler, and because enrollment is down and we don't know if there will be enough tuition to keep preschool afloat next year."

"So, where are we going?" My entire body stiffens as Ingrid plows through another yellow light.

"I made some appointments to tour potential auction venues. Becky says we need to raise fifty thousand dollars if we want the new playground, because we have to cover the embezzled monies first. If we don't get a new playground, you'll need a new preschool."

Fifty thousand dollars! Holy crap, preschool is doomed, but I'm not saying that out loud when Ingrid is already driving like a woman possessed. Instead, I say, "How can you raise that much money at the auction?"

"I've called in lots of favors to get some amazing items for the live auction and auction baskets. That reminds me, I have to set a date to assemble the baskets." Ingrid sips from a glittery tumbler that says "Boss Mama." "There will be a raffle at the auction for a year of discounted tuition, and I'm taking portraits of the kids and selling them in cheap frames for twenty bucks."

"Maybe it would be easier to catch the thief and embezzler and make them pay back everything they stole."

"I don't know how to catch the thief or embezzler." Ingrid honks several times at a minivan. "But with a suitable venue, I know how to throw an awesome auction; and if I throw an awesome auction, maybe we can raise fifty thousand dollars and save preschool. Massage?"

Ingrid holds up a control pad attached to my seat. Of course Ingrid tricked out her passenger seat with a heated vibrating massage cushion. She also added a velvet seatbelt cushion, an essential oil diffuser clipped into an air vent, and pink glittery coasters inside the cup holders.

I press a button on the controller and several nodes knead my shoulders and back while my bottom warms. Maybe having Ingrid back in my life is not so terrible. "Where's the first venue?"

"Here," Ingrid swerves and parks behind a hearse.

We are parked outside a decrepit pink building nestled between an auto repair shop and a mortuary. Ingrid assesses the situation, says, "Absolutely not," and swerves back into traffic.

"I thought we had an appointment?"

"Time is money!" Ingrid accelerates as if we are fleeing a crime scene.

The second potential venue, a seafood restaurant, is a few blocks away, and the owner meets us as we park. He is wearing a white apron smeared with blood. Ingrid stiffens but follows him to the back, where the owner pushes open a creaky wooden gate to reveal a romantic patio with fairy lights strung overhead and a gorgeous view of the rolling San Gabriel Mountains. Unfortunately, the entire patio reeks like the river otter exhibit at the Los Angeles Zoo.

As the owner lists buffet options, Ingrid says, "Sorry, this won't work for our needs," and without further explanation, she speed walks away, gracefully leaping over a suspicious puddle in her black heels.

We visit a few more venues that Ingrid dismisses for various reasons (bad acoustics; lousy ambience; next to a playground that will remind everyone of our termite fiasco). The last potential venue is a grimy building on a busy street. "Oh no," Ingrid groans, "it's even worse in person."

Ingrid drives down an alley that ends in a parking lot. At the far end, there is a pink Volvo station wagon parked next to a brick wall with old wooden barn doors, one of which is cracked open. I walk over to investigate and glimpse an enormous camphor tree, its branches decked with lanterns and large metal stars. I wave Ingrid over.

"Could we have the auction here?"

"This garden is perfect," Ingrid gushes. "I wonder why it wasn't on the website?"

I push the barn doors open and step into the garden. We can set up the auction items on the brick patio, use the lawn surrounded by ferns for dinner, and put the bar on a raised platform that surrounds the massive tree. With a venue like this, Ingrid can easily raise fifty thousand dollars.

"I'm sorry, but I'm in the middle of an appointment," a trim woman with bobbed hair says as she approaches us. She is dressed even more impeccably than Ingrid in a pink tweed suit.

"We have an appointment at 10:45," Ingrid says.

"That's strange. I only have one bride scheduled today, and she's already here."

"This is for the preschool auction," Ingrid says.

"Auction?" The lady frowns, and then her brow relaxes. "You must have an appointment with Rose City Banquet Hall. This is Oswald Garden. It's confusing, I know, but our guests enter on the other side of the garden and use a different parking lot."

"Idiots!" A woman with a cane stands by the garden entrance. She is dressed like a nun, minus the habit. "You went to the wrong place!" She shakes her cane at us. "I told you! Come up the ramp! This way!"

Ingrid casts a last look at the garden and asks, "Do you have any availability on April thirtieth?"

"That's the day booked for this bride's wedding," the woman says as she gestures toward a few women standing on the other side of the camphor tree.

"We couldn't afford it anyway," Ingrid says to herself.

I notice the pink Volvo station wagon again as we exit and say, "I think that's Miss Blaire's car."

"No," Ingrid says. "She drives a black Audi."

We follow the woman with the cane back to the white building. "The garden would have been out of our budget anyway," Ingrid murmurs as we walk up the ramp to the building's side entrance. The walls are cracked, the paint is badly chipped, and the ground is filthy. "Oh god," Ingrid moans.

"The auction will be at night." I adopt the tone of a motivational speaker. "No one will see the details."

Ingrid shakes her head. "We should cut our losses short and not waste money on a dump like this."

The old woman pushes open an emergency exit door, and we enter a foyer whose walls and ceiling are painted black. Ingrid's gaze bounces from a crack on the ceiling to broken floor tiles and back to the crack.

"The decorations will pop against the black backdrop." I embrace my new calling as Ingrid's personal motivational speaker. "We can string up Christmas lights. Remember Dorm Prom?" Ingrid organized an end-of-year dance for our freshman dorm. "You made the crappy common room feel like the Met Gala. You can work with this."

Ingrid's face brightens a little.

"The bar goes here," the woman points with her cane. "Come." She limps toward another set of doors that open with a push bar, and we enter a room the size and height of a gymnasium with a stage perfect for the live auction and plenty of space for schmoozing and dining. Ingrid nods and says, "I can work with this."

A violent banging echoes through the room, and I leap closer to Ingrid.

"That is Joe," the woman says.

"Joe?" Ingrid asks.

"Joe lives in the alley. Sometimes he gets upset and bangs on the doors with a metal bat."

The banging continues for another twenty seconds and then the whacks lose their potency, dwindle, and cease. My nerves are shattered.

"How often does Joe get upset?" Ingrid asks in a strained voice.

"All the time, but if you give him fifty dollars, he will leave for the night."

Ingrid moans quietly.

"Can you give us a moment?" I drag Ingrid away for a conference.

"Tiny Geniuses Academy would never host an auction here," Ingrid says.

"Yes, but Tiny Geniuses Academy does not have a fundraising director with your talents."

Ingrid snorts derisively.

"I'm serious. Remember that fundraiser you organized for the women's health center when we were freshmen? You raised ten thousand dollars from just the JV football team."

Ingrid's posture improves a little.

"We improvised at the book fair and look how much money we raised."

"True," Ingrid says.

"And you already have a bunch of awesome ideas for raising money at the auction."

"I do."

"I'll handle Joe," I promise. "We totally got this."

27

"You can't be serious about the auction?"

"It's a preschool tradition!"

"It's pandering to the capitalist consumer agenda."

Our new room mom Natasha overheard Ingrid telling some moms about the auction venue, and now Natasha is trying to convince Ingrid to cancel the entire affair.

"We are raising money for preschool." Ingrid is beyond exasperated. "How do you think Mountain View pays for things? With fairy dust?"

"We pay tuition," Natasha says. "We shouldn't be spending money on an auction venue to raise more money."

Miss Blaire, who was hurrying back to the front gate after coming to tell Miss Lucy something, stops mid-step. "Auction venue? I thought we were having the auction at preschool this year?"

"Elodie and I found a magnificent but affordable banquet hall yesterday," Ingrid lies easily. "We can raise much more money there than at preschool."

"Where is it?" Miss Blaire asks.

"Over on Oak Avenue. Rose City Banquet Hall."

Miss Blaire runs a jerky hand through her hair. "Is that by Oswald Garden?"

"Yes," and now Ingrid sounds exasperated with Miss Blaire. "But its entrance is on a different street."

"That's right," Miss Blaire says. "I better get back to the gate."

"Why would she care about the venue?" I wonder aloud. "She'll be in Bulgaria."

"She cares," Natasha says, "because Mountain View is supposed to be above all the capitalist pigs." Natasha moves her hands around a lot, making her bangles bounce between her elbows and wrists. "I care about Mountain View, too, so I'm changing Easter this year."

"What?!" Several parents standing outside Miss Lucy's class exclaim like a Greek chorus.

"For the potluck, there will be no gluten, sugar or dairy, and everything must be organic."

I grind my molars together.

"For the egg hunt, everyone will drain the yolks and whites from a dozen eggs and dye them naturally. None of those plastic eggs that people fill with candy and toys."

"How do we dye eggs naturally?" Maude twists her necklace back and forth. "That sounds a lot like cooking."

"It's a school-wide egg hunt," Genevieve says. "Using real eggs won't work."

"Plastic eggs further the consumer culture and destruction of the planet!"

"Where's Becky?" Ingrid storms away, heels clicking against the courtyard concrete.

Wednesday morning, Natasha stands next to the sign-in sheet, holding a clipboard, much like our original room mom Charlotte did on the first day of school. Natasha thrusts the clipboard toward me and says, "Will you sign this?"

I knot my fingers together and refuse to take the clipboard. "What is it?"

"It's a petition to reform the school's egg hunt. Plastic eggs with treats destroy the environment and contribute to childhood obesity."

I shake my head. "It's a childhood rite of passage. I'm not signing it."

Outside our classroom, Ingrid foams with indignation. "Can you believe the nerve?"

"Elodie," Maude whines, "can't you be room mom again? Why did you quit?"

I stiffen and plaster a smile on my face. "Let's give her a chance to come to her senses. How many parents will actually sign the petition?"

That night, as I am bathing Madison in our pink clawfoot tub, Ingrid texts:

Natasha is threatening to sue preschool.

I wrestle Madison into pajamas and let her shimmy into the thing that is barely a tutu so I can call Ingrid. "I don't think a lawsuit would have any merit."

"Preschool can't afford to be sued," Ingrid laments. "We'd have to hire a lawyer. We'll never get a playground."

"One parent should not be able to ruin the entire school's egg hunt!"

In her weekly Sunday email, Dr. Konig announces the egg hunt is canceled.

The next morning, a week and a half after Becky gave my room mom crown to Natasha, I glare as she struts past me in the courtyard in her baggy green harem pants.

"Can't you tell Dr. Konig you reconsidered, Elodie?" Zelda's mom Paula pleads. "You can't let Natasha be our room mom."

"I agree." Maude's eyes bulge — partly because she is jittering with anxiety, but mostly because her ponytail is scraped back so severely. "We need you, Elodie. Miss Lucy needs you."

Genevieve loops an arm over my shoulder. "You're the best room mom in the world, but if you don't have the time for it, I understand."

I hate lying to Genevieve. I hate lying to all the parents, but if I tell them the real reason I "stepped down" as room parent, they will think less of me. Yet all this worrying is draining and I'm sick of it. "I didn't resign." I raise my chin. "The executive board voted I should not be the room mom anymore."

"What?" "What the hell?" "Why on earth?" The moms splutter and protest.

"Becky has had it out for me all year. She's convinced I'm the preschool thief."

"But you aren't!" Genevieve looks offended. Bless her.

"I know I'm not, but Debbie talked about it on her podcast and badmouthed preschool for letting a known thief be a room mom."

"Debbie," everyone says in a collective sigh of defeat and contempt.

"I wish I could still be room mom," I say, "but Becky wants Natasha."

Then I have a lightbulb moment, and I can't help it. My face lights up.

"What are you so happy about?" Genevieve narrows her eyes.

"I'll email later."

. . .

"This is a terrible location for an egg hunt."

"What? Why?" My stomach churns. Is there some hidden danger? Did I pick a park built on a nuclear waste dump?

"There is nowhere to hide the eggs!" Luke says.

"Those bushes are promising." Danforth Sr. points at a thorny tangle. He's wearing a ripped *Star Wars* t-shirt and flip-flops and arrived a few minutes ago on his skateboard. He looks shorter than usual standing next to my husband.

I exhale with relief. "They are preschoolers. We just spread the eggs out on the lawn."

"What?" Luke's face falls. "You mean I left work early for a fake egg hunt?"

"It's not fake. It's just scaled down to the participants' abilities."

"But I can hide Madison's eggs on Sunday, right? I'm putting one in the exhaust pipe of my car. Then I thought I'd bury one—"

"What? Luke! No! She's not even three yet."

Seriously. Sometimes I feel like I'm raising two children.

Ingrid summons Luke and Danforth Sr. to help with the eggs, and I whip out a yellow balloon and get to work. Ingrid, Genevieve, and I commandeered several concrete picnic tables a few hundred feet away from the playground, and before us, a huge grassy field sprawls waiting for plastic eggs filled with treats.

I tuck my tote bag beneath the table, safe from the preschool thief, who at this point could be anyone.

"That's smart." Genevieve places her bag next to mine, and Dr. Konig and several other moms and teachers follow our lead.

Two nearby tables are laden with sweets and a vegetable platter with limp celery and pale carrots. I contributed bunny shaped sugar cookies, cheesecakes that look like nests, and chocolate chick cupcakes. (I swear, I am detoxing from Pinterest next week.) Natasha would not be pleased. After I emailed about the after-school egg hunt, she emailed, "I am disappointed that you are slaves to the sugar agenda." Luke and I had an excellent laugh over that barb — while eating ice cream, of course.

Natasha, Usurper Of Room Mom Crowns, Wearer Of Many Bangles, and Enemy Of Joy, is not attending our illicit egg hunt, but pretty much everyone else is. By "everyone else," I do not mean "the families in Miss Lucy's class" but ALL the preschool families, teachers, and Dr. Konig, who at the present moment is inspecting the dessert spread while wearing a navy pencil skirt, sensible beige pumps, and bunny ears. I meant to limit this speakeasy egg hunt to Miss Lucy's class, but Genevieve wanted to bring her older son Huck, then the parents of Huck's friends begged to come, and now the entire preschool, minus Natasha, has assembled at a park a block away from preschool.

I hand Madison a balloon chick, and she clutches it to her chest. Though it has been a few weeks since the book fair, she has not yet shown any signs of tiring of mama's balloon talents. I twist white and pink balloons into a bunny as children gather around me. Grubby hands snatch at the balloons, but Dr. Konig and several teachers swoop in and wrangle the kids into a line. Miss Blaire stands by my side and plays *Let It Go* on her ukulele while I create a warren of balloon rabbits.

I spot a motherless Arlo waiting in line for a balloon and scan the area for Debbie's resting bitch face while twisting a blue balloon into a bunny. She is not hovering near the dessert table where parents are chatting, nor is she mingling with the parents clustered beneath the shade of a few maple trees. That must mean Debbie is... as if on cue, a breathy high-pitched voice squeals, "Luke! You are too funny!"

The balloon I'm holding pops.

Debbie is following Luke around the baseball field while he and Danforth distribute eggs. For today's festivities, she selected a sexy bunny costume that would be appropriate for the Playboy Mansion. During her most recent podcast episode, she debated whether she would wear her leather bodysuit with the fishnet stockings or "keep it classy" with a pink bodysuit with lace trim. I am happy to report she went with the pink bodysuit, though I would not describe her ensemble as "classy."

"Can I get a duck?" A young child begs.

"Yes!" I say in a voice pitched a bit too high. "One duck! Coming up!"

Ingrid climbs on top of a picnic table between the remains of a carrot cake and the untouched veggie platter, wielding a megaphone. Now her outfit — a floral print dress, blue cardigan and neutral heels — is classy. Maybe Ingrid could give Debbie some wardrobe lessons after the egg hunt. "Parents, we are going to have the children line up in between Miss Blaire and Miss Lucy." Ingrid gestures toward the empty baseball field where the teachers are standing.

A screech of feedback rips through the air, and half the children cover their ears with their hands. Becky, wearing a weighted vest over pastel workout clothes, climbs up on to the picnic table, knocks over the veggie platter, and seizes the megaphone. So much for an unofficial, unsanctioned preschool egg hunt. "Parents, every child may collect six eggs. SIX eggs. Got that? Six eggs! So please, count whatever they collect and return any extras."

"It's hunt time!" I grab Madison's pink basket and offer it to her.

"I have to poop!"

I blink at Madison, utterly confused by this announcement, because this is the first time Madison has shown any interest in potty training. Last weekend, I put a pink plastic potty in the Womb Room while she was watching *Frozen*, and she kicked it over.

"Then go in your diaper." This is not the time to start potty training.

"No!" Madison stamps her tiny foot. "I want to go on the potty!"

"Just go in your diaper. It's time for the hunt."

This makes logical sense. What preschooler chooses the potty over an egg hunt? Then again, when has logic ever worked with my preschooler?

"Potty!" Madison demands as she clutches her butt and bounces on her feet.

"Okay, potty," I say and take Madison's hand as we march toward the bathroom facilities, which are several hundred yards away. Madison will poop in her diaper halfway to the bathroom and then we can return to the hunt. I'll give her a fresh diaper after she has collected her eggs. I organized this speakeasy egg hunt. My daughter will not miss it.

My daughter misses the egg hunt.

I will spare you the details of the horrors that happened in the park's public restroom. Let's just say a public restroom is not the ideal place to begin one's adventures with potty training. Let's also say I have seen things I can never unsee and now bear permanent psychological scars.

When we make it back to the field, the children are hunched over their baskets, sorting through their loot.

"You missed the hunt!" Luke jogs toward us. Debbie follows, her breasts bouncing vigorously in the "classy" pink bodysuit.

"Madison had to use the bathroom."

"She used a toilet?"

I shrug. I cannot even begin to recount the horrors that transpired over the last ten minutes of my life. Like I said: permanent psychological scars.

"I saved plenty of eggs for my favorite girl." Luke scoops Madison up, puts her on his shoulders, and heads for the field, weaving his way between chocolate-smeared children. This leaves me alone with my favorite podcast host.

"I suppose I should thank you." Debbie toys with the strand of pearls that accents her cleavage. The necklace with the blue diamond is allegedly still stolen.

My entire body tenses. "What? Why?"

"With my insurance proceeds, I bought even better jewelry. As an influencer, I have to keep my selfies fresh. Plus, a lot of the brands I feature sent me gifts to make up for the Trunk-or-Treat burglary."

It was not a burglary. I learned that in Criminal Law many years ago, but that's not the point that concerns me. "Debbie, I did not steal your jewelry."

Debbie is about to say something else, presumably rude and inflammatory, but Genevieve runs over and says, "Have you seen my bag?"

"Your bag?"

"The Trader Joe's reusable tote? I put it under the table with your bag and now it's gone."

"Oh, no," I moan.

"The thief," Genevieve finishes my thought. "Well, at least I had my phone with me."

Dr. Konig strides over in her sensible beige pumps. "I left my purse with yours, Elodie, while I was helping with the balloon animals. Did you move it somewhere?"

I'm going to cry.

28

A peacock fans its feathers and sashays toward me.

"What do you want?" I snap. I'm wearing black leggings, a black oversized t-shirt and my favorite shabby grey cardigan. My soul is a wasteland, so I wanted to dress the part. When Madison saw my outfit, she grimaced and said, "Mama, you need some pink."

The peacock shakes its feathers while turning in a slow circle, to display its blue tush, but I refuse to be intimidated and return to my study of the map at the entrance to the botanical gardens. I have been meaning to come here ever since we moved to Pasadena, and after dropping Madison off at preschool, I decided today was the day.

"What do you suggest?" I ask the peacock, tucking a loose lock of brown hair behind my ear.

The peacock struts toward me as if to say, *Behold the glory of my feathers!*

Is the peacock trying to seduce me? I abandon the map and walk, letting the garden reveal its wonders to me, not wanting to add "accidentally mated with a peacock" to my growing list of problems.

I amble along a black paved road past an enormous lawn and fountain that sprays water twenty feet into the air until the road reaches an area of dense vegetation. A tiny sign informs me I have reached the "Prehistoric Forest." The temperature cools ten degrees thanks to a canopy of tree branches that blocks most sunlight. Vines wrap around the trunks of taller trees, and palm fronds litter the ground. A stegosaurus might wait beyond the path's next curve.

The *Game of Thrones* theme song yanks me back into the present. It's my new ringtone.

"Hi, Mom," I answer as I step over an enormous root.

"Hi, sweetie. How are you?"

Well, let's see. On Friday afternoon, we eventually located Genevieve's and Dr. Konig's purses, along with several more, behind a trash can near the playground. The thief had stolen their wallets while the egg hunt distracted parents, and of course, left my bag untouched. Debbie wasted no time in accusing me. I explained repeatedly that I missed the hunt because Madison needed to go to the bathroom, but even I knew how lame my excuse sounded. After all, everyone could see Madison's diaper beneath her pink tutu. Becky thinks I organized the egg hunt to plunder unattended bags, Luke thinks we should find a different preschool, and Liz Huffenby made sure everyone knows the gory details. So, in answer to my mom's question, I am wallowing in some dark feelings, including sadness, rage, despair, frustration, helplessness, more despair, and abject woe.

"I'm good."

In the background, several voices babble, and my mom says, "I'm talking to Elodie."

"Put her on speaker!"

"She's our sister!"

"Don't hog her, woman!"

My mom sighs and switches our call to speakerphone.

"Hi, everyone." I've left the prehistoric forest and entered a garden that reminds me of an English landscape. Stone paths wind around bushes manicured into bulbous shapes, and Mr. Darcy and Elizabeth Bennett might stroll by at any moment.

My siblings hoot a chorus of greetings, and Ferris says, "Where's Maddy? We want to talk to our niece!"

"She's at school."

"I still can't believe she's old enough for school," Colette says.

"She'll be three in less than a month."

"Any birthday plans?" my mom asks.

"Yes," I say, grateful for the distraction from the s-show that is my life. "We're having a party the Saturday before her birthday. She wants a pink moon bounce, pink cake, pink decorations, and Elsa. I booked the best Elsa impersonator in L.A. County and we have a pink castle jumper, and of course I will bake too many cupcakes. I jut wish you guys could be there."

"Me, too," my mom commiserates.

"We should go!" Cormac says.

"The circus will be in South Carolina," my mom says.

"We are so overdue for a vacation," Ferris whines.

"We're going to Colorado first for that billionaire's event." Colette says. "Colorado isn't that far from California."

"It's just her third birthday," I hurry to say before my mom feels even worse than she already does about missing her only grandchild's birthday. I do not expect my family to drop everything and come to Pasadena for a party. It's been a long time since we were together, but it's not their fault the flu ruined our December plans.

Our call ends when the ringmaster summons everyone for a pre-show meeting. During our call, I felt better, but now, on top of my general sense of impending doom regarding preschool, I also feel homesick. Sometimes, I feel destined to spend my entire life feeling that way. As a child, I was homesick for somewhere I had never lived, a place with a permanent address and the same kids at the same school, year after year. Now I have that life, but I am homesick for my circus family. I'm planning to visit them this summer, but that seems so far away. If only Madison and I could get on the next flight to wherever they are, but I can't leave Pasadena now, not with Debbie's latest round of accusations. She'll tell everyone that I dipped into wallets during the egg hunt to buy the plane tickets. That's just the sort of theory that Detective Becky would find plausible.

Somewhere ahead, a thundering sound roars, and I round the bend and stop in my tracks. A waterfall that looks like a Maui postcard tumbles down the rocky side of a steep hill, lush with moss and ferns, and then divides into two waterfalls that cascade into a clear pool. Several people are taking selfies, and I join them, angling my phone so the photo includes as much of the waterfall as possible while still avoiding the effect of a triple chin.

Feeling renewed, I promenade in the general direction of the parking lot. I take photos of flowers and peacocks and end up at a cafe where I buy myself a Diet Coke and blueberry muffin. I sit at a bistro table outside and enjoy my snack while reading a book. A peacock lurks nearby, waiting for crumbs. When I finish my chips, I check my phone and find a deluge of text messages from assorted preschool moms. Ah, what fresh new hell is this? I read Genevieve's message first because she has the healthiest perspective on what constitutes a crisis.

> Can you believe all this drama? First the egg hunt and now Debbie's latest episode.

A chill runs down my spine. I pull up Debbie's podcast and sure enough, the *Centerfold Mama* posted a new episode this morning. It's eight minutes long. I can listen while I drive back to preschool.

Stomach churning, I barely notice the peacocks perched above the exit and reluctantly hit play after buckling my seatbelt.

> *Hey there, mamas and papas, I have got to vent about this mom at the Prince's preschool.*

My stomach lurches.

> *Her name is Tricia.*

Is "Tricia" code for "Elodie"?

> *Tricia has a kid in the Prince's old class and has gained so much weight that this morning, she was wearing her old pregnancy jeans! I could see the elastic band and heard her telling a friend that she's embarrassed to be wearing them when she's not pregnant. Can you believe it? Her kid is two, and she still owns maternity jeans? WTF?*

> *It's moms like Tricia who make life tough for moms like me. Men expect us to get fat just because we had babies.*

*Why do you think men cheat? Because of moms like
Tricia.*

I turn off the episode. I cannot listen to another second of Debbie's body shaming rant. There is a mom named Tricia with a kid in Miss Ellen's class. She was so gracious when I accidentally opened her car door. Somehow, this latest podcast rant feels worse than Debbie's accusations that I'm the thief or her blatant attempts to seduce Luke. A woman's body is sacred. Motherhood is tough enough and plenty of us have trouble losing the pregnancy weight. Great for Debbie and her bikini model body, but she does not get to prop up her self-esteem by shaming other moms.

Upon parking my car at preschool, I take several deep calming breaths. My rage feels a little less rage-y.

A red Ferrari pulls into the handicapped space and out pops Debbie, wearing a skintight backless dress, stiletto heels, and resting bitch face. I clench my steering wheel and stare at Debbie through narrowed eyes. Debbie would say that I am aggravating my frown lines and it's high time I invest in Botox, but Debbie can go [CENSORED] and [CENSORED] and then [CENSORED] with a dead bear.

I get out of the car, slam my door shut and storm toward preschool, rage and anger and loathing racing through my arteries and igniting my senses. A little voice tells me to calm down and act pleasantly, but my rage snuffs it out. I am not interested in anger management or calming breaths or fitting in or being pleasant and nice.

I want Debbie's head on a pole.

As I enter the preschool courtyard, Tricia, eyes red and watery, slumps on a bench outside Miss Ellen's classroom. One mom offers tissues while another says, "She's awful. Ignore her. Just ignore her."

I agree. Debbie is awful. But I can't just ignore her. Not this time.

Debbie stands outside Miss Lucy's classroom, hip thrust forward while aiming her boobs at Danforth Sr. To his credit, Danforth is backing away. As I approach, Debbie says, "So then I told my trainer that my pre-baby body is not good enough! What do you think?" She turns and gives her booty a shake. "Couldn't my derriere use some extra squats?"

Danforth Sr. clears his throat, mutters something about the office, and beats a hasty retreat. Smart man.

Maude bounces on her feet. She sidles up to me and whispers, "Did you hear Debbie's latest episode?"

I grind my teeth. "I listened to the first few minutes but couldn't stomach the rest."

"It's awful. Poor Tricia. She's humiliated."

"Debbie shouldn't be saying those sorts of things on a podcast."

"I know," Maude says. "But what can we do? We have to ignore someone like that."

There's that word again: ignore. It makes my blood seethe.

Across the courtyard, several more moms console Tricia.

Debbie shakes her buns for Josh, our token stay-at-home dad, and then says in a fake whisper, "Isn't it pathetic how some women let themselves go?"

THAT.

IS.

IT.

"Just shut up already," I say in a loud, ringing voice. The parents standing outside Miss Lucy's classroom go quiet. "No one wants to hear your foul filth."

Debbie huffs. "On the rag? You look bloated."

Now the parents outside the neighboring classrooms go quiet.

"I'm sick of listening to you say malicious things about other parents. This is a preschool, not your sorority."

Debbie tosses her hair over her shoulders. "I don't say malicious things."

A fresh wave of fury surges through me. I feel like Daenerys, Mother of Dragons. No — I *am* a dragon. "I won't count off all the malicious things I've heard you say this year, but don't play stupid. Stop saying nasty things at preschool, and stop saying even nastier garbage on your podcast."

Debbie makes the sort of noise that the popular girl in a high school movie makes when annoyed. "I can say whatever I want. Haven't you heard of the First Amendment?" Debbie smiles smugly, but she does not know what she has done. By mentioning the First Amendment, she has unleashed my inner lawyer.

"Oh, yes." The entire courtyard has gone quiet by now. "I learned all about the First Amendment in law school. I also learned about libel and slander. Ever heard about them? Did you know juries can hold you liable in a court of law when you slander someone?" I feel eight feet tall. "Did you know people can file lawsuits against you? And seek damages? Do you have any idea what sort of damages Los Angeles juries like to award for emotional distress? You'll have to pawn more than your jewelry to deal with legal expenses."

I pause. Debbie is speechless. Parents from other classrooms have drawn a little closer. If this is the motherhood circus, today I am the ringmaster, popping off on the lion tamer. Everyone is watching, and I do not care.

"The slander on your podcast is beyond egregious." Sparks practically fly out of my nostrils. I have no idea if the things I am saying are true. I never worked on a case involving slander, and it has been years since I studied for the bar exam, but Debbie does not know that. "If I were you, I would delete your little podcast before you get slapped with a dozen lawsuits. There could even be a class action." Now I know that last bit is wrong, but again, only one of us went to law school, and it's not Debbie.

"Well," Debbie says in a shaky voice, "I'm entitled to my opinions."

Mr. Joe opens the classroom door and the other doors around the courtyard swing open. The courtyard fills with the shouts of children being reunited with their parents. As we wait to collect our children, I lean close to Debbie and whisper, "Go ahead and tell yourself that if it helps you sleep at night."

Later that day, I check Debbie's podcast, but it does not appear in my feed. Debbie deleted every episode. It's as if *Centerfold Mama* never existed.

29

"Oh butterscotch," Miss Lucy says. "I printed templates for today's craft project, but left them in the office. Miss Elodie, do you mind getting them for me?"

"Not at all!"

After a week's absence for spring break, it is great to be back at Mountain View Co-op Preschool. I enjoyed my lazy mornings with Madison and our outings to the zoo, aquarium, and children's museum, although the highlight of the week was our trip to Target to buy big girl undies. I assumed she would want the *Frozen* themed undergarments, but she picked Dora the Explorer, Peppa Pig and Minnie Mouse. The girl likes options — except when it comes to pink tutus. There might have been a bit of a scene when I steered her toward a rack of tutus and suggested we buy a new one, and I might have bought Madison a stuffed animal to calm her hysterics. Lesson learned. I did not object to her tutu again for the rest of spring break, even when paint and pancake batter dripped all over it.

Despite all the fun I had with Madison, I still missed my

friends. Genevieve and her boys went camping; Ingrid and the Danforths spent the week in Lake Tahoe; and Maude visited family in Florida. Even Extremely Pregnant Chloe left town to attend a family reunion in Palm Springs. I nearly texted stay-at-home dad Josh to schedule a playdate, but decided I was not that desperate for adult companionship.

Today I'm volunteering, and I had my yellow apron tied on before any other parents arrived. I chatted with all the parents, minus Debbie and Ashley. Then during circle time, Paula and I exchanged several meaningful glances whenever Josh sang the songs with a falsetto. I wish I had a video of it.

Out in the courtyard, Becky is whisper-shouting at Monica while doing squats. She ignores me as I stroll by. I hum to myself and suppress a smile. Becky should beg me on bended knee to be Miss Lucy's room mom again. I vanquished Debbie! I'm a hero! Where's my medal?

I step into the office and barely recognize the place. The orchids have been moved to the white L-shaped reception desk, and the couches, love seat, chairs and coffee table have been shoved together into a corner. In their place, someone erected a studio for a professional photo shoot. On one metal stand, there is a white umbrella with a large lightbulb, and on another metal stand, there is a box with silver fabric. A black backdrop hangs from a frame of PVC poles, and a cart is loaded with makeup pots and brushes. Maude clutches a large rectangle of shiny fabric and tilts it at random angles.

"Say cheese!" Ingrid stands next to a tripod, places the tips of her index fingers on the corners of her mouth and pushes her lips into an exaggerated smile. A child sitting on a stool in front of the backdrop bursts into tears.

I sidle over to Ingrid and Maude. "Auction photos going well?"

Ingrid gives me a withering look as she coaxes the crying child off the stool and ushers her next victim into place. As part of Operation: Get Preschool A New Playground, she is taking portraits of each kid to sell in cheap IKEA frames at the auction. She texted several moms about her latest plan last week and begged us to help her take the photos. I was relieved when I checked my calendar and learned I was already scheduled to work my volunteer shift. With all due respect to my freshman roommate, she is now occasionally bearable, but I would still rather spend my morning managing snotty preschoolers than listening to her dolphin laugh.

"Say cheese!" Ingrid demands.

"Booger!" the boy shouts.

Charming.

"Let me try," I suggest. "Say hooray!"

The boy scowls. "Balloon!"

"This is impossible," Maude moans. She is wearing a puffy jacket zipped to her neck, but is still shivering. "We have to take over a hundred photos, and the kids won't cooperate."

"Balloon!" the boy shouts again, his face twisting into a petulant scowl.

"Yes," Ingrid says in her most coddling voice. "This is the balloon lady. Doesn't she make wonderful balloon animals?"

"Ba! Loon!"

"Oh!" I say. "I'll be right back!" I sprint to my car. Okay, it's more of a jog-walk, but in my heart, I'm an Olympic athlete. I return a couple of minutes later, armed with my balloon making supplies, which have been languishing in the trunk of my car since the egg hunt debacle. I pump up a balloon and twist it into a dog.

The little boy grins as I hand it to him. Ingrid snaps a photo, checks the preview screen and exclaims, "Perfect!"

Dr. Konig watches from behind the jungle of orchids on her desk. Her white blouse is so crisp, she must have ironed it this morning. Diplomatically, she says, "Perhaps Elodie should help with the photos and Maude could take her place in the classroom?"

Maude grabs my yellow apron and departs with Miss Lucy's templates. I do not mind being drafted into balloon lady duty. Yes, Ingrid will assault my ears with her dolphin laugh any moment now, but thanks to my crazy circus skills, Ingrid might raise a couple thousand extra dollars at the auction. It will not be enough to stop preschool's free fall into financial ruin, but hey, it's a start.

Ingrid and I fall into a peaceful rhythm. I banter with the kids and fulfill their balloon animal dreams while Ingrid snaps their portraits and ticks their names off her list. "This reminds me of the time freshman year that you wanted to take a group photo of everyone on our floor," I say, as Ingrid boosts a girl onto the stool. "You had a fancy camera and tripod even then."

Ingrid grimaces. "Zoe convinced half the floor to boycott the photo."

My stomach flips and flops.

"I could never figure out why Zoe despised me so much." Ingrid snaps a photo.

"Seriously?"

In a perplexed tone of voice, Ingrid asks, "Do you know?"

"Yes." I hesitate and then lower my voice. "I don't want to talk about it here."

"Elodie! You can't do that. Now I'm stressed." Ingrid knots her fingers together, forgetting all about the children waiting to have their pictures taken. "I've always wondered what I did. Zoe had a vendetta against me."

"You s-p-i-k-e-d her drink at the Halloween party. That's why she got so d-r-u-n-k."

"What?" Ingrid does a double take. "I would never do something like that!"

"But that's why she danced t-o-p-l-e-s-s on the table."

Ingrid's ears are almost as red as her hair. "She did that because she pounded six s-h-o-t-s of v-o-d-k-a in twenty minutes."

Blood pounds in my ears. My lungs constrict. Zoe has been my best friend since college, but I believe Ingrid.

A little girl breaks the silence. "Can I have a balloon unicorn?"

"Of course," I say, and turn back to Ingrid. "But what about Craig? You stole him from Zoe."

"No, I didn't." Ingrid laughs with relief. "I was dating Craig and Zoe knew it because I told her. I didn't tell you because you thought he was a womanizer."

"He was a womanizer."

"I know! He h-o-o-k-e-d-u-p with Zoe the weekend I went home for my grandma's funeral." Ingrid brushes a little girl's hair before positioning her on the stool. "Then Zoe bragged about it to me. That's when I came to my senses and dumped Craig. I still don't get why Zoe hated me so much." Ingrid's voice trails off.

"Me neither," I confess. All these years, I despised Ingrid on Zoe's behalf when all Ingrid ever did was laugh like a dolphin. Okay, Ingrid can also be pretentious and condescending, but that's just her way of dealing with her insecurities.

"Is that why you hated me?" Ingrid whispers.

"Well..." I feel pathetic and petty. "Yeah... that... and you made me feel bad about my freckles."

"I love your freckles!" Ingrid protests. "How did I make you feel bad about them?"

"Because you asked if I had ever tried lemon juice to lighten them."

"That was because I was obsessed with my complexion. My mother always told me that a single freckle would ruin my face, but I was jealous of your freckles. They are so wild and gorgeous. I'm sorry I made you feel bad."

"I'm sorry I didn't ask for your side of the story about the Halloween party."

We are on the verge of a teary, cinematic moment when Becky barges inside, frowning at paperwork while doing bicep curls with a ten-pound weight. She mutters to no one in particular, "The playground contractor emailed this morning with a memo of new rates." I make a balloon dragon for a three-year-old with glasses. Becky mutters numbers to herself and makes calculations out loud. Then she notices me.

"What is she doing here?" Becky storms over to the impromptu photography studio.

"She's helping," Ingrid says condescendingly.

"We talked about this." Becky gives me the side eye while switching the ten-pound weight to her other hand. "You need my approval for any volunteers helping you in the office. Especially her." She looks meaningfully at me. "You know we are dealing with a delicate situation."

Translation: they still don't know who the embezzler is.

"Elodie is my savior, Becky." Ingrid says her name like it's a swear word. "None of the kids would smile for the camera. They were crying, and Elodie's balloon animals cheered them up. Now the pictures are amazing, and I'll be able to sell them for a huge profit at the auction. I didn't have time to get your approval."

Becky's nostrils flare. I blow up a yellow balloon which she regards suspiciously, as if I might use it to embezzle from preschool. Oh, Becky, if I was that smart, do you think I would embezzle from Mountain View Co-op Preschool? Wouldn't I would set my sights on a bigger target? For example, Tiny Geniuses Academy and the U.S. Treasury both come to mind.

Miss Blaire wanders into the office with a sniffling Arlo. She swept her blonde hair into a messy but elegant bun, and her complexion glows so radiantly, I am a crone in her presence. Arlo looks like he stepped off the pages of a parenting magazine with his suede sneakers, dark jeans, leather jacket and hair styled upwards into a swoop. The outfit sends out "teenage delinquent vibes" but tears stream down both cheeks as he sucks his thumb. Poor kid. It's not his fault Debbie is his mom.

"Miss Blaire!" Becky effuses.

Miss Blaire opens a cabinet and removes the first aid kit. She has not even registered Becky's presence. "What do you think, Arlo? Do you want a Spiderman bandaid or Paw Patrol?"

"Spiderman," Arlo whispers.

Becky hovers over Arlo as Miss Blaire pats a scraped elbow clean with a wipe. "Are you excited about your wedding? I'm so sorry we can't make it."

"I didn't expect anyone from preschool to go," Miss Blaire says in her silvery, Disney princess voice. "Not after my fiancé insisted on Bulgaria for the wedding!" She laughs charmingly.

That was not the impression I got from Miss Blaire's

fiancé on Thanksgiving. If memory serves, he did not even know the wedding is in Bulgaria; but Thanksgiving had its fair share of excitement, and I only have a hazy memory of my chat with Steve.

"At least we can make it to your bridal shower!" Ingrid positions a child for the camera.

"Bridal shower? You're having a bridal shower? Why wasn't I invited?" Becky says in a strangled tone.

"I wish I could have invited everyone, but my mom said I had to keep the guest list to under a hundred. That's why I only invited the moms from Miss Lucy's class."

"You could make an exception for the co-op president," Becky teases, but there's a note of desperation in her voice that makes me cringe.

Ingrid comes to Miss Blaire's rescue. "If she makes one exception, she'll have to make a thousand."

Becky's shoulders droop as Miss Blaire puts away the bandaids and leads Arlo away. Becky follows but pauses at the door and says, "Ingrid, do not leave any parents unsupervised in the office."

Ingrid and I exchange eye rolls and continue working. After another half hour, she announces, "We're making good progress. I'm going to take a bathroom break after I take these kids back to Miss Ellen."

I blow up my next balloon. My fingers ache, but it's a good ache.

A frazzled mom pops into the office. "Meredith, I'm so sorry, but the sink is acting up."

Meredith bounds to her feet, plunger in hand. Her hair, once purple, is now a vibrant shade of aqua. "I'm on my way!"

The office phone rings, and Dr. Konig answers. "Yes? Yes... Of course." She stands and hurries out of the office, with no explanation, but no doubt on important director business.

I count my balloons. I have created a reserve of thirty. Then I calculate the number of kids we can photograph before the end of school. I have more than enough balloons and return my pump to my tote bag.

"What the hell?" Becky enters the room while doing a set of sideways lunges. "Where's Ingrid? Where's Meredith and Dr. Konig? Why are you alone in the office?"

"Ingrid went to the bathroom," I say defensively. I have done nothing wrong, but my stomach lurches.

Becky glares at me while doing sideways lunges toward Meredith's desk. "What is this?"

"What is what?" I do not care if this woman is the most powerful parent at Mountain View Co-op Preschool. I'm sick of being her prime suspect in the ongoing preschool thief saga.

"Why is this computer unlocked? Only board and staff members are supposed to have access to the computers."

I do not like this woman. "I don't know," I snap. "But I haven't been near the computer all day. I've been making balloon animals. A parent needed Meredith to unclog the sink, Ingrid went to the bathroom, and Dr. Konig got a phone call and left."

"It's very suspicious that you are available to help Ingrid with auction photos and then you ignore my warning and stay in the office alone with full access to an unlocked computer."

My vision narrows and my skin feels hot. "What are you insinuating? Why is it my fault Meredith left her computer on?"

"I think you are the embezzler," Becky hisses, "and Ingrid is too blind to see how you are manipulating her."

Ingrid returns with a fresh batch of children.

"Ingrid!" Becky barks. "Elodie is done helping with auction photos."

"Don't be preposterous." Becky is about to protest, but Dr. Konig returns, so instead she side lunges away.

"Ignore her," Ingrid says. "She's way out of bounds."

Ingrid might as well be offering advice to the wall. I am too busy wondering whether I could strangle Becky with a balloon noose.

30

"Oh my god," Genevieve grabs my arm. "The signature cocktail is a cranberry orange mimosa."

"That does not sound at all dangerous."

The cocktail's name is written on a chalkboard next to a wooden bar manned by two barmen who are younger versions of Bradley Cooper and Taye Diggs. We have just entered a stone courtyard surrounded by pillars. We walk past a tiered fountain whose water falls into a basin filled with rose petals and deposit our presents on a ten-foot-long table that is already piled with presents, including more than a few Tiffany Blue boxes wrapped with big white bows. After perusing Miss Blaire's five wedding registries, I ordered a gift from Target. No points for guessing where Ingrid purchased her gift.

"Where have you been?" Maude joins us in the drinks line. She looks nice in her black pants, black sweater, and black pea coat — okay, so her outfit is better suited for a winter funeral than a spring bridal shower, but in makeup and tailored pants, Maude exudes less misery than she does at preschool. She holds a glass of champagne in one hand and a plate of melon prosciutto skewers in the other. Someone is making the most of her break from the motherhood circus.

"We had trouble finding a parking spot and Ingrid thought the valet was stoned," I explain. We carpooled to Miss Blaire's bridal shower, Maude driving herself and six moms in her minivan and four of us riding with Ingrid. Natasha declined our invitation to carpool because she does not support events held for the collection of material goods, and no one invited Ashley or Debbie.

Maude nods and then squeals, "Bacon wrapped dates!" and hurries after a waiter.

When we reach the front of the line, Genevieve and I order the signature cocktail. Armed with our fancy beverages, we wander the crowd of milling women. I went to a blowout salon with Ingrid this morning, so I am feeling pretty fabulous in my little black dress and emerald green cardigan. I even put on eye shadow and lip gloss. Genevieve eschewed the blowout salon, insisting that she had already picked a fedora for the occasion. I am jealous of the ease with which she pulls off her fedora, even at a bridal shower on a wind-swept bluff with an unobstructed view of the Pacific Ocean.

A briny breeze fills my lungs, and I sigh contentedly. "This is so much better than a three-year-old's birthday party."

"Poor Paula," Genevieve agrees.

Paula sent invitations to her daughter Zelda's birthday party two and a half months ago. Then, a few weeks later, we received invitations to Miss Blaire's bridal shower on the same day. Paula was devastated, but it was too late to reschedule: the deposit for the posh indoor playground was steep and nonrefundable. I, meanwhile, am secretly gloating because all the moms are planning to attend Madison's party next weekend.

"She was so bummed to miss," Genevieve continues, "I promised her we would organize a mom's night out."

"Except no Debbie." My blood freezes as Maude rejoins us. Fighting my rising panic, I ask, "Have you seen Debbie?"

"No," Maude shudders. "I bet she is with Ashley."

As if on cue, Ashley flounces over in a slinky white dress. "When is Debbie getting here?" she demands in an accusatory tone.

"I assumed you drove here together," I say.

"No, but she promised me yesterday she was coming!" Ashley whips out her phone and checks her text messages while stalking away from us.

"If she's not here, she must be—"

"Oh god." Bile rises up my throat. "She's at Zelda's birthday party."

"With all our husbands," Maude whispers.

"What's wrong?" Ingrid walks over with a Diet Coke, and I explain the situation.

"I'm texting Paula," Ingrid says without hesitation. She types a message and a moment later, her phone pings back. "Worst case scenario," Ingrid reports and tilts her screen so we can read for ourselves.

> Oh god, Debbie is here. Her shorts are so tiny, I can see her butt cheeks. She is flirting with all the dads.

So this is how my marriage ends. While I go to a bridal shower, Luke elopes with Debbie. Okay, okay, I am exaggerating. Today they will disappear into the bathroom for ten minutes of illicit passion while the preschoolers eat cake. In a few weeks, they will elope after Debbie announces she is pregnant with Luke's child.

Why did I let myself feel so smug about vanquishing the preschool succubus? Sure, I convinced her to delete the filth she calls a podcast, but she is still a swimsuit model with plans to seduce a married preschool dad AND I PROVOKED HER. Debbie is the sort of person who seeks revenge. Sweet baby Jesus, I might as well have painted a target on Luke's penis and sent Debbie an engraved invitation to wreck my life.

I type a quick text to Luke.

How's the party?

Maybe Luke forgot about the party, or maybe Madison threw a tantrum and refused to get dressed, or maybe there's a mountain lion prowling our neighborhood and Luke can't risk venturing outside to the car.

A woman who is an older version of Miss Blaire taps the side of a glass with a metal knife until the crowd quiets. "Thank you, everyone, for coming to my daughter's bridal shower today! Please join us down on the lawn for lunch."

The assigned seating chart separates the preschool moms. Ingrid and Genevieve join a table with an excellent ocean view; Extremely Pregnant Chloe toddles toward a table of older women; and Ashley and Maude disappear somewhere in the middle of the sea of guests. I am banished to a table with a gaggle of young women that is not even on the lawn but a neglected patch of dirt.

The young women go quiet as I approach.

"Hi, I'm Elodie." I wave and glance down at my phone. No messages from Luke.

"I'm Fiona," the young woman seated to my left says.

She has curly hair and is wearing a gorgeous knit blue dress with a scalloped neckline. "We are the B-squad."

"The what?" I ask. Is this some new slang millennials use?

"'B' as in backup," the woman seated on Fiona's other side grumbles. She is wearing a pumpkin orange dress that is not doing her any favors. "We were in the same sorority and thought we were friends, but lately, Blaire has been treating us like her backup squad."

"It's like she only invited us today to get more presents," a third woman with a long neck pouts.

"How many place settings do you need?" Fiona says. "I know Blaire is marrying into a wealthy family, but thirty place settings from Tiffany's seem excessive."

She has a point.

"I bet she's just returning the settings for money," the woman in the pumpkin orange dress sulks.

"I don't know why I am surprised," Fiona sighs. "Given the way she talks about her actual sister."

"What?" I yelp.

"Blaire's sister is a waitress and drives an old pink Volvo, and Blaire talks about how her sister is such a disappointment to their parents."

Is this the Miss Blaire that preschool knows and loves?

"Are you going to the wedding?" I ask Fiona after a waiter delivers our plates of salmon, roasted potatoes and caesar salad.

Fiona shakes her head. "I'm in law school. I have exams and then my summer internship, plus I can't afford a ticket to Bulgaria."

I nod sympathetically and resist the urge to warn her against a legal career.

The woman with the long neck says, "Blaire gave me a

number for the hotel, but I swear, the person on the phone was speaking Spanish, not Bulgarian."

After the main course, every table gets a roll of toilet paper to create a wedding dress. Fiona, the law student, directs everyone while weaving peonies from the mason jar centerpiece into a crown. As I plunder the centerpiece for flowers, my phone rings with an incoming FaceTime call. It's Luke.

I hurry back to the cocktail courtyard and answer. Luke's face fills the screen. Behind him, twisty slides and tunnels snake around a ball pit. His glasses sit askew and his silver hair is rumpled — from chasing Madison down playground slides or spending a little private time with Debbie? In a hushed voice, Luke asks, "Is it okay if I take Madison home early?"

"What's wrong?" My adrenaline surges.

"I'm trying to be polite, but I can't take that Debbie woman any longer. I'm sorry, Elodie, I don't want to criticize other moms, but she has been inappropriate all year. Remember that outfit she wore to the Christmas concert? And I didn't want to bother you when you had the flu, but she kept harassing me that week." He runs his fingers through his hair, rumpling it even more. "Doesn't she realize we are parents at a preschool, not characters on a soap opera? Why are you smiling? This is serious."

I arrange my face into a solemn expression, but inside, I am throwing a dance party. Debbie disgusts Luke! He said she is inappropriate! Hallelujah! As casually as possible, I say, "If you think it's best to take Madison home early, that's fine with me."

"Thanks. I think—" and then Luke looks away as a commotion breaks out behind him. "Oh my god, watch this."

Luke flips the camera view. Debbie, wearing an outfit reminiscent of the one Julia Roberts wore during the opening sequence of *Pretty Woman*, complete with thigh-high boots, towers over Danforth Sr. but Danforth is not intimidated. He wags an irritated finger at Debbie while saying something I can't hear.

"I have every right to be here!" Debbie shrieks.

"Not if you are going to act like you are on spring break!" Danforth Sr. booms.

From the sea of tables, amidst the flurry of women turning toilet paper into wedding gowns, I spot Ingrid. We make eye contact and I gesture for her to join me. She sprints to the courtyard.

"I was just having fun! We don't have to be boring because we are parents."

Ingrid races up the stairs. "What is it?" I tilt the phone so she can enjoy the show.

"You are trying to turn a three-year-old's birthday party into an orgy! Can't you take a hint? No one is interested. What does your prenup say about cheating?"

"That was low," I say.

"Good," Ingrid grins.

Debbie stomps away from Danforth Sr., yanks Arlo away from the table where he is eating birthday cake, and marches toward the exit. The camera flips and Luke's face reappears. "I guess we can stay at the party," he says. "Hi, Ingrid."

"Hi, Luke. Tell Danforth he was amazing."

When I return to the B-squad's table, Miss Blaire is inspecting the toilet paper wedding gown that Fiona created. The woman with the orange dress, now obscured by layers of toilet paper, turns slowly in a circle. This white dress suits her more than the orange, even if we made it from bathroom products. "The winner!" Miss Blaire declares, and everyone at our table cheers. The mother of the bride hurries over and hands everyone a pink gift bag. I peek inside and stifle a yelp of pure joy. The bag contains fancy bath salts, a fancy candle, a fancy loofah and a fancy face mask. If Miss Blaire's family can foot the bill for this swanky affair, maybe they also want to buy Mountain View Co-op Preschool a new playground.

"Wow," I tell Fiona as we sit down again. "That dress," I nod toward the toilet paper creation, "is almost as gorgeous as the one you are wearing."

"Thank you." Fiona blushes and touches her dress's scalloped neckline. "I knit this when I was supposed to be studying for my criminal law exam."

"You made that?"

Fiona's neck flushes. "Knitting is my therapy."

"What else have you made?"

Fiona pulls up her Instagram feed and I drool over her hand knit scarves, sweaters and socks. I sigh. "I always wanted to learn how to knit and took a class in college but my scarf was so horrible, everyone laughed at it."

"I'll teach you." We exchange numbers, and I follow Fiona on Instagram. Then we spend the rest of the bridal shower swapping law school horror stories. We hug goodbye when the bridal shower ends.

Ingrid describes Debbie's eviction from the birthday party to the other moms as we hike back to her Mercedes SUV. Between the cranberry orange mimosas and Debbie's rejection, we are downright giddy. I do not even mind getting squished into a middle seat between Genevieve and Brooke Rust.

Halfway back to Pasadena, Ingrid's phone rings, and the name "Becky" appears on the elaborate console. "Ugh, I'm sick of that woman." Ingrid hits a button and sends Becky to voicemail purgatory.

Ten seconds later, Becky calls back. Ingrid groans and accepts the call.

"Did you send me to voicemail?" Becky barks.

"I'm driving," Ingrid says.

"We are having an emergency closed meeting Monday morning after drop-off."

"Another one? What's the emergency now?" Ingrid pauses. "This better not be about the auction."

"The auction is the least of our concerns. We need to deal with that friend of yours. Elodie."

Genevieve rests her hand on top of mine.

"Elodie is not the thief or embezzler!" Ingrid makes a heart-stopping lane change.

"Then why was she snooping on Meredith's computer when you were taking auction photos?"

"What? Becky, you know she wouldn't do something like that."

"I'll explain Monday. We have a genuine crisis, and someone's head needs to roll. I don't care if Elodie is the thief or embezzler, but we have to do something or Mountain View is ruined. See you tomorrow."

After a long moment of silence, Genevieve says, "What does Becky have in mind?"

31

"The sink in Miss Lucy's room is clogged," Mr. Joe says, standing just a foot inside the office.

"On it!" Meredith grabs her plunger, jumps to her feet, and surveys the office, which Ingrid has transformed into auction command central. Between the folding tables, baskets, and donated items, there is not a lot of room to maneuver so after studying the situation, Meredith crawls under a folding table, climbs over a filing cabinet, tiptoes around a tower of wicker baskets and is still nowhere near the door.

"Godspeed!" Meredith tosses the plunger toward Mr. Joe. "Give it a few swift plunges and then hold the plunger down for thirty seconds before switching to the twist-plunge I showed you last week."

Mr. Joe eyes the plunger skeptically and retreats.

If the fire inspector pays Mountain View Co-op Preschool a surprise visit today, Ingrid is going to have a lot of explaining to do.

I stuff a wad of shredded paper into the bottom of a wicker basket. Let the record reflect: I don't want to be here.

Becky thinks I'm embezzling, so spending additional time near the computers does not strike me as the wisest of moves, but Ingrid and Genevieve insisted I would look guilty if I did not help with today's efforts to prepare for the auction.

"I can't believe you're here when you have Madison's party in a few days." Maude wrestles with a sheet of clear cellophane. "There is so much to get done."

"I've already done most of the prep. I just need to bake a cake on Friday."

Confession: I started making checklists for Madison's third birthday party the day after Christmas, including checklists for decorations, food, and party favors and a master checklist for all of my checklists.

"Yes, but you are hosting at your home," Maude frets, shivering despite her UGGs and fleece jacket. "I would be on my hands and knees scrubbing the floor every free moment. Then I'd have to clean all the windows, polish the banister, sterilize the counters..." I nod but after Gavin Rust's party (raw chicken in the sink, pig parts in the freezer, vomit all over the birthday cake), I think the parents will be thrilled so long as I do not have a wild animal chained up in the backyard. The bar is really, really low.

Ingrid hurries into the office and inspects our progress. She wants to be here micromanaging our work, but Becky's special emergency board meeting is happening right now in the upstairs room. Ingrid cannot help herself, but I wish she would stay upstairs where she belongs. Becky wants someone's head to roll, and everyone knows that "someone" is me, so Ingrid needs to make sure that doesn't happen. While I stew, Ingrid takes an empty basket, pops in a pair of large ceramic mugs, adds a few bags of coffee and a French press, fluffs the shredded paper, tucks in a gift certificate for a coffee tasting party, and voilà, the coffee gift basket is ready for cellophane if Maude ever cuts off a sheet.

"How is it going up there?" I whisper. Subtext: what are you doing here when Becky is turning me into a sacrificial lamb?

"So far, so good," Ingrid breathes. She flashes me the thumbs up before joining a group of parents preparing the paddles for bidding during the live auction. She puts down her clipboard and demonstrates the proper way to use the glue stick to a pair of befuddled dads.

"We should bid together on the wine tasting package," Genevieve says as she inspects the finished baskets.

"There's a wine tasting package?"

"There's no basket for that," Ingrid calls from the paddle station. "It's part of the live auction."

My phone rings, and I answer while measuring out a yard of silver ribbon. "Hello?"

"This is Martha from Premium Party Rentals calling to confirm your moon bounce rental for the thirtieth of April."

"What?" I raise my voice over the hubbub of chatting parents, hoping I heard wrong. "I reserved a moon bounce for this Saturday."

"No, you didn't," Martha from Premium Party Rentals intones. "You reserved the pink mermaid palace for the last Saturday in April."

"No! I don't want a pink mermaid palace on April thirtieth. I need it for April twenty-third."

"Just a moment." A computer keyboard clacks. "The pink mermaid palace is unavailable this Saturday."

"Okay." I take a deep breath. "What about a different pink moon bounce?"

More tapping. "We don't have any pink moon bounces

available. We have our standard red, yellow and blue castle. Would you like to reserve that?"

"No, cancel the reservation," I say, and hang up. Madison requested a party with a pink moon bounce, Elsa impersonator, and lots of cake, and so help me God, she is getting a pink moon bounce, Elsa impersonator and lots of cake. We live in Los Angeles County. I can track down a pink moon bounce rental before Saturday.

"Who was that?" Ingrid asks. The dads appear to be applying glue in a way that meets Ingrid's professional standards.

"The party company that was supposed to bring the bouncy castle to Madison's party on Saturday. They screwed up the date."

"That reminds me! I need more chairs for the auction."

Ingrid pulls out her phone as Becky appears at the office door and snaps, "Ingrid, I need you upstairs. Remember?" She places extra emphasis on the word "Remember?" and an invisible hand squeezes my heart. But no, I will think happy thoughts. I trust Ingrid and Monica. They will not let Becky steamroll the board into expelling my family. Everything is going to be fine, fine, fine! Look at me, finding happy thoughts despite Becky's best efforts to crush my spirits.

Ingrid thrusts her phone toward me. "Can you call? Tell them we need forty more chairs and then bring my phone upstairs." She hits a number on speed dial and I take the phone.

"Premium Party Rentals, this is Martha," says a flat zombie voice. Oh joy, the company that screwed up my daughter's birthday party is also handling the auction.

"Hi, I'm calling about Mountain View Co-op Preschool's rentals."

"Just a moment." Lots of typing. "Yes, three hundred chairs, forty-five tables and three hundred place settings for inside, and for outside, forty tables, three hundred chairs, and three hundred place settings." This strikes me as odd. Then I remember Ingrid is using the ramp outside the venue to display some of the auction baskets. Wow, she is super organized.

"We need forty more chairs, please."

"For indoors or outdoors?"

"Indoors," I guess. If I am wrong, we'll move the chairs.

Martha clicks away on her keyboard and then confirms the rental for the auction. She hangs up, and I set Ingrid's phone down on the table. If she thinks I am taking her phone upstairs during Becky's special emergency meeting, she has another thing coming. Instead, I busy myself with the auction baskets.

"What are you doing?" Genevieve has abandoned her post and stands next to me with her brows furrowed into an expression of deep concern.

I am using a toothpick to clean the baskets. "There are little smudges of dirt in between the—" I pause, not knowing the words for the different parts of a wooden basket. "There's dirt," I finish lamely.

Genevieve peers at the baskets. "Come on, relax."

"I *am* relaxing."

"You're worried about the meeting upstairs."

"No, I'm not."

"Yes, you are."

I stab myself with the toothpick and throw it on the ground. "Wouldn't you be freaking out? Becky thinks I'm embezzling from preschool!"

The entire room stops talking and turns toward me.

"We know it's not you," Maude says, and the other parents nod their heads enthusiastically.

"Yeah, but you guys are not on the board. Becky hates me."

"Becky is crazy," Genevieve says, "but everyone else is sane. Well, Ingrid is crazy in her own special way."

I laugh and wipe away a few tears. I did not realize I was crying.

"You've done a lot for the school this year," Genevieve continues. "You saved the Easter egg hunt, and you raised tons of money at the book fair with your awesome balloon animals. The board would have to be total idiots to think you embezzled."

"But Becky wants a head to roll," I sniffle.

"Then shouldn't you be up there?" Genevieve says.

"I'm not on the board."

Maude says, "But shouldn't you have the chance to defend yourself?"

My inner lawyer goes on high alert.

"You should be there!" Genevieve urges.

They are right. I *should* be there. Every defendant gets her day in court!

I grab Ingrid's phone and storm outside. Vienna Vega, the annoying older kid who longs to bolt up the Forbidden Stairs, blocks my path. She is bigger than ever. Is this kid really a preschooler? She scowls at me, but I am not in the mood for her shenanigans. "Step aside, please," I say in a voice that leaves no room for negotiation, and she squeaks and scampers away. I am no longer the meek room mom from last September but the fierce ex-room mom on a mission and no kid is going to stop me from defending myself against Becky's bogus accusations.

I march up the stairs, planning to throw the door open.

Alas, someone propped it open, depriving me of a dramatic entrance. No matter! I stride inside.

Board members sit on folding chairs arranged in a U-shape, and a folding table littered with yellow legal pads, white binders, empty muffin wrappers, and a gavel is at the top of the U. The executive board members sit behind this table. Well, Monica, Yolanda, and the secretary, whose name I forget, sit behind the table while Becky stands behind her chair, doing calf raises.

"This is a closed session," Becky hisses.

"Ingrid needs her phone back." I wave the phone in the air. Ingrid smiles faintly as I push inside the semi-circle of folding chairs to return her phone.

"You can go now," Becky says, switching to squats.

"If the board is discussing me, I have a right to defend my character."

Becky ignores me.

"Elodie is right," Monica says. A few other parents murmur their agreement.

"Fine," Becky huffs and sits. She picks up the gavel and strokes it absent-mindedly. "Elodie, I have brought a motion to expel your family from Mountain View Co-op Preschool."

"I'm not the thief," I say, "and I did not embezzle from preschool. I wouldn't even know how. If you let me explain —" I look at the board members, one by one, but few will meet my eyes.

"Then why were you using Meredith's computer on Friday?" Becky says.

"What?" My mouth hangs open. "I never even went near her computer."

"I caught you in the office alone on Friday and you were using Meredith's computer."

"No, I was on the opposite side of the room."

"But you were in the office alone?"

"Yes, but—"

"So you admit you were in the office alone after I said you needed supervision?"

"Well, yes, but I didn't go near the computers."

"Are you calling me a liar?"

"Yes?" but the word comes out as a question. I was not prepared to counter a complete and utter lie by Becky.

"That's the sort of thing a thief and embezzler would say."

Several board members nod.

"Well, it's true," I stammer. "I didn't even realize I was alone in the office..." My voice trails off. Ever since the playground collapsed, parents have been panicking and registering for different preschools. Preschool cannot afford a new playground if there is a thief and embezzler on the loose; and no one wants to send their child to "that tragic preschool with the collapsed playground." If they expel my family, the gossip mill will take care of the rest. People will believe the thief/embezzler situation has been handled, and the board can use auction profits for the long-awaited playground. Parents will register for next year. And since it's my word against Becky's, no one is going to believe that the president blatantly and shamelessly lied to pin the blame on me.

"Shall we vote?" Becky holds up the gavel and twirls it in the air.

I stand my ground, although I am too upset to speak.

"All those in favor of passing the motion to remove Madison Jones from Mountain View Co-op Preschool because her mother is not a desirable member of the community?"

A flurry of hands rise. I count seven ayes but don't know if that is good or bad. I can't do math at a time like this.

"All those opposed?"

Ingrid, Monica, and four other parents raise their hands. Six nays, seven ayes.

"The motion passes." Becky strikes her gavel against the folding table. "Please be sure to empty your daughter's cubby on your way out."

32

L uke and Madison find me surrounded by several batches of cooling cupcakes in our pink kitchen. "Who wants waffles?" I say with false cheer as I slather batter on the iron.

Luke takes a backward step. "How many people are coming today?"

"I don't know!" I'm not doing a good job of keeping the hysteria out of my voice. Today is Madison's birthday party. All the invitees, except for Natasha, RSVP'd "yes," but that was before: before Becky brought a motion to expel my family from Mountain View Co-op Preschool; before the board agreed with her sham justification; before the rumor mill spread the word that I was the preschool thief, embezzler and a horrible human being not to be trusted around children. No one has changed their RSVP, but that does not mean they are coming. Coming to Madison's party risks being guilty by association. I don't expect my friends to do that though now that I think about it, they probably aren't my friends anymore. I am no longer a mom with a growing circle of friends but an outcast reduced to sending pathetic texts to her lone mom friend who is somewhere in the woods of Alaska, communing with bears and shit like that.

"I don't know who is coming!" I say again, flipping the waffle. "But I want options for our guests!"

"I guess the kids can work up an appetite on the moon bounce." Luke rubs the back of his neck. "When is that coming?"

"Between eight and ten!" And then, my stomach plummets.

Ohhhhhhhh.

Myyyyyy.

Goddddd.

I forgot about the moon bounce.

My eyes dart toward Madison. She is under the table, singing to herself. "We don't have a moon bounce," I whisper.

"No moon bounce!" Madison scurries out from beneath the table and glares at me. "Why not? I want a moon bounce!"

"We'll fix it, we'll fix it." I quickly explain what happened to Luke. After Becky's motion passed on Monday, I forgot about the comparatively minor moon bounce crisis, but at least I am on theme for the week (the theme being "how to wreck your daughter's childhood").

Luke calls every party company he can find online while I burn the first and second waffles. Madison is hangry. "Moon bounce!" she screams as I tear the third waffle into bite-size pieces.

That's when Elsa calls.

"Hello?" I press my phone against my ear with my shoulder as I pick burnt pieces of waffle off the iron with tongs.

Whoever is calling hacks, wheezes and sneezes in rapid

succession. I cringe. A very hoarse voice rasps, "I'm sorry—" cough, cough, "—but I won't," hack, wheeze, "—be able to make it today."

"Who is this?" I ask sharply, wondering which of my former friends is betraying me first.

Another coughing fit, and then the voice croaks, "Elsa."

"Elsa?" I don't know anyone named Elsa, except the Disney princess—oh crap, it's the Elsa impersonator. "No, you have to come, I booked you over two months ago."

"I have a one hundred and four degree fever. I'm not coming."

"Can someone else come?"

"The other Elsa is triple booked today."

"What about Ariel? Belle? Snow White?"

"I'm sorry," Elsa hacks some more. "Call Bob." She hangs up.

Bob? Bob? Who the hell is Bob? Luke leaves a message with yet another party rental company while watching me for signs of an imminent nervous breakdown. I don't need a mirror to know I have crazy eyes and being surrounded by scores of cupcakes in a pink kitchen heightens the effect of a woman on the edge. I ought to take a few deep breaths and have breakfast. Instead, I call the company that arranged our Elsa impersonator.

An hour later, I am too defeated to even manage a nervous breakdown. I could not locate an Elsa, Anna, Moana, Jasmine or even Cruella Fricking de Vil though I did get a lead on a Cookie Monster, but I fear it might be the Cookie Monster who often lurks outside the L.A. Zoo and smells like a wet stray dog. I may be desperate, but even I have to draw the line somewhere.

Luke departs for the party store and returns with an excessive number of helium balloons. I festoon the front yard with pink streamers, garlands, and bunting. When I planned this party, I decided balloons were enough. Anything more seemed excessive since our Victorian house is already on theme with its garish pink exterior. But something inside of me cracked when the board passed Becky's motion, and I spent the past several days filling that crack with party decorations. That is why I am now sprinkling homemade pink confetti on the lawn while Luke orders the pizza. What will the neighbors think when no one comes to Madison's party?

I shower, drag my hair into a ponytail, don the Elsa shirt I bought special for today, and plaster a big phony smile across my face. I can do this. Sure, I am crumbling inside, but I can pretend like nothing is wrong for my daughter's sake. Madison puts on the Elsa shirt that is the smaller version of my own and beams. Then she asks when Elsa is coming. I tell her the truth, and Madison sobs as I carry her outside. She squirms out of my arms and crawls beneath some bushes. Fantastic. Now her rag of a tutu will be covered in mud. Let's just have one of those airplanes write in cloud letters, "Elodie Jones is the world's worst mom!" and call it a day.

Genevieve and her boys arrive five minutes to eleven. "Sorry we're early! The boys couldn't wait!" She bears a large pink gift bag, and upon seeing the present, Madison army crawls out from under the bush.

Over the next fifteen minutes, our guests arrive: Ingrid and both Danforths; Maude, Sven and Emma; Brooke, Josh and Gavin Rust; No Longer Pregnant Chloe and her clan, including a newborn tucked into a grey sling; and Paula and Zelda, both wearing their hair in pigtail buns. Luke texted Debbie and informed her she was not welcome at our home, but Ashley came with her husband, the neurosurgeon, and their daughter, Sophie. Everyone is here. My friends are still my friends. They have not abandoned me.

"I've started a petition," Ingrid announces, showing me a stack of papers on her clipboard entitled, "Bring the balloon lady back!" and beneath the title, Ingrid wrote a lengthy description of the story behind our departure from preschool. "I have seventy-three signatures already!" I hug Ingrid and cry.

Moms surround me. Someone rubs my back. Someone else says, "Becky is an idiot. Becky is such an idiot." I laugh and wipe away the tears.

"You should come back on Monday," Genevieve says. "What is Becky going to do? Call the cops? Miss Lucy wants you back."

"So does Dr. Konig," Ingrid says, "and the board members are embarrassed by the way Becky manipulated them."

My spirits lift — barely.

Even if Ingrid orchestrates Madison's return, people will still think I am the thief and embezzler. I will be banned from volunteering at school events, and I can kiss my room mom career farewell, which is for the best, because I am a disaster. I can't even throw my daughter a respectable birthday party! No moon bounce, no Elsa. The children are bored, and everyone will bail before the pizza arrives. Speaking of which, where is the pizza? It should have been here ten minutes ago. What else could possibly go wrong?

A noisy truck parks in front of our house. Two guys get out and unload an enormous pile of striped plastic sheeting. A neighbor must be tenting their house for termites. That's it. I'm canceling the party.

"Is this the Jones house?" one man calls out. Luke hurries over and they confer. Then Luke and Danforth Sr.

move the folding tables and chairs into the driveway as the men from the truck drag the enormous pile of striped plastic on to the front lawn. I stare and try not to drool. My brain cannot handle this influx of new information.

"A moon bounce!" Genevieve claps. "Boys! Madison got a moon bounce for her birthday!"

Luke comes over grinning. "It's their circus themed moon bounce. They were delivering it to a party in Los Feliz, but that party cancelled at the last minute."

The driver of the truck activates a generator and the moon bounce takes shape. All the kids laugh, clap, and dance — except Madison, who has turned her back to the moon bounce. My heart aches. It's too little, too late. The sudden expulsion from preschool already traumatized my daughter. No moon bounce can save her birthday.

Madison bolts and takes off down the sidewalk. My daughter is running away. I am such a lousy mother that she is taking her chances with the wild. I chase after her, but then I freeze.

"Grandma! Grandpa!" Madison shouts as she sprints toward a pink and blue RV parked at the end of our block. My younger brother Ferris does a back spring toward her, picks her up and tosses her to my older brother, who tosses her on my dad's shoulders.

Ladies and gentlemen, boys and girls, children of all ages: the circus has arrived!

33

"I hope we didn't overstep by coming," my mom says apologetically. After the party, she changed out of her full pink tutu and shimmery leotard into jeans and a simple blouse. "But once your brothers got the idea of making a surprise appearance at Madison's birthday party, I couldn't stop them."

I set two empty wine glasses on the pink counter and pour us some chardonnay. Everyone else is watching television in the Womb Room, so my mom and I retreat to the front. I hesitate to call it a living room because it is still mostly used as a play space for Madison, but at least the moving boxes have been unpacked and cleared away. There are also two new mismatched armchairs I bought at an estate sale, and in between the chairs, I put a t.v. tray I rescued from the curb. Ingrid would not approve of my interior decorating, but every pink wall needs to be painted white before I invest in anything else.

"Are you kidding?" We settle into the mismatched armchairs. "That was the most bitching birthday party ever."

I am not exaggerating. My family put on a performance that involved juggling, a unicycle, and a breathtaking array of acrobatic flips. They set up a tether line between two trees on our parkway, and my mom performed a tightrope act. When Madison tried to join her, Cormac put her on his shoulders and walked across the tether line, backwards and forwards, while Madison laughed with joy. My sister Colette and her dog, a poodle named Lady LaLa, ended the show with a routine that involved dancing and jumping through a ring of fire.

The pizza guy looked very confused when he pulled into our driveway.

After inhaling a slice of pizza, Madison climbed into the moon bounce, only to emerge a moment later with a scowl on her face. She wiggled out of her tutu and then noticed me. "Why are you watching me?" she demanded.

"I thought you were upset," I said.

"I am upset," she said. "This tutu makes it hard for me to jump." Then she took the tutu and unceremoniously dumped it in the trash. When she was back inside the moon bounce, I rescued the tutu from the trash — partly so I can save it in a box of baby mementos but mostly so Madison would not put it back on with fresh pizza sauce stains.

"It was perfect," I tell my mom. "Better than what I had planned." My voice wobbles. "Thank you." I wipe away a few tears.

"Honey," my mom pats my hand. "What's wrong?"

I try to answer, but my voice hitches and turns into a sob. I bury my head in my hands and cry for several minutes while my mom stands and drapes herself over me, holding me just like she did when I was not much older than Madison. When the storm passes, I sit up, brush back my hair, and say, "It's been a rough week."

"Tell me about it." My mom settles back into her seat and reaches for her wine.

I tell her everything from Becky, Debbie, my parking lot mishap and Trunk-or-Treat to yearning to be room mom but thinking I was not good enough because I never went to school myself. Then I tell her about Zoe going off the grid in Alaska and my pathetic stream of texts and learning that Ingrid didn't spike Zoe's drink, so all these years, I hated my freshman roommate for no valid reason. I tell my mom about my mental health, my psychiatrist's concern that being room mom will set my recovery back a decade, the mortification of losing my job as room mom, and my unrelenting fear that I am ruining Madison's childhood. As I talk, my mom rubs my arm and nods her head. I do not stop until I describe our expulsion and Ingrid's petition to get us back.

"But even if Ingrid gets Madison back into Mountain View," I conclude, "Luke won't be okay with that, and he's right. Becky fanned the rumor mill. I'll always be worried that the parents are gossiping about me."

My mom exhales loudly. "That sounds like my worst nightmare."

I laugh grimly.

"I was always grateful that I didn't have to deal with motherhood politics. It's very brave that you were room mom."

"It's not that big a deal," I mumble.

"Sure it is! It's like the circus. It's easy to be in the audience and criticize the lion tamer because the lion refused to jump through a hoop. Anyone can do that. Most people live their life in the cheap seats. Very few people get into the ring, but you did. Let the other parents gossip. If they stay in the audience, their opinion doesn't matter."

I open my mouth to protest, but stop as I remember

making balloon animals at the book fair and Easter egg hunt. I did not stay in the audience. Even when Becky stripped me of my job as room mom, I stayed in the main ring, doing my best to partake in the motherhood circus.

"I know that the school drama sucks," my mom continues, "but you are flourishing in Pasadena. You seem happier than you have ever been in your life. Even if that monster Becky kicked you out of preschool."

I ponder my mom's words for a moment. "You're right. I am happier than I've ever been in my life." Then my stomach lurches. "My psychiatrist doesn't think so. He thinks I'm undermining my mental health by being a stay-at-home mom."

My mom leans over and puts a hand on my arm. "Do *you* think you are undermining your mental health?"

I take a moment and consider. "No." I pause. "I think I'm ready to wean off Zoloft, but my psychiatrist keeps insisting that he will be the judge of that. He acts like I'm on the verge of imminent collapse and he's the only thing between me and disaster."

"Do *you* think you are on the verge of imminent collapse?"

"No."

"Do *you* think he's the only thing between you and disaster?"

"No."

My mom refills her wine glass. "It sounds like your psychiatrist is an idiot."

One week later, the day before the auction (which I will not be attending, because Becky is evil), I follow Dr. Dankworth to his office and ease myself onto the couch, which has gained even more doilies since my last visit. Dr. Dankworth collapses into his seat and goes through the motions of extracting and lighting a cigarette. He inhales, blows several smoke rings, and says, "When did you last have sex?"

"Excuse me?" My cheeks flush hot. We had sex last night, thank you very much, but I don't want to tell Dr. Dankworth that. My sex life is something sacred between me and Luke.

"Oh, so you aren't having sex?" Dr. Dankworth leers at me. "The Zoloft is killing your sex drive."

My nerves skitter and bounce. How much longer must I endure this man's torture? I do some quick math: my appointment with the new psychiatrist is in July; today is the penultimate day of April; and only a few pills rattled in my Zoloft bottle this morning. I have to suck it up for a few more months. "No, I don't think Zoloft is killing my sex drive."

Dr. Dankworth gives me a disbelieving smirk and takes a drag of his cigarette.

"We had sex last night!" I have to tell Dr. Dankworth this, or he will change my prescription unnecessarily, but I also just betrayed my husband. And I dislike the way Dr. Dankworth studies me now, as if he is imagining me and Luke in the throes of our passion.

"When was the time before that?" He balances the cigarette on the edge of the closest ashtray.

It was a few weeks ago. We had some of the best sex ever after Luke told me, during Miss Blaire's wedding shower, that he was sick of Debbie's advances. I felt like a new confident, sexy woman, but then I had my period, followed by another yeast infection, and if this is TMI, please go read *Pride & Prejudice*, but remember: the Bentley girls all menstruated and got yeast infections even if Jane Austen skipped those bits.

"A week ago? Two weeks ago?" Dr. Dankworth watches my face closely. "Three weeks ago?"

I cross my arms over my chest. "I had a yeast infection and couldn't have sex."

"Wait, wait, wait, wait, wait!" Dr. Dankworth puts up a hand as if he is talking to a defiant toddler. It is as orange as his face. "There's always anal sex."

My mouth falls open.

As far as possible.

I am a cartoon character.

"A red-blooded heterosexual man cannot abstain from sex for weeks on end just because his wife has a yeast infection. It goes against all our biological instincts. A man has needs. SEXUAL needs. Do you expect your husband to be monogamous?"

"Yes," I say, my voice unsteady.

Dr. Dankworth launches into a monologue about the sexual needs of the modern man, and I glance at the photo of his wife and his kids, *but it is gone*. There are new photo frames with school portraits of his children, but no sign of the wife. As Dr. Dankworth talks about lubricant, I vomit a little in my mouth and notice that his wedding band is missing. There is an obvious white ring of skin on his otherwise orange hand. Maybe I am speculating here, but I suspect Dr. Dankworth's marriage recently derailed, and he blames his wife for being "sexually stale" (the phrase he just shouted) rather than diving into the waters of personal responsibility.

"Your husband needs to feel challenged," Dr. Dankworth says, "but he also needs to know he is giving you the best orgasm of your life. Ask any sex therapist. They will tell you the same thing, but I'm telling you this for free! You also need better grooming. Have you tried Botox? What about makeup lessons? The freckles are cute, but men don't want cute. They want sexy."

He continues his tirade, pausing occasionally to take a drag of his cigarette. I am powerless, trapped on the itchy couch, forced to listen to this asshat blather on and on about sexual appetites and the things women must do to satisfy their men while stoking the flames of desire.

Then I hear my mom's voice in my head, as if she is sitting next to me. "It sounds like your psychiatrist is an idiot."

My mom is right.

This man is an idiot. I am not a fragile woman teetering on the brink of disaster but a fierce bad ass with awesome freckles who is done with this sorry excuse of a psychiatrist. I stand.

"I'm still talking." Dr. Dankworth gestures for me to sit down with his cigarette.

"I'm done listening." I hoist my tote bag over my shoulder.

"What?" Dr. Dankworth stumbles to his feet and knocks over a stack of files. He lunges for the files and instead knocks his laptop off his desk. He trips and catches the laptop right before it hits the ground. "You can't walk out in the middle of a session!"

"Oh yes, I can," and I do exactly that.

I pause at the reception desk and survey the crowded waiting room. The usual nature program about mountain goats blasts on the television. The patients look at me. They must think I am a lunatic. I don't care. Everyone should unleash their inner lunatic from time to time. I say, "I can't believe how long I have put up with this b.s." Then I turn to the receptionist. "Please send me the bill for today's session, but please be advised that I will not be paying it."

"You can't do this!" Dr. Dankworth runs out of his office, still clutching his laptop.

"Watch me."

A woman in the waiting room cheers, and several patients rise to their feet. "She's right, this is b.s.," a guy with a baseball cap says. A woman wearing purple yoga pants shouts, "Amen!"

I march out the door and stomp down the stairs. The man with the baseball cap and the woman in purple pants join my escape, as well as a half dozen other patients.

Dr. Dankworth follows. "You can't just leave! You have appointments!"

Various patients shout back. "Yes, we can leave!" "You treat us like garbage!" "I'm reporting you to the medical board!" I, however, have said enough.

In the parking lot, I stop long enough to high five the patients who followed me out of Dr. Dankworth's evil lair. Then I get in my car while Dr. Dankworth shouts obscenities. As I pull out of the driveway, I glance in my rearview mirror just in time to see Dr. Dankworth throwing his laptop to the ground.

n hour before the auction, Ingrid is still trying to convince me to come. Her latest text reads:

You paid for a ticket! Anyone can come! You don't have to be an official preschool family!

I am not going anywhere near the preschool auction. I have to preserve my last scrap of dignity, thank you very much, and besides, Becky will never let me cross the venue's threshold, even if I helped secure it.

Luke is playing poker tonight with some high school friends while Madison has a sleepover with my in-laws. And me? I am going to have a bubble bath in our pink clawfoot tub, eat cheese for dinner and watch *Bridget Jones's Diary*.

I turn on the water and pour in my fancy bubble bath. (If you tell Madison about it, you are dead to me.) I wrap my hair into a bun and check social media while the tub fills. The first photo that appears in my Instagram feed is Miss Blaire in a flimsy wedding gown. I forgot she is getting married today in Bulgaria. In the photo, she is eating french fries while looking both glamorous and cute. My thumb moves to like the photo and I notice Fiona, the leader of the B-squad, posted it. I read Fiona's caption:

In-N-Out in Bulgaria??? Officially dead to me.

There's no way the California fast food franchise opened a location in Bulgaria. I bring the screen closer to my face and confirm the fries look like In-N-Out fries, but surely restaurants serve fries in Bulgaria...

I scan the comments.

Didn't you know that "Bulgaria" is code for "Pasadena"?

And then:

How many "friends" did she snub? Raise your hand!

Fiona thoughtfully tagged the accounts of Miss Blaire's bridesmaids, so I click on the first, but it's private. Foiled! I click on the second and bingo! This bridesmaid has a public account and already posted a dozen wedding photos.

I scroll backwards in time and see the bride and groom kissing and exchanging vows, Miss Blaire walking down the aisle, and Miss Blaire in a limousine, looking winsome while fingering a necklace resting against her perfect clavicle. Photos of the wedding party appear, and my jaw drops.

The wedding party posed in front of a waterfall that tumbles down the rocky side of a steep hill lush with moss and ferns. It is very familiar. Maybe I saw it during my Maui honeymoon — HOLD EVERYTHING. I toggle over to my Instagram account and check the selfie I took during my walk at the Arboretum.

It's the same damn waterfall.

Maybe there is an innocent explanation. Maybe Miss Blaire took wedding portraits in Pasadena before flying to Bulgaria. No need to jump to sinister conclusions. I check the caption:

> Makeup and hair are done. Taking photos now at the Arboretum. See everyone in an hour when Blaire and Steve get hitched!!!

Unbelievable. So Miss Blaire *is* getting married in Pasadena after telling everyone at preschool she was getting married in Bulgaria — but why? I hate to be cynical, but maybe she wanted the gifts without the guests. Between the bridal shower and wedding, Miss Blaire raked in thousands of dollars from parents whom she never really invited to the nuptials. She probably returned gifts to pay for that gorgeous venue. Not cool, Miss Blaire, not cool.

My body hums with a surge of energy. Miss Blaire is a con artist.

This wedding looks expensive, and if Miss Blaire exceeded her budget, maybe extra wedding gifts were not enough to make ends meet. Maybe she dipped into purses and wallets for wedding funds. She mentioned making money as an "influencer" but that's not a foolproof plan. Maybe Miss Blaire felt mortified when she could not raise money with social media and was too proud to scale back or borrow money.

I have no proof.

I should take my bath now.

The other parents will never think ill of Miss Blaire. She's the institution.

Which made it easy for her to slip around undetected.

My mind races back over the past school year. The morning I patrolled the parking lot, Miss Blaire seemed startled to find me there. She thought all the board members were upstairs listening to her future father-in-law's playground pitch and had left the parking lot unattended. I bet the "smoothie in the car" trick was a ruse to give her access to unattended cars before the security cameras' installation.

The time Becky accused me of stealing from the Trunk-or-Treat refreshment stand: Miss Blaire was there. The time money disappeared from my wallet: Miss Blaire was the one carrying my bag to the office when she should have been with the kids. The book fair: Miss Blaire helped. The egg hunt: Miss Blaire could have rummaged through unattended purses while parents were filming their precious darlings.

Miss Blaire is the preschool thief.

But I could scream, because I have no evidence. I don't even have solid proof her wedding is in Pasadena.

Oh! I scroll back to the wedding photos. The bride and groom stand beneath a big camphor tree hung with lanterns and metal stars. I know that tree. I know that garden. It's the charming garden that shares a parking lot with our auction venue. OH MY GOD! The pink Volvo! The day we toured auction venues, someone parked a pink Volvo station wagon outside the garden, but Ingrid said it was not Miss Blaire's car. Now I remember where I saw that car before: in the preschool parking lot the day I opened Tricia's car. Miss Blaire said she was borrowing it from her sister. She must have driven to the garden venue with her sister the day Ingrid and I were there and the venue was not available for the auction because Miss Blaire had already booked it for her wedding.

I jump to my feet, excited to tell everyone that the perfect Miss Blaire is getting married next door to the auction that she "hated" missing, but freeze. Just because Miss Blaire is getting married next to the auction venue does not mean she is the preschool thief. I have a motive, but I do not have proof she committed the crime. Preschool parents will just resent me for casting suspicion on sweet Miss Blaire.

I scroll through social media, bothered by a nagging feeling that I am missing something important, but the thing I am missing is a firm grasp on reality. I will never clear my name, and we will never return to Mountain View Co-Op Preschool. I scowl at the photo of Miss Blaire in the limousine when it hits me, and I zoom as close as possible to Miss Blaire's clavicle.

I know how to clear my name.

Ten minutes later, I leave my car with the valet and bless Ingrid for insisting on this expense. I run up the ramp, dashing past parents in suits and dresses. Folding tables draped with black fabric cloths line the wall, and the auction baskets are on display, each paired with a clipboard and bidding sheets. The sheets are all blank.

I spot Ingrid, sitting on the ground at the top of the ramp, sobbing. "You came!" she wails in between sobs.

I forgot about her texts. She thinks I am here to party. I should comfort her and ask why she's crying, but I don't have time for pleasantries. I pant, "Is Debbie here?"

"Who cares?" Ingrid hiccups. "It's a total disaster! All this work!" She sweeps an arm toward the tables. "And no one is bidding! They're worried about the embezzler. No one wants to donate money to a school that is doomed." Something bangs, and an unshaven man in filthy clothes beats the handrail with a metal bat. Ingrid hiccups. "I forgot to bribe Joe."

I grab Ingrid by the shoulders. "Ingrid. This is important. Is Debbie here?"

"Of course she is. Would she miss an opportunity to dress up?"

I run inside. The room is packed with parents milling around with drinks. Maude and Paula are posing with inflatable electric guitars in the photo booth; stay-at-home dad Josh is playing Pac-man at one of the arcade machines Ingrid rented; Ashley's husband, the neurosurgeon, is leering at a woman wearing a backless gown; and as the woman in the backless gown turns, I spot her resting bitch face. I push through the crowd toward everyone's favorite former podcast host.

Debbie sees me coming. "Ew, what are you doing here?"

"I have to show you something." I grab her hand, but she pulls away.

"Debbie, I swear, you want to see this."

Debbie rolls her eyes but follows me to the main door.

"Elodie!" Genevieve, seated at the check-in table, jumps to her feet and follows. We pass Liz Huffenby, who abandons the drinks line and hurries after us, confident she has spotted juicy gossip.

Becky sees me, mid-sip, and sprays red wine all over Ashley's slinky white dress. Ashley shrieks but Becky is already pursuing me, shouting, "What is she doing here?!"

"This better be good," Debbie huffs as we cross the parking lot.

"You have no right!" Becky hollers.

"Leave her alone!" Ingrid stomps after Becky, her indignation squashing her sobs.

The refrain of *Y.M.C.A.* blasts from the garden venue.

The barn doors in the brick wall are open. A few teenagers lurking outside extinguish a joint and run back into the wedding festivities.

"I'm not wedding crashing," Debbie hisses.

Yes, I think, *but wait until you see the bride.*

I stand on tiptoe and scan the crowd for Miss Blaire. She has to be here. The wedding is in full swing.

The impeccably dressed lady steps in front of me. Tonight, she is wearing a black tweed skirt and jacket. "I'm sorry," she says, "I think your event is in that building." She waves toward the auction.

"We wanted to say hello to the bride," I say. "Miss Blaire teaches at our kids' preschool."

"Miss Blaire is getting married in Bulgaria." Becky pulls me away from the garden.

The lady smiles. "How lovely! Blaire is about to cut the cake, but I'll tell her you stopped by." There is the sound of a plate breaking, and she hurries away.

"Excuse me," Liz Huffenby says. "Did she say Miss Blaire is about to cut the cake?"

As if on cue, Miss Blaire, in a slinky wedding gown, walks into view, with the camphor tree behind her.

"OMG, it is Miss Blaire," Liz Huffenby says.

"She looks radiant," Becky whispers.

"That bitch stole my necklace!" Several wedding guests turn as Debbie storms into the party and makes a beeline for the bride.

Miss Blaire is laughing, head thrown back, the better to showcase the large blue gem surrounded by tiny clear diamonds hanging around her neck. Then she sees Debbie and stops mid-laugh, her face contorting into surprise and horror. A guilty hand flies over the necklace.

"You stole my necklace!" Debbie roars.

"This is mine," Miss Blaire stammers. Her lips and chin tremble.

"That's a family heirloom! It belongs to my husband's great-aunt! She loaned it to me! And she has given me hell!"

"It was a gift," Miss Blaire whimpers. "I swear I didn't steal it."

"A gift?" The groom is on high alert. "From who? You said you found it at a vintage store."

Miss Blaire looks toward her bridesmaids, but they are shuffling away from the train wreck in progress.

Meanwhile, Debbie has pulled out her phone. "Here!" She displays the phone for the groom and all the guests standing nearby. "That's me, wearing the necklace." She lowers the phone and swipes. "Here! That's my husband's great-aunt Joan wearing the necklace right before she loaned it to me. It's in her insurance policy. I can prove Miss Blaire stole it."

Miss Blaire lowers her head. Tears stream down her cheeks. She raises a shaking hand, unclasps the necklace and hands it back to Debbie.

"I'm sorry," Miss Blaire sobs. "I was going to give it back."

The groom staggers into a nearby chair, and a bridesmaid fans him with a program.

Debbie snarls a few choice words and puts on the necklace.

Behind me, someone clears her throat. "And the wallets and purses?" Liz Huffenby strides forward, her long red fingernails playing with the strap of her dress. "And the money that went missing during Trunk-or-Treat? And the book fair? That was all you?" Liz Huffenby is sating her own lust for gossip, but I appreciate her thoroughness. She will make sure everyone knows about Miss Blaire's confession before the auction is over.

"I'm sorry," Miss Blaire weeps.

"Would you like some cake?" The mother of the bride appears with cake-laden china plates. Ingrid and Becky both accept slices. The mother of the bride leans toward us and whispers, "I am so sorry. I was wondering where Blaire was getting the money for all the extra expenses. How could she pay for a string quartet on a preschool teacher's salary? She will pay everything back. Please," she pleads, "don't take this to the police."

"It's a shame we will have to fire Miss Blaire," Ingrid says wistfully, admiring the wedding. "She has excellent taste. She chose the same chairs and place settings I picked for the auction!"

"Oh!" I gasp. "That's how the money was being embezzled!"

35

"Will the new playground be too fancy?"

"Too fancy? There's no such thing!" Ingrid tilts back her head and shrieks like a dolphin. I do not stiffen or wince. I like her laugh after all. It's endearing.

Ingrid and I are standing in the preschool courtyard. It's the last day of school, and she is showing me the playground blueprints. Genevieve peers over our shoulders and gasps. "I thought we were going with the basic model?"

"That was before Elodie figured out how Miss Blaire was embezzling money from preschool, silly."

Miss Blaire ordered tables, chairs, place settings and even food from the party company that preschool used for the past decade. When the school treasurer reviewed the accounts, she skimmed over any entries from the party company, assuming they were legitimate expenses. No wonder Becky thought Ingrid was exceeding her auction budget! Miss Blaire was piggybacking tens of thousands of dollars of wedding expenses on Ingrid's event. A good accountant would have caught this, but we are not running a Fortune 500 company. We are a co-op preschool powered by the volunteer hours of dedicated parents. Occasionally, we might have a treasurer with less than stellar credentials.

Miss Blaire's father-in-law, founder and CEO of Terrain de Jeux, saved the wedding by announcing his company would pay back the monies embezzled, and donate a deluxe playground to Mountain View Co-op Preschool. Debbie was about to protest, but Ingrid elbowed her aside and graciously accepted the offer. Preschool is coming out ahead. Our humble co-op could never have afforded the structure that Miss Blaire's father-in-law is donating.

"Is there room for six slides?" I fret.

"Trust me," Ingrid says, "there's room for all the slides and the rock climbing structure, monkey bars, and suspension bridges. We will have the best playground in Pasadena!"

"Even better than the one at Tiny Geniuses Academy?" I tease.

Ingrid rolls up the plans and swats me playfully. After the auction, she toured Tiny Geniuses Academy and announced, "It doesn't feel like home." Danforth Jr. will be in Madison's class again next year. Ingrid is going to be the co-op president.

Speaking of the co-op president, Becky did not speak for five days after the auction. (I'm not complaining.) When she recovered her power of speech, she grabbed random parents at school and apologized for not realizing Miss Blaire was the thief and embezzler. I had to listen to her excessive apologies no less than eleven times. I almost wished my family was still banished, because every time I stepped onto campus, Becky ambushed me. Once, she even cowered at my feet and sobbed. That was a little gratifying, but mostly awkward. Two weeks after the auction, for her swan song,

Becky sent a school-wide email announcing her resignation from the presidency and board.

Next year, she just wants to be a room mom.

My room mom crown was restored at the auction. Liz Huffenby sprinted back to the venue after Miss Blaire admitted to being the preschool thief and embezzler. Within minutes, every parent at the auction was in the loop. People bid on neglected auction items and by the evening's end, Ingrid had raised more money than the last three auctions combined. Meredith's plunger will get a lot less action next school year. The plumber arrives tomorrow.

Before the live auction, Dr. Konig, wearing a frilly white blouse with her navy pencil skirt and sensible beige pumps, took the stage. After some welcoming remarks, she went off-script and thoroughly mortified me. "As you probably know by now, we have apprehended the preschool thief." Several parents cheered. "It was not, as some board members believed, Elodie Jones. I would like to apologize to Miss Jones. You have added so much to our community this year."

"We love your balloons animals!" an anonymous dad hollered.

"Yes," Dr. Konig beamed. "We are excited to welcome the Jones family back — if they will have us."

I nodded from my seat, tears filling my eyes.

Dr. Konig continued, "We love Elodie's balloon creations and all the contributions she made at Trunk-or-Treat, the book fair and, of course, the egg hunt. She has also been a very dedicated room mom."

I blushed so hard, I wondered if I could give myself a sunburn.

"Some hasty and unfortunate action was taken as to Miss Elodie's role as room mom, and she was replaced without the entire board's approval. I spoke with our board members, and I am thrilled to reinstate Miss Elodie as Miss Lucy's room mom."

The parents seated at my table jumped to their feet and applauded wildly. Genevieve made ridiculous cat calls, and Ingrid winked. Natasha, the interloper room mom, was absent. She had boycotted the event "as a protest against capitalism."

"Mama!" Madison tugs at my hand. She's wearing a pink shirt, pink ballet flats, and a blue tutu. Since turning three, she has amassed a collection of tutus and wears them in rainbow order. Tomorrow will be purple. "Miss Lucy needs you!"

Madison leads me to her classroom. She does not know that she missed two weeks of school. Someday, when she is older, I'll tell her all about The Miss Blaire Affair. We'll go out for a fancy dinner, share a bottle of wine and oh my god, my baby will someday be old enough to drink wine. I can't. I'm sorry, I can't think about this yet.

"Surprise!"

Miss Lucy's classroom is filled with parents. Mr. Joe hands me a bouquet of colorful flowers, and Miss Lucy hugs me and slips me a box of chocolates. "This is the good stuff," she whispers. "Don't let Madison see it."

Genevieve raises a juice box into the air. "Thank you, Elodie, for being our intrepid room mom!"

The parents clap as I blush and dip into something that resembles a curtsy. Debbie abstains from clapping and elbows Ashley when she joins the ovation. Natasha is not here. She is boycotting the potluck because there's gluten in the mac and cheese, food coloring in Genevieve's sugar cookies, and the juice boxes will be the downfall of civilization. She also does not approve of the Target gift cards I gave the teachers for the end-of-year class gifts. Something about pandering to the capitalist agenda. I did not read her email closely.

Debbie heads over to the buffet where Luke, Danforth Sr. and a few other dads are discussing boring sports stuff. They block Debbie's path to the Le Croix and she has to ask them several times to move. The men shuffle to the right while continuing their heated debate. None of them so much as glance at Debbie's derriere. She wilts visibly, but I do not gloat because I am a highly evolved woman who extends compassion and grace to all her fellow moms.

Just kidding. I have grown a lot this school year, but not that much. I am gloating shamelessly.

Lucky for Debbie, she will have a fresh batch of dads to seduce next year. I overheard her bragging to Ashley about the beach house she convinced her husband to buy in Malibu. Arlo will attend a prestigious preschool with an ocean view. My prayers are with Malibu moms.

"I hear you had quite the year!" Miss Jenny, the new assistant teacher, says, as I use the back of my hand to wipe chocolate off Madison's face. Dr. Konig hired her to be a substitute teacher during Miss Blaire's honeymoon, but thanks to Miss Blaire's confessions on the night of the auction, the post became permanent. She's only been here for a month, but Madison adores her. The kids barely registered Miss Blaire's sudden departure. (The dads, on the other hand...)

I received a check in the mail last week and a note of apology from Miss Blaire's husband:

My wife is too overwrought to write this letter. She
wanted a deluxe wedding and was too embarrassed to ask
me to cover the expenses her parents could not afford, but
we want to make amends. Blaire tells me she took several

*hundred dollars from your wallet. I hope this amount
covers your losses, plus interest and a little extra for your
inconvenience.*

Sincerely,

Steve

I laughed out loud when I read the bit about my "inconvenience" and considered tearing up the check. Then I tucked it into my wallet and scheduled a posh spa day.

I easily have time for said spa day because my new psychiatrist only wants to see me every three or four months. She had some cancellations, and I saw her in mid-May. She agreed that my mental health is better than ever and I am ready to wean off Zoloft. In fact, I started weaning last week. But I know that between my psychiatrist and gynecologist, and all the other health care providers in Pasadena, I will get the mental health support I need, including any prescription refills.

During the last minutes of the school year, Miss Lucy gathers the children on the rug one last time to present awards. Danforth Jr. receives a certificate for Best Dressed, Arlo is recognized for Best Hair, and Madison gets the award for Future Tightrope Walker. Her grandparents will be so proud. I tear up as Madison stands and accepts her certificate. My baby has finished her first year of preschool. Oh my god, I am going to be a wreck when she graduates from college.

"So will you be room mom next year?" Maude asks as we collect the last haul of art projects.

"Maybe," I say coyly, though I am just relieved preschool is not in danger of closing. The Monday after the auction, dozens of parents crowded into the office with their down payment for next year. There is a lengthy waitlist for classes.

"No, she can't be room mom," Ingrid says. "She is taking over as the fundraising director."

I am about to protest when my phone rings. I go to silence the call but stop when I read Caller ID.

"Zoe?!" I weave through the crowd of parents and children, stumble outside and find a relatively quiet spot.

"Elodie! Oh my god, I just finished reading your texts. I am here! I am ready to troubleshoot! Where should we start?"

"There's nothing to troubleshoot. Is everything okay with you? I thought you were off the grid until August?"

"That was a nightmare. I couldn't take it anymore. I love the grid. Who leaves the grid with adolescent twins and a preschooler? I'm getting my hair done in Juneau." A hair dryer roars in the background. "Tomorrow we are flying back to New York. I can't believe you had to deal with Ingrid all year!"

"She's been fine."

"Fine? How is that possible? Ingrid is in league with Satan."

"Maybe," I say noncommittally. I need time to figure out how to tell Zoe that Ingrid is my friend. Actually, I need time to figure out my friendship with Zoe. For starters, we have to have a serious conversation about the Halloween party and her lies about Ingrid.

"And the co-op president thinks you are the preschool thief?" Zoe continues, oblivious to my inner turmoil.

"That was a big misunderstanding. Ancient history."

"But they expelled Madison?"

"Another big misunderstanding," I say nonchalantly. I spent most of the school year waiting for this phone call, desperate to fill Zoe in on the preschool drama and listen to her sage advice, but now that we are talking, I want to end the call as soon as possible so I can rejoin my Pasadena mom friends for our last hurrah with Miss Lucy.

"Wow, I'm impressed. I've been worried about you all year."

"You have?"

"Of course, Elodie. You were a total head case our first year of college. I get it. You grew up in the circus. College was a tremendous culture shock, so I thought Madison's first year of preschool would trigger freak outs for you. And Ingrid was there! It's like history hit the copy and paste button and you repeated an entire year of your life."

Yes, and no. The universe might have conspired to bring Ingrid and I back together, but I have grown and changed a lot since our freshman year of college. Ingrid was not at the root of my suffering; *I* was. Ingrid genuinely thought it was cool that her roommate grew up in the circus. I, however, was so insecure about being Elodie Flimbizzle, I assumed she was trying to humiliate me whenever she asked me to make balloon animals or juggle. She wasn't. She just appreciated my quirks more than I did. But now that I am Elodie Jones, room mom extraordinaire, I am also ready to embrace Elodie Flimbizzle, the bad ass balloon lady.

From somewhere inside Miss Lucy's classroom, Ingrid shrieks like a hysterical dolphin.

"Was that Ingrid laughing?"

"Zoe, I have to go." Zoe will feel betrayed on a deeply personal level when I tell her Ingrid and I are friends now, but maybe that's for the best. "I'll call you tonight."

When I rejoin my friends, Ingrid is wearing Genevieve's blue fedora. "Nope," I say, switching the hat back to

Genevieve's head. "I have one friend who looks good in a fedora, and I'm sorry, Ingrid, but it's not you."

Ingrid's dolphin laugh fills the room. Somewhere in Juneau, Alaska, a tiny piece of Zoe Ziegler's soul dies, but that's okay. It's not like the Zieglers are moving to Pasadena.

"Also," I continue, "I want the record to reflect that I will never be the fundraising director."

Ingrid pats my shoulder. "I was joking. Tricia is taking over fundraising." She pauses. "But the position for family activities director is still open."

"Family activities director?" I ask warily.

"The family activities director is in charge of all the school-wide events for parents and kids, like Trunk-or-Treat and the Easter egg hunt. Evan Mumford was the family activities director, remember?" Ingrid sips her Diet Coke. "That's why we didn't have movie nights or bingo this year."

Movie nights? Bingo? My heart patters wildly.

"That sounds like something I'd enjoy," I admit.

"It's so many events," Maude says. "That would be a lot to juggle."

Ingrid, mid-sip, laughs and chokes on her Diet Coke and Genevieve has to beat her on the back several times.

"Oh my god, what?" Maude self-consciously touches her face. "Is there a big booger hanging out of my nose? Why are you laughing at me?"

"She's not laughing at you." I pat Maude's shoulder. "She's laughing at me because I can actually juggle."

"Oooh, how many things?" Genevieve asks.

"It depends," I hedge.

"Depends on what?" Brooke Rust asks, her mouth full of one of my brownies.

"It depends on whether I'm riding a unicycle or if any of the items are on fire."

Genevieve, Maude, and Brooke stare at me.

"Also," I add, "if I'm balancing something on my head, that changes the physics. It's all about focus and staying in the flow."

"No wonder you're such a good room mom," Maude breathes. "If you can do that, planning a potluck must be easy for you."

If she only knew the grief that first potluck caused. Then again, another room mom might have quit at the first sign of adversity. Motherhood can be quite the circus. Maybe my unconventional childhood prepared me for motherhood more than I ever thought possible.

ACKNOWLEDGMENTS

I can never thank enough the wonderful teachers at Hastings Ranch Nursery School. Miss Angie, Miss Alyson, and Miss Julie — thank you, thank you, thank you for being such wonderful teachers and friends. I'm not going to try to list all the other people who made HRNS such an amazing place because somewhere in between Miss Jen and JLK, I am bound to miss someone, but if you are looking for a preschool in Pasadena, you can't go wrong with our co-op.

Oops, I do have to mention a couple more people from our preschool years! Allison Perez and Laura Karas, thank you for always bringing levity and a dash of irreverence, even when the shit was hitting the fan.

Many profound thanks to my disposable lint roller for keeping my leggings somewhat respectable, and also to TikTok, for being a cornerstone of my mental health.

Even profounder thanks to my editor Elise Hitchings, who gave some excellent advice to improve this book. (But she didn't read these Acknowledgments, so she's not responsible for my tendency to ramble...)

Kalea Dunkleman - how many times did you listen to me talk about this book? SO MANY TIMES. How many times did you encourage me to write this book when we were hanging out at Chateau Wilkes, making sure our kids did not torment Rosie during pod? Too many times to count. I can't thank you enough for being such a supportive, encouraging friend.

Stefanie Greenwood, thank you for your awesome artistic eye and all your help designing my book cover. You the bomb!

Katie Conner, for all the listening, TikTok's, rants, and sanity checks.

Michelle Chaldu, starting back in Purple Door, you have been the Monica paving the way for the rest of us. I expect lots of reports from middle school.

And my book club! Annie, Adrian, Katelin, and Sarah - best book club ever. You've listened to me talk about this book for a year and a half now. Good news - now I'll be talking about the sequel.

The Magic Castle Cousins - thank you for your humor, love and our intense pop culture discussions.

I am really not good at writing pithy Acknowledgments. Probably should have settled for "thanks to everyone who supported me through the writing of this book" and been done with it. Though if you have read this far, wow, you are awesome. Also: if you have not tried ketchup on your scrambled eggs yet, you are missing out. Delicious.

My sister-in-law Sara, thank you for insisting you would read this book even though you usually read non-fiction.

Matt and Katherine, best damn siblings.

Mom and Dad: you might not be acrobats, but you bent over backwards to give me a wonderful childhood

Pippa and Julian, I love you SO MUCH and being your mom is the most magical part of my life.

Last but not least, I could never have written this without the love and support of my husband, Nathan. Who was always ready to help, from brainstorming ways to embezzle from a preschool to answering pesky grammar questions. Love you, MP.

ABOUT THE AUTHOR

Courtney Henning Novak lives in Pasadena, California with her husband Nathan, their children Pippa and Julian, Hamsty the hamster, and an assortment of aquatic creatures. She loves cooking, crafting, and tackling DIY projects that only occasionally end in total disaster. She has been a room mom since Pippa started kindergarten. Contrary to popular opinion, Courtney did not grow up in the circus.

www.CourtneyHenningNovak.com
Instagram: @Courtney.Novak
TikTok: @courtneyhenningnovak

Made in United States
North Haven, CT
28 July 2022

21914876R00173